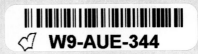

Hamesh Shahani

about the author

Anna David is the author of the novel *Party Girl* and the editor of an upcoming anthology about reality shows. She's the sex-and-relationship expert on G4's *Attack of the Show*; appears every month on *Red Eye* on Fox News; has popped up on the *Today* show, *Hannity & Colmes,* CNN's *Showbiz Tonight,* MTV, E!, and VH1; and has been published in the *New York Times,* the *Los Angeles Times, Playboy,* and *Details,* among many others.

bought

ALSO BY ANNA DAVID

Party Girl

bought

a novel

ANNA DAVID

HARPER

NEW YORK • LONDON • TORONTO • SYDNEY

HARPER

HarperCollins books may be purchased for educational, business, or sales promotional use. For information, please write: Special Markets Department, HarperCollins Publishers, 10 East 53rd Street, New York, NY 10022.

FIRST EDITION

Designed by Cassandra J. Pappas

Library of Congress Cataloging-in-Publication Data is available upon request.

ISBN 978-0-06-166918-7

09 10 11 12 13 OV/RRD 10 9 8 7 6 5 4 3 2

For my mom, Gail David-Tellis

Until we lose ourselves, there is no hope of finding ourselves.

—HENRY MILLER

Shake your money maker.

—JAMES BROWN

bought

chapter 1

I TURN FROM THE GORGEOUS, thoroughly indifferent bartender to Rebecca. My lips make actual contact with her cheek, and for a second I worry that she thinks I've completely invaded her space—or, even worse, that I'm known as the creepy girl who transforms air kisses into cheek kisses and everyone discusses this when I'm not around. But she's talking so fast that I don't have time for a full-blown fit of paranoia.

"Emma! Oh my God! Can you believe this house?" she asks. "I mean, an actual Neutra? And did you hear Liz Smith is supposed to be coming?" She pauses and then takes a sip. "Can you believe the way they've just gone all out?"

"I know." I'd just been asking myself when it became acceptable for baby showers to have male guests, not to mention take place at mansions with koi ponds, trees carved into sculptures, multiple bars, valet parking, and hot waiters only pouring drinks while they waited for their big break. As the bartender—who I suddenly realize I saw in an Old Spice commercial last week—

finally hands me a glass of champagne, I wonder what ever happened to the notion of a bunch of girls sitting around decorating onesies and discussing the various merits of names like "Tristan" or "Sally."

"So how are you?" Rebecca asks, but doesn't wait for an answer. Instead, she gestures toward a pile of toys—which include a giant playhouse and stuffed reindeer larger than me—that guests have left. "My God, how spoiled is this kid going to be?" She looks thrilled by the notion.

"Very." I take a gulp of my drink, hoping she doesn't notice how uncomfortable I am. The first time I met Rebecca, we talked for an hour straight and I was excited that a manager—someone who represented successful writers and directors—would be so open to me, a lowly party reporter. But when I ran into her at an Equinox yoga class the next week, she'd acted so distant that for a second I wondered if she suffered from amnesia and had been in some sort of a blackout when we'd been chatting. Now I get that she's only periodically sweet, and that's usually when no one more important is around. On a conscious level, I don't want to be her friend—I see that she's shallow and snobby, a girl who'd ditch her blind grandmother while walking her across the street if it meant being able to lick the bottom of Gwyneth Paltrow's shoe—and yet I still seem to want her approval. Maybe I start to view myself the way I know she sees me—as filler—and somehow allow that to define me. Or perhaps I want to be like her, wish I could stand there and appear aloof and patronizing, ache to be able to speak the secret code that people like her—people who automatically know when they're standing in a Neutra house and aren't embarrassed to sacrifice themselves entirely in order to suck up to celebrities—seem to come by naturally. "This is some baby shower," I add.

Mercifully, Steve walks up with a camera. A friend from college who, seemingly overnight, turned into a hugely successful movie producer, Steve is both the soon-to-be father of the sure-to-be-spoiled baby and probably the only person in this environment that I can be myself around.

"How are you?" he asks as Rebecca makes her way over to Bart Jacobs, the lumbering CAA agent throwing the party for Steve and his wife.

"Any sign of him?" I say in lieu of a response.

Steve shakes his head and sighs. The poor guy's grown understandably weary of hearing about my never-ending obsession with Matt, an agent he introduced me to seven months ago who ended up pursuing and then dumping me once I was hooked. "Please don't let him get to you," Steve says, throwing a protective arm around me. "He's honestly not worth it."

"I promise I won't," I lie, just as Steve's wife, Celeste—who, in typical Hollywood form, barely looks pregnant at six months—comes up and greets me.

As she and Steve kiss, I wonder why it seems to be so easy for some people to figure out how to have and maintain relationships when it's always been unspeakably difficult for me. Then Will Smith and Jada Pinkett start meandering over and Steve whispers under his breath that this is his cue to be "on" and he and Celeste embrace them. Rebecca and Bart are by now engaged in a relatively impassioned conversation about how adorable Jada looks and how amazing she is and how there really hasn't ever been anyone as talented as her. I can't tell if they're saying all of this in the hope that Jada has supersonic hearing abilities and can actually listen to them while she's talking to Steve and Celeste or they're so excited to be around her that these feelings are just spouting out of them uncontrollably.

I interviewed Jada Pinkett on a press line at a premiere—some big and blockbustery summer extravaganza that Will was in. She'd been sweet, which means that she seemed to notice I was a real person and not just a creature whose only skill and purpose was to press the PLAY and RECORD buttons on a tape recorder at the same time. But I'd already made the mistake of thinking that just because I'd interviewed a celebrity on her way into an event, that meant I knew anything about her or that she'd remember me. Once, after a particularly chummy Q&A session with Kate Hudson, I actually believed we might be friends—especially when, a week later, she came up to me shrieking, "There you are!" as I stood near the press table for the Global Water Event at the Egyptian Theatre. I threw my arms open, thrilled to receive the hug Kate was clearly about to give me—only to realize that she was really screaming at Naomi Watts, who was to my left.

So I opt not to contribute to the Jada conversation and glance around instead: Peter, a producer friend of Steve's, is standing with a female agent who's rumored to have thrown a desk—with some kind of Herculean strength she possesses whenever she loses her temper—at not just her current assistant, but also the two previous ones. I decide to drop my present—a pair of baby socks with stuffed ducks on the end that seemed adorable until I saw the reindeer and giant playhouse—into the pile of massive gifts while no one's looking. As I turn around, Brooke, an independent film producer with lots of nips and tucks—and the personality to match every single one of them—calls my name. I walk over to her and when her air kiss produces actual slobber on my cheek, I feel relieved that if anyone's dissecting those who can't manage cheek kissing, her name is sure to come up before mine.

She immediately launches into a story about an Australian actor she was seeing for a month who moved in and then left her for a yoga teacher. "He'd told me he wanted to get married," she sighs. "Granted, I knew it was only for the green card—but still, a yoga teacher? I mean, how is that supposed to make me feel?"

I'm not sure what to say. I could tell her that it seems like dating actors is a recipe for disaster best attempted only by other actors or masochists and that citizenship-craving foreigners probably don't make solid romantic partners, but since my dating life is about as exciting as that of Star Jones—pre–gastric bypass surgery—I doubt I could say anything that she doesn't already know. While I'm not unattractive—and if I lived in Des Moines or somewhere in Canada, I'd probably be considered hot—there are so many tall, body fat–less, perfect-looking female specimens arriving in Los Angeles every day by the boatload that to be just a brunette on the short side with neither enormous breasts nor long legs is to feel hopelessly plain. We all have different ways of coping with this harsh reality—Brooke's seemed to be to make her face and body into a shrine to the miracles of surgical procedures—and mine, I guess, is to try to be as realistic as possible.

"Are you seeing anyone?" Brooke suddenly asks.

"No," I answer, and of course, that's when I see Matt. And I not only feel my pulse speed up but also hear it pound in my ears and I'm annoyed because I'd known he was going to be here so there's no reason for my heart to be racing like I'm on the last leg of a sprint. I have no intention of speaking to him—in fact, I hope to make sure he doesn't even see me—so I silently tell my overly anxious nervous system to calm down. Taking a step toward Brooke so that a piece of shrubbery carved into the shape of Buddha is blocking his view of me, I smile at her. "Are you?" I ask.

Brooke looks at me strangely. "The Australian just moved out yesterday, remember?"

I nod. *Focus,* I tell myself, trying not to notice the confident waves and "Hey, man"s Matt is throwing around the party. "Right," I say.

There's a girl standing next to Matt and, despite my nearsightedness, I can make out perfect boobs (probably fake but expensive enough that they look real) and lots of shiny dark hair. Oh, God. I quickly dig through my purse, retrieve my prescription sunglasses, put them on, and immediately wish I hadn't when I realize that I'm looking at the dictionary definition of what you don't want on the arm of the guy you're obsessed with: a stunning Eurasian creature whose blue-and-white striped dress looks like it was custom-made to fold around every contour of her body and whose every hair and eyelash is so perfect that it seems impossible to believe she doesn't have a makeup and hair team nearby. As I put my glasses away, I notice Matt place his hand on the small of her back and feel a stab in my heart. Watching as he brushes his brown hair out of his eyes, I want to run over and do it for him, remind him how much he once liked me, and insist that he explain what changed and how he was able to exit my life so quickly. Instead, I act like Brooke has just said something incredibly funny and giggle loudly. I can't think of anything to say so I ask her, "A yoga teacher, huh?"

Brooke stares at me like I'm insane. But since nearly all of my brain cells are focused on keeping myself hidden from Matt and looking like I'm having the time of my life in case he does decide to glance over, I have too few left over to worry about Brooke. "Where did she teach?" I ask. "City Yoga?"

"City Yoga sucks," Brooke says and then launches into a diatribe about a teacher there who adjusted her ass inappropriately. Although I'd never admit it to her, the whole thing sounds like wishful thinking on her part. I'm just grateful that it gives me time to look occupied while my mind is somewhere else.

Not counting when I've hidden from him on press lines, this

is only the fourth time I've seen Matt since he broke up with me six months ago. The first time—at a *Variety* party Steve brought me to—he'd given me a cursory glance and the kind of greeting you might expect a movie star to give to a fan who had been arrested for stalking him, and I almost burst into tears on the spot. While of course I essentially *had* been stalking him—obsessively reading about the deals he made on industry Web sites and driving by his house on Blue Jay Way when I was feeling particularly infatuated—he didn't have any way of knowing about that and I was stunned at how easily he was able to look through me. Even worse, his indifference only seemed to fuel my preoccupation with him all the more. The second and third times I saw him, I ignored him as well.

Brooke is talking about how the girls in her yoga class are more interested in wearing the latest lululemon jog bra than in any kind of spiritual enlightenment as I wonder if I'm ever going to get over Matt. A successful agent, he'd swooped up to me at Steve's birthday party, drowning me in attention and compliments—making me feel, through his interest in me, like I was finally in on a well-kept secret that the brightest and shiniest people have known since the beginning of time. Our first two dates were movie perfect: comfortable, lively, curious conversations in elegant restaurants followed by knee-weakening kisses. The next week, he started taking me to events with him and introducing me around ever so casually—"You know Emma, right?"—and calling me a few times a day. The attention made me feel giddy, like the situation or event—the world itself—ha been created solely for me and a few other hand-selected luc people to enjoy. So I slept with him during our third wee dating and, shortly after, he zipped out of my life as quic he'd entered it—getting increasingly distant after about a eventually e-mailing me one morning and explaining though he thought I was a "great person," "work pressures" were making it impossible for him to be able to keep "hanging out." The message I'd left for him on his cell phone all but begging him to reconsider—suggesting that we simply slow things down and see each other less—had yet to be returned.

I'm aware of the fact that Brooke is talking, something about chakras being bullshit and mantras even worse and I realize I've somehow gotten her to transfer her hurt feelings about the Australian into anger at yoga and New Age crap in general. But the topic doesn't sustain her for long because she's suddenly jutting her head in Matt's direction and saying, "Hmmm—look who's here." I want to kill her, distract her, repeat the words "downward facing dog" over and over so that I can get her back to remembering her rage for the Aussie-stealing yoga teacher, but I know I don't have the guts to do anything more than nod. "Did you hear he's going to be made a partner?" she asks.

"Yep," I say. I'd discovered this news during my Matt Internet stalking.

"Isn't that amazing?"

"It sure is." I'd read once in a magazine that you were only supposed to be sad about a guy you dated for half the amount of time you were with him, but I'm well past that with Matt and my obsessive depression is showing no signs of abating. And while I'd acted cavalier at the *Variety* party by pretending to be as indifferent to him as he was to me, the avoidance seemed to leave bruises on the inside.

"Didn't you date him?" Brooke suddenly asks.

Although I'm pretty sure she's certain of the answer—I remember the exact two times that Matt and I ran into her when we were together—I also understand that she's only asking so I'll spill details. Gossip is Brooke's lifeblood and she needs a steady infusion of it to keep the collagen-filled lips, Restylane-injected forehead, and the rest of the machine running smoothly. "I did," I say, downing the rest of my glass of champagne.

"Me, too," she says, clicking my glass. "Winter of 2004."

"Really?" I ask, surprised, even though I shouldn't be. Although I hadn't realized it when I dated him, my Internet research on Matt had turned up indisputable evidence that the guy got around.

"Oh, yeah," Brooke answers with far more proprietary bravado than I'd like, her blond bangs glinting in the afternoon sun. "He did the full-on 'you're the woman I've been waiting for' trip on me—I even had lunch with his mother—and then the next thing I hear, he's at his company Christmas party shoving his tongue down the throat of some chick who had, like, one line on *Entourage*." She fills her glass with champagne from a bottle I notice she seems to have pilfered from the bar. "A Christmas party he'd told me was canceled because the agency was taking the money they would have spent on it to give to the homeless." She takes a sip and shakes her head. "I mean, who lies about homeless people?"

I don't say anything. Based on the fact that I'm practically crippled with jealousy over her story—he'd never asked *me* to meet his mom—I see that nothing good can come out of my mouth right now. I do, however, allow Brooke to pour me more champagne.

Then Rebecca comes over and tells us what an "inspiring" conversation she just had with Jada about owning her womanhood, and while Brooke grills her about it, I take my eyes off Matt and the girl and examine the party: a slew of men in forced and uncomfortable casual wear and their taller, long-haired wives ar girlfriends—all of whom are awash in labels and aglitter w diamonds. They're the same women I always see on Robe Boulevard, ducking into Surly Girl to get whatever bag th let du jour was photographed holding that week before strolling over to Alice + Olivia to buy armloads of the latest low-waisted pants. The couples seem to be visual representations of the fact that successful men in this town are only interested in committing to yes-women with zero aspirations—pretty empty shells who can oversee the nannies and cleaning ladies with Botoxed excellence and liberally use the black Amex to help make their lives look perfect. Gazing at all of the trainer-sculpted calves resting in Balenciaga pumps that are currently digging into Bart Jacobs's lawn, it occurs to me that the reason I've always judged these women so harshly is that I never actually thought I was alluring enough to join their ranks.

"I have to admit," Brooke says as she looks over at Matt and the girl, "it *is* satisfying to see that he's clearly run out of respectable women in this town and now has to resort to whores."

Rebecca laughs. "He probably still has her from yesterday and they pulled an all-nighter."

Brooke smiles. "Of course. I bet she thought she could drum up some new business here."

I look from one of them to the other. "What are you talking about?" I ask.

Brooke and Rebecca both glance at me with surprise, like they'd forgotten I was there. "Sorry," Brooke says. "You're right. I shouldn't call her a whore."

"Why not?" Rebecca asks. "That's what she is."

"Call *who* a whore?" I ask.

"She's *not* a whore," Brooke looks at me sharply. "She's . . . more like a yuppie prostitute. A temporary girlfriend."

"A *what*?" My eyes feel like they're about to pop out of their sockets.

Brooke shrugs. "Well, she's not a kept woman because she has more than one client, and she's not a hooker because she accepts gifts and not cash. She's like the date who hangs out for as long as you want her to, or the girlfriend who will go away at your word." She turns to Rebecca. "What's that called again?"

"A whore," Rebecca spits out.

"Come on," Brooke says, annoyed. "What's that other word for it?"

Rebecca sighs and says they might as well just call it what it is and Brooke tells her that's not the point and that she's trying to think of a specific word, while I point to Matt's date, still in shock. "Her?" I ask. "That girl? A yuppie prostitute? *Matt's* yuppie prostitute?" While she's inarguably the most attractive girl at the party, there's nothing about her, outwardly, that suggests she's any different from your average baby shower guest.

Rebecca puts a finger to her lips and shushes me as Brooke grabs my pointed finger. "Honey," Brooke says, "not for the entire party."

Brooke then asks Rebecca if she told her the story about how she saw Hugh Jackman walking up Runyon with his dog and Rebecca tells her she did but she wants to hear it again and I just stand there, trying to wrap my mind around the fact that the guy I'm obsessed with is walking around this baby shower with a girl who's supposedly being compensated for the experience.

Of course, I'm not completely naïve. I know that there's more to prostitution than what you see on Hollywood Boulevard. I still remember the size of the Yves Saint Laurent and Chanel packages the skinny girl in my freshman dorm at Skidmore received from her "benefactor," some New York businessman. The girl—who sat next to me a few times in art history class and always seemed to be doodling into her notebooks instead of writing down anything the professor said—hopped into a limo on Friday evenings and was delivered back to Saratoga Springs promptly every Sunday night. But I'd imagined this benefactor as some fat, oily, probably married freak—not a hot young guy who was about to be made a partner at his talent agency. "But . . . how?" I manage to utter.

Brooke gazes at me like I've just informed her that I can't remember my own name. "Look, how long have you lived here?"

"My whole life."

"Not the Palisades." She points at the ground. "*Here.* In town."

I think for a second. "A little over two years."

"Well, it's time you woke up then. These girls are everywhere. I mean, when you go to the gym or Starbucks in the middle of the day—Christ, when you drive down Santa Monica Boulevard at times when people should be in their offices—why are there always so many young girls everywhere? How are all those women with their Mercedes convertibles loaded with shopping bags paying their rent? Do you think they're all trust funders?"

"I guess I always just assumed they were actresses."

"All of them? Get real."

"But still, why would Matt . . . ?" My voice trails off.

Brooke glances at Rebecca. "Who knows?" she asks. "Maybe girls like that are better in bed."

Brooke returns to talking to Rebecca about the sweat that she saw running down Hugh Jackman's pecs as I regretfully consider my bedroom skills—particularly my blow job technique. "Technique" is probably too optimistic a word for it, really; every time I go down on a guy, I sort of alternate between feeling like a bulimic being gagged in order to upchuck and worrying that I'm not sucking my teeth in enough and am thus leaving bite marks the way Tanya Larkin was rumored to do in high school. "So who is she?" I ask.

"Jessica Morrison," Brooke says, lowering her voice, even though no one's standing near us. "Got to town a few years ago, determined to fuck her way into an acting career. But then, lo and behold, discovered that the casting couch really just left you with a velvet imprint on your ass. Besides, turned out she wasn't all that interested in actual auditions or having to be on sets and, you know, *work* all day. So she fucks for a living."

"But she takes gifts and not cash?" My voice sounds high, like I've just inhaled helium.

"Sometimes the guys take her shopping. Maybe they pay her rent—I heard she lives at the Royale—or make her car payments."

"Apparently, she's quite popular with our crowd: both Rob Silver and Cary Crayn have used her," Rebecca adds. She examines her fingernails. "She's always at the Starbucks on Santa Monica near Doheny."

Brooke nods. "Oh, yeah. I've seen her there for years."

I'm shocked. "You've known about this for *years*?"

"Well, sure," Brooke says, glancing over at Jessica distastefully. "But that doesn't mean I expected to be, like, socializing with her."

Rebecca shakes her head. "Matt should really know better than to bring someone like that to something like this."

Brooke suddenly snaps her fingers. "Wait! I just thought of the word: courtesan! That's what she is: a modern-day courtesan." She smiles. "A courtesan with contracts."

"Contracts?" I ask, helium voice still intact.

"Apparently," Brooke says, "she makes each client sign a contract stating exactly what he's giving her."

"Are you serious?" I ask. "How do you know all this?"

They both shrug. "It's like, how do you know that everyone wants to buy a house on one of the bird streets?" Rebecca says. "You just know."

"But did you hear it from a reliable source?"

Rebecca laughs. "You're always such a journalist."

I smile, only wishing this was true. "I collect quotes from celebrities on press lines."

"Oh, but you're not going to be doing that for long," Brooke says, touching my shoulder with something close to affection. I don't know if she's saying that because she wouldn't associate with someone who did my job for very long or because she actually believes it.

"I just don't get why those guys would need a girl like her," I say. "I mean, why would men who can get anyone they want pay for sex?"

Brooke sighs. "Oh, honey," she says. "They're not paying her for sex. They're paying her to *leave*."

chapter 2

I WATCH JACK MAKE his way over to our assigned spaces on the Race to Erase MS press line and decide not to mention that he's late. Given the fact that he and I have been relegated to the spots right next to the hotel entrance, a passive-aggressive hissy fit from him may already be brewing, and I have no interest in being the one responsible for pushing him over the edge. I still haven't fully recovered from the last time we were at the end of the line, when he muttered, "But I'm from *Entertainment Weekly*" about fifty times in this sort of astonished whisper, as if he couldn't believe the world hadn't parted to create a direct path for him to heaven because of his impressive credentials.

As soon as he reaches me, Jack points to a yellow lacy dress-encased butt about twenty feet away. Tilting his head ever so slightly, he asks, "Did she stop to talk to you?" I wish, briefly, for a time machine so that I could travel back to Jack's childhood and tell his mother to hold him more or do whatever might have stopped him from developing into this overly conscientious, ever-smiling rodent. I glance at the butt in discussion—or, more accurately, the butts standing around that butt chattering away—and determine that he's talking about Teri Hatcher.

One of Jack's favorite activities is to show up on press lines about ten minutes late, apparently so that he can torment me by pointing out who I'd failed to speak to before his arrival. And, true to his sixth sense, he'd managed to find someone that had zoomed past me—the whole *Desperate Housewives* cast had—in her race to erase MS, or zeal to look like she was, anyway. Jack never seemed to let such slights stop him—"Charlie!" I'd once seen him yell at Charlie Sheen, his gaze as unblinkingly positive as a Scientologist on a conversion mission, "You'll stop here now!" Publicists always instruct us to let the celebrities who don't want to be interviewed pass on by and not to bother them once they've stepped off the carpet, but Jack never let a simple thing like propriety stop him from suctioning his lips to a star's ass.

I gaze down the line and notice that the arrivals seem to have come to a standstill, save for one lone, unrecognizable woman making her way toward us. You never know if a respite like this means that the event is a wash or if most of the celebrities are simply waiting in their limos until the last possible moment so they don't look too eager or uncool. Glancing down at my barely used tape recorder, I realize that it better be the latter since I haven't gotten any quotes beyond some disingenuous claims from a few C-listers about how much this particular event meant to them. Maybe the tall, cheesy-looking woman walking down the line will say something outrageous or funny enough to make up for all that. The only problem, of course, is that I don't know who she is. She seems to scream reality star, but I have no idea if we've watched her kick Vicodin, vie for Tila Tequila's love, or not be declared America's Next Top Model. Jack, who seems to have been born with an extra chip in his brain that's devoted to retaining every possible fact about legitimate celebrities, has-beens, and never-weres alike, surely knows. But since it gives him entirely too much pleasure to know things I don't, I can't bring myself to ask him.

"She's from *Rock of Love*," he suddenly offers while squirting white cream from a BriteSmile tube onto his finger and rubbing it on his teeth. I resist a sudden, shocking urge to push his hand into his mouth so that he accidentally gags himself on tooth whitener.

Before *Substance* hired me as a freelance party reporter two years ago, I thought covering events sounded like one of the most glamorous and exciting activities a person could be lucky enough to participate in on her way to becoming a feature writer. The idea of only coming into the office once a month for staff meetings and spending my nights gallivanting around with the glitterati seemed almost unfathomably cool. I'd imagined filling articles with elegant prose composed of my witty exchanges with George Clooney at the Oscars and intense conversations with Angelina Jolie about the deep meaning behind every last one of her tattoos and children. I didn't know then that the fastest way to distance yourself from someone was to add a tape recorder and notepad to your person. And I hadn't realized that party reporting wasn't a stepping-stone to anything—besides more party reporting.

I watch the *Rock of Love* woman pretend not to care when the *Entertainment Tonight* host ignores her. It's hard not to feel bad for people like her: they get all dressed up and gamely answer questions, seemingly unaware of the fact that in a year or a month or a week, no one's going to remember their names or care about their opinions on anything. And they'll miserably pursue the limelight like rats gulping down sugar water because they remember how good it felt the first time.

"That's a great outfit," I say as she walks up to me. She looks genuinely thrilled—I'm surely the only person to compliment her all night—and when she tells me that she went shopping with her mom for it, I want to throw my arms around her and advise her to leave Hollywood now. Instead I ask her how she got ready for tonight's event and listen as she tells me that she just gave herself "a quick douche." While this is going on, I see that Jack has somehow lured Teri Hatcher back to the press line and seems to be engaged in a lively interview with her. The *Rock of Love* woman is laughing hysterically as she's telling me something I'm not listening to because I'm too busy wondering how Jack managed to pull this Teri Hatcher thing off.

I know it shouldn't matter to me that I'm horrible at a job I hate, but somehow seeing how giddy Jack is about the whole thing—all but watching "I made it" emanate from his every fake-baked pore—makes me think that not being able to get good quotes from celebrities on press lines is somehow indicative of major character flaws on my part. But then I remind myself that I only do this because it will lead to my being a feature writer. It's become something of a mantra for me, but two years into this job, with a slew of rejected or ignored feature ideas on my desktop, I have to start wondering how accurate the statement actually is.

Teri flits away before I can grab her, but by then Don Rickles has turned up so I instead listen to him say things I don't think are funny into my tape recorder. Surely Maureen Dowd never had to fake-laugh as Don Rickles joked about drunk Irish Catholics and sleepy Mexicans? When I'm done, I watch Jack take his turn with Don Rickles—which involves them doing some sort of secret handshake that Jack probably learned about on a Don Rickles fan site—and wonder what will become of me if the *Substance* editors continue to ignore or reject all my feature ideas. Will I evolve into a press line lifer, like the woman from the *San Fernando Sunshine* paper—who's about sixty-five, has chronic halitosis, and seems not to sense that her existence could have been more fulfilling than asking inane questions of people who see her as nothing more than a nuisance?

Sandwiched between other reporters who seem willing to sell not just their own soul but also anyone else's in order to get the best quotes, I usually pray for the earth to swallow me whole before someone I know walks in and sees me on this side of the velvet rope. The addition of Jack a few months ago—a former Florida gossip reporter new to Hollywood—seemed oddly inevitable, the rancid cherry on top of my melted sundae. Disturbingly, and for reasons still unclear to me, on every single press line since, Jack and I had found ourselves placed next to each other—like we were two perfect-for-each-other singles that everyone desperately hoped would end up together. Since Jack clearly hadn't contemplated the private parts of a woman since he'd emerged from his own mother's, this scenario seemed less than likely, so I had to guess that it was all just a terrible coincidence, or at least evidence that the universe really did hate me.

"Yo, kiddo, wassup?" I hear as Antonio envelopes me in a hug and drowns my olfactory senses in a cloud of Drakkar Noir. Antonio is either a real-life Mafioso taking a break from a life of crime to freelance for the *New York Post* or on a mission to seem like he is, and I've never managed to figure out which. He's also the only person I've met on these lines who doesn't seem to consider interviewing celebrities roughly as important as negotiating with terrorists in the middle of plane hijackings. While he's nothing like anyone I've ever known before—and if I were to, say, introduce him to my mother, she would surely be confused, concerned, and deeply in need of both a shower and a Valium—he's the closest thing I have to a friend in the whole event-covering world.

"You get anything juicy?" Antonio asks as Jack smiles thinly at him. I don't think it's fair to say that Jack dislikes Antonio, or vice versa; it's more that they're so far from each other on the spectrum of what human beings can be like that they barely comprehend each other. "Nothing," I tell Antonio. "You?"

Antonio shakes his head, sniffles, and wipes his nose. "Jack shit." I think about what a fine expression "jack shit" is and wonder if whoever came up with it knew the Jack standing next to me, or at least somehow predicted his existence. "Nobody's sayin' anything interesting. They're probably all beat up from the Chrysalis Ball last night. Or the thing at the Chateau. I hear that went until the wee hours." Antonio's talking a mile a minute and I know what that means.

Growing up in the Palisades meant attending a school where at least half the kids were on drugs. While I wasn't exactly in their crowd, I'd been to enough parties—where the parents were out of town and the mirrors on the tables—to understand when people were on cocaine. Even at Skidmore, where pot seemed to be the substance of choice, there was usually someone doing coke at the off-campus parties or local bars and they always acted the same: blathering nonstop out of mouths that seemed so dry I'd want to pour water into them myself, and sniffling or incessantly wiping their noses. The first time I'd seen Antonio displaying those telltale signs—last year, at the Celebrity Pet Awards in the Valley—I'd thought maybe I was imagining things, castigating him in my mind when perhaps he was just extremely dehydrated, chatty, and coming down with a cold. But when that became his standard mode of behavior—and he started constantly disappearing, saying he was "going to the bathroom" every ten minutes or so—I'd felt certain he'd picked up a legitimate coke problem. And for months now, I'd been trying to decide if I knew him well enough to say something to him about it.

"I'm gonna take off," Antonio is saying, looking at his watch. "You get anything good, you call me, you hear?"

"Sure thing." I smile weakly. Antonio had recently started leaving events before most of the celebrities arrived and, as a result, I'd gotten into the habit of e-mailing him whatever quotes I got and didn't need. While this was surely an infraction of about twenty journalistic rules, I figured that was okay since there was nothing remotely journalistic about what we were doing out here. Antonio gives me a mock salute and scoots off.

Jack waits about half a second to announce, "God, Teri was amaaaaaaazing," stretching the word as long as he can. I wonder if this even requires a response as it occurs to me that interviewing Teri Hatcher might have been dicey, anyway. For all that *Substance* is inarguably one of the best publications out there—regularly picking up National Magazine Awards, with a slew of contributing editors who are household names—we also don't shy away from mocking celebrities at every opportunity, which doesn't always sit so well with the ones who take themselves seriously.

And an oh-so-serious one, the French actress Maxine Benoit, is walking toward me now. I can't make out if the sneer currently on Maxine's face is personally directed toward me or the *Substance* sign at my feet but it makes me suddenly feel incredibly nervous. Still, I smile brightly and ask her how she prepared for tonight's event.

"How?" she asks, her brown eyes crinkling in disgust.

"Yes, how," I say, trying to smile the way Jack does—with blank, unmistakably phony enthusiasm.

"I do the Ralik's Sandor technique," she says, pulling her black wrap higher up on her tiny shoulder.

Plenty of times, when I get home from events and start transcribing my tapes, I realize that I don't have a clue what on earth the people I was interviewing were talking about because I was too embarrassed to explain at the time that I didn't have a clue what they were talking about. And tonight's turnout had been so sorry that a quote from Maxine Benoit might actually end up being relevant. I glance at Jack to make sure he's not paying attention and note that he's smiling as he gazes off into the distance, like a baby with gas. "I'm sorry," I say to Maxine. "What's the Ralik's Sandor technique?"

She glares and enunciates as much as a woman with an extremely strong French accent can. "I *said* I do the *Alexander* Technique."

I gaze at her blankly, running over the possibilities in my head. Is it a face mask? A deep-conditioning treatment? I order myself to stand up to her. "I'm sorry," I say. "What's the Alexander Technique?"

She blinks, looking as if she's trying to decide whether to shoot me with an AK-47 she's hiding in her dress or have some celebrity journalism bureau take my tape recorder away. "Do you have a dictionary?" she asks. I nod brightly, ready to explain that I even have an online dictionary on my phone. "Well then, go *look it up*," she snarls as she saunters away.

Embarrassingly, tears start stinging my eyes and one even drops down my cheek. God, why do I have to be such a wimp? I tell myself that she's a nasty French actress who probably has hairy pits and secret rolls of fat from too many croissants and I should in no way let her make me cry. Then I accept the fact that it's too late for that so I amend the statement and tell myself I should in no way let Jack see this horrible French actress make me cry. The tears dry instantaneously—every now and then, being overly concerned with what people think of me comes in handy. Then I imagine myself befriending some important French director who has the power to give Maxine Benoit a part she really wants and running into Maxine while the powerful French director friend and I are doubled over in hysterics over something I've just said. In my fantasy, I'm telling Maxine with a casual shrug that it's too bad she didn't get whatever role it was she was so desperate for and that she should maybe try comforting herself with the Alexander Technique, whatever the hell that was.

"It's something actors do—a body alignment thing," Jack says. He's now finished interviewing Maxine himself and we're waiting for more people to walk down the line.

I want him to go far, far away. "I'm sorry?" I say.

"The Alexander Technique."

I contemplate telling him that I knew that and just couldn't understand Maxine's indecipherable way of speaking—adding that if I was the one who'd moved to a new country, I'd probably be trying to tone down my native accent and make more of an effort to assimilate. Instead, I smile. "I should probably try it," I say. Noticing that the only people coming down the press line now are the gold case–opening girls from *Deal or No Deal*, I put my tape recorder in my bag.

"Leaving already?" Jack asks.

"Yep. How much longer are you staying?"

"Well, I'm going inside the event. Aren't you?"

Of course I'm not. When my boss, Lauren, gave me this assignment, she told me that no reporters were actually being allowed in. And although I know that I don't want to be there—that it will be filled with Maxine Benoit and many American versions of her, as well as a slew of celebrities acting like they're absolutely dedicated to finding a cure for MS and not just grateful for the photo op and a chance to look like do-gooders—I nonetheless develop exactly what Jack had been hoping I would: a massive inferiority complex.

"Nope," I say. I don't let myself ask him how he was able to finagle a ticket. "But have fun."

"I will." He smiles. "I hear there's a great gift bag, so I'll hopefully be able to make a solid chunk of change. Look out for it on eBay!" He gives me his BriteSmile smile and a thumbs-up.

chapter 3

I'M SCANNING THE AISLES of natural colas and corn syrup–free juices, cursing the fact that I decided to stop by Whole Foods instead of the regular market. "Where's your Diet Coke?" I ask the blond guy in the apron walking by.

He stops and cocks his head as he balances the gallons of water he's holding against his thighs. "First time in a Whole Foods?" he asks.

I examine him. While I don't tend to get deeply engaged with supermarket checkout types, his face—an ode to Aryan features and innocence—is undeniably cute. "Is it obvious?" I ask.

He smiles and I notice a gap between his two front teeth. "I can usually tell the ones who've just made the transition from Ralph's or wherever because they think the Fresh Grind peanut butter machine is an invention up there with the telephone. Or they're bitching because they can't find those hundred-calorie packs that, from the looks of them, they like to eat by the truckload." He smiles again and adds, "Or they're asking for bad things like Diet Coke."

"And what's so bad about Diet Coke?"

"Nothing, if you don't mind being loaded up with aspartame." He smiles. "Which, for the record, causes brain tumors in rats."

I look at the vein busting out of his arm and then at his face. "Meanwhile, who needs a peanut butter machine when you can just buy a jar?" I'm not sure if I'm genuinely curious or if I simply want to keep talking to him.

He laughs, but it's really more of a guffaw than anything. I'd only heard the word "guffaw," as a matter of fact, but hadn't actually known what one sounded like until this exact moment. "Are you sure you live in L.A.?" he asks.

"I know, I know," I say. "I'm the least healthy person in town, I think." It's not an unfamiliar topic to me; every time someone offers me a wheatgrass shot and my stomach turns over at the very thought, I realize how out-of-place my eating habits are for my environment. Glancing at the organic grapefruit juice, I add, "I really blame my parents. When I was little, our house was filled with junk food: Lucky Charms and Cocoa Puffs, Lays potato chips and Milano cookies. Then, one summer when I was at camp, my mom read this diet book written by some sadist named Dr. Pritikin and I came home to meals of like, lentils, whole wheat pasta, and branches." He laughs and I wonder what I'm doing confiding my junk food history to a guy who works at Whole Foods. Yet I find myself continuing, "If they'd put me on the lentils and branches plan from the get-go, it would have been all right. But my formative years were defined by frozen pizzas and KFC."

The guy looks bemused. "Wow, they really tortured you," he says.

I start walking toward the deli section and he follows me. "It's true." I watch his arm muscles bulge as he carries the water. "It was like Guantanamo Bay, but with TV viewing privileges."

"Guantanamo Bay, huh?" he says, raising an eyebrow. He puts the water down as we reach the end of the deli line. "An unusual reference for an actress."

I laugh. "Why does everyone in L.A. always assume that if you're relatively young, female, and not physically deformed in some way, you must be an actress?"

He folds his arms across his chest and gazes at me. "Come on. You're in Hollywood. You're in Whole Foods—albeit for the first time. And you're beautiful. After working here for almost a year, I can tell you those are some mighty convincing statistics."

I look down at my cart, unsure of what to say. Because I have a little sister who's always been breathtakingly gorgeous and I'm the girl who's always sort of but not quite looked like Lilly, I tend to be completely thrown whenever someone compliments my appearance. "Thank you," I manage, wondering if the red-haired girl in spandex in front of me in the deli line is listening to our conversation.

"Hey, you're blushing," he says.

"Really?" Now I actually feel my face darken. I once heard that since blushing is the one thing people can't fake, the way to test a woman's virtue in the eighteenth century was to see if she blushed if anything inappropriate was said. And where I come from, flirting with someone like him is most definitely inappropriate, though I don't know how virtuous that makes me.

The fact is, it's been ingrained in my head from the time I was a fetus that the only men I should socialize with are ones who have MBAs, law degrees, houses with four-car garages, secretaries, and investment portfolios. Tomato-weighers, as Lilly called supermarket employees, were people who told you where the oatmeal was. "Well, thanks for the aspartame warning," I say lamely, wondering why a Whole Foods manager isn't coming over and telling this guy—who I suddenly notice is wearing Birkenstocks with socks—to get back to work.

"Excuse me, where can I find the tofu?" I hear someone ask and I realize with surprise that it's Ethan Harrington, a *Substance* senior editor from the L.A. bureau who either doesn't see me or just doesn't think I'm worth acknowledging.

As my Whole Foods friend tells him to go to aisle seven, I suddenly find myself saying, "Hey, Ethan. How are you? I'm Emma, a *Substance* freelance party reporter." He looks immediately embarrassed so I decide not to tell him that I've seen him at events I've covered over the past few years or remind him of the fact that we actually had a conversation once in the office kitchen about how a liberal arts education essentially qualified you to do nothing.

"Oh, right," he says. "How are you?" Before I answer, he adds, "Well, good to see you. I should . . ." He motions to his cart and starts to wheel it away.

I don't know if it's because being called beautiful has given me extra confidence or I've simply realized I can't survive many more interactions with Jack, but my hand suddenly finds its way to his cart. "I've actually pitched you some ideas," I say as he turns around. "A piece on the failure of the MTA system in L.A. And another one on the hypocrisy of the celebrities who go to charity events but never donate any money. Also one on the people who get handicapped signs under false pretenses so they can park wherever they want." I opt not to mention the three other ideas I've sent him over the past couple of years, or bring up the fact that I'd peppered the magazine's other two senior editors with similar e-mails.

To my delight, he looks intrigued. "That handicapped one sounds interesting."

I glance at my Birkenstock-and-sock-wearing friend, who's now busying himself arranging breakfast burritos. "Did you know that all you need to get one of those handicapped placards is a signature from a doctor on some one-page form?" I ask.

"Really?" Ethan appears surprised.

"Really. Apparently people have their acupuncturists and plastic surgeons sign them."

He seems to mull this over. "The dishonesty of the overentitled in a city built on overentitled dishonesty," he says. "I like that." Then he adds, "I have to admit, it doesn't ring a bell. Might have gone to my spam folder. You want to resend it?"

"There's really no point," I say. "Last week, the *L.A. Times* did the story."

"Did they?" He looks at me and, for the first time, I actually feel him take me in. "Look, your ideas—even the handicapped one—are a little tame," he says. "Our readers tend to thrive on the salacious and surprising. But you're on the right track, so when you come up with something with a bit more bite, e-mail me. Then call to follow up. Let's not let the next one slip through the cracks."

"Great," I say, thrilled. "I will. Thank you."

"No problem. Sorry for not recognizing you."

"Don't worry about it." As he starts walking away, I suddenly notice that within a five-foot radius, there are at least three drop-dead gorgeous women: in addition to the spandexed redhead in front of me in line, there's a beautiful blonde wearing only a sarong and bikini top examining a jar of barbecue sauce and an Amazonian brunette at the salad bar on my left. It's eleven thirty on a Wednesday and none of them are wearing wedding or engagement rings, nor do they seem like they're running from the office to grab a quick snack. I consider what Brooke had said about how so many of the women in town are getting by and suddenly realize that the piece with a bit more bite is standing right in front of me—in fact, it's all around me. "Actually, I think I already have another idea for you."

He looks back. "You think you have it or you have it?"

I think of Jessica and her supposed contracts, the Skidmore girl and her benefactor, and the three women standing here—one of whom is now wandering away, her perfect ass making the sarong sashay in a way the designer had probably only dreamed it could. I know that telling Ethan I want to write about modern-day prostitution because the girls doing it are everywhere is useless until I find out more information and figure out an angle. But I also see that this is the story I need to pitch. "The germ of an idea."

"Well, consider me a bit of a germophobe," he says and then winces at his pun. "By which I mean develop it some more and then get in touch with me." He smiles and starts moving down the aisle.

"Okay," I say to his retreating back. Excitement prickles my spine as I turn around.

"So you *are* an actress," I hear.

While I should have no interest in continuing to flirt with this Whole Foods guy—I mean, really, I should be offended and annoyed that a stranger is standing here eavesdropping on the biggest career opportunity I've ever had—something about him intrigues me. "What's that supposed to mean?"

" 'Oh please, Mr. Editor guy,' " he says in falsetto, " 'take a chance on me. You know you won't regret it.' "

I laugh, not sure whether I'm more amazed that he has the balls to give me a hard time or that I'm letting him. The whole thing reminds me of Matt—how he would mock the way I sounded when I was nervous. Even though I used to be embarrassed that he could sense my anxiety, it always felt flattering and vaguely intimate—like it was evidence that we were close. "Look," I say, "if you're going to be making fun of me, don't you think it's only fair that I know your name?" I hold out my hand. "I'm Emma."

"I picked that up," he responds, shaking it. "Danny."

He doesn't let go and I feel immediately uncomfortable. "Well, I better go," I say, grabbing my hand back. I can only imagine how much I'm blushing now.

"Okay." He folds his arms again as he continues to look at me. "Come back and see us real soon." He smiles. "Ideally, before the brain tumor diagnosis."

chapter 4

Classical music blares from the speakers of Mom's SUV at such high decibels that it seems amazing she hasn't blown her eardrums out entirely. "Hi, honey," she says as I open the car door and get in.

"Can I turn it down?" I ask, hand on the volume, as she pulls into traffic.

"Of course," she says. "I always forget that you don't like Mahler."

I sigh. I've never liked Mahler or Beethoven or Mozart or any of the composers, German or otherwise, that she and Lilly adore, although I'm not sure if the classical music appreciation gene was left out of my system when I was born or if it's a learned dislike because of how passionate my mom and sister are about it. Mom's response to my aversion is to simply pretend it doesn't exist, which means that she's either surprised or feigns surprise when I don't want to subject myself to levels of her music loud enough to rouse the dead.

"I'm so glad you could come with me, honey," she says once we pull up at a home décor store on La Brea. "We don't see nearly enough of you."

I open the car door, shake off the fur from Mom's golden retriever that has attached itself to my pants and shirt, and try to fight the guilt that always seems intent on weighing me down whenever Mom makes one of her "we don't see nearly enough of you" comments. She and Dad live half an hour away—fifteen minutes when there's no traffic—in the house I grew up in and the fact that I only make it over there once a month for family dinners eats me alive with shame. My little sister, Lilly—home from Harvard for the summer—is the polar opposite. She lives to spend every minute she possibly can at the house with Mom—handing her a trowel when she's gardening, whipping up amazing desserts by her side in the kitchen—whereas simply accompanying Mom to get tiles for the bathroom she's remodeling is currently threatening to send me into a miasma of misery.

"So, have you met anyone special lately?" Mom asks as we walk into the store.

I sigh and wonder if Mom really thinks it's possible that I've met a guy in the three days since she last asked me the same question, or if she only queries me in this way to drive me slowly insane. "Nope."

Miraculously, my one-word response seems to be enough to satisfy her. "So how's Claire?" She picks up a teacup and examines it.

This topic isn't actually much of an improvement. "Fine," I say in a tone that probably makes my "Nope" sound welcoming. I'm really not sure what's gotten into Claire—or, even scarier, me. We'd been best friends since we met in third grade, but as soon as she met and married her Financial and Managerial Accounting T.A. from USC and transformed herself into his full-time yes-woman, she and I had less and less to say to each other. We used to get together every week and then every month, but right now we're just down to phone conversations that seem to frustrate and annoy both of us and occasional get-togethers to watch TiVo'd episodes of *The Real World*.

Maybe people and relationships are just in a constant state of change, I think as I watch Mom point to a red-and-green-colored tile and clearly charm the saleswoman—a put-together blonde with a short bob. Mom and I used to be close. But the more Lilly becomes the fulfiller of all parental expectations, the further away Mom felt.

"What do you think, Em?" Mom asks, her copper hair shiny, her brown eyes alert. She's holding up the tile from a few feet away while the saleswoman grins at me as if to say, *Aren't you lucky to have such a chic and charming woman for a mother?*

"It's pretty," I respond, but my voice is small and my tone disingenuous. The fact is, I've never been terribly interested in decorating, primarily because I don't have the money to spend on tiles—not to mention brand-new couches and tables. Even though, technically speaking, I was spoiled rotten as a kid, extravagant gifts were always followed by lectures from Dad on how I better take good care of whatever it was because of how much it cost—until I felt horrible for having motivated him to purchase it in the first place. And while I was surprised when he suddenly explained after I graduated from college that the "parental piggy bank has closed," I had to admit that it was something of a relief. Scraping by on the thirty thousand dollars a year *Substance* gives me isn't easy—and my credit card bills are fairly high—but it's preferable by far to the torment my parents' generosity often caused. Since none of this is ever discussed and Mom seems to live in a world where everyone can drop thousands of dollars on tiles, I act like this is true for me as well.

"Oh, I'm so glad you like it!" she shrieks, nodding at the saleswoman, who seems to be glancing at me in confusion, as if she's trying to make sense of my lack of enthusiasm over this exciting tile purchase. Mom looks at her. "I'll take fifty of them!" She turns to me brightly. "Emma, we're going to line the back bathroom walls with them . . . won't that look exquisite? Like it's a room from a Spanish castle?" I nod and smile, trying to shake off my mood as I walk outside. Someone once told me that if you keep forcing yourself to smile, eventually your brain chemistry will change and you'll actually start feeling happy, but right now this seems highly unlikely.

Mom comes out a minute later, high from her purchase, seemingly oblivious to how far away I feel from her. "Ready?" she asks, giddy, perhaps envisioning long, satisfying shits in her Spanish castle-esque bathroom as Beethoven plays. I have a brief fantasy that the two chubby-for-L.A. women—probably tourists—walking toward us suddenly recognize me as a major writer and ask for my autograph before telling my mom how proud she should be of my many accomplishments. Instead, one of them sneezes—essentially on me—as they move past and the other yells, "Gesundheit!" seemingly at the top of her lungs.

Mom unlocks the car and I slide into the passenger seat. "Guess what?" I say as she starts the ignition. "I'm going to write a story for *Substance* about a new kind of kept woman." I realize that this is a borderline delusional way to summarize my Whole Foods encounter with Ethan Harrington. And I hadn't made any progress on my idea beyond calling Steve to plug him for information about Jessica and learning that he was shocked as hell to hear that there had been a hooker at his baby shower. But I want to tell Mom something that will make her believe in me, or at least believe that I haven't been wasting the past few years blistering my feet on press lines.

"Really?" she says, sounding distracted. Mom is a painter who's never sold any of her work—she claims that commerce would sully her art—and she seems to buy into Dad's belief that anyone who wants to make money needs to go into law, like him, or some other soul-depleting pursuit. The sense I get is that Mom and Dad are simply waiting for me to wake up to the fact that writing makes a far better hobby than career, in much the same way they silently tolerated my high school passion for the Grateful Dead.

"They don't take money—just gifts," I say. "But they have lots of different clients."

"That sounds interesting." Her tone is one that an adult might use with a four-year-old who'd announced that Play-Doh was actually paste. I know she couldn't possibly be listening because there's no way she'd allow the topic to simply float in the atmosphere without comment.

"But they're still, essentially, hookers," I say, finally getting the reaction I want when her head swivels over to me sharply.

"Excuse me?" Her eyes blink rapidly.

I notice that we're on the verge of colliding with a lesbian couple crossing the street holding hands. "Mom, the road!" I yell.

She looks back ahead and swerves, narrowly missing the lesbians, who are both giving us the finger. "They're more like yuppie prostitutes," I continue. "They have a lot of clients but rather than charging money, the men pay their rent or buy them clothes or something. It's an arrangement." Watching her take this information in, I suddenly feel horrible. Mom means well and it's pathetic that, at twenty-nine, I'm trying to make her uncomfortable simply because she's not giving me the validation I want.

We're silent until she pulls up in front of my apartment, where she gives me the smile that never fails to win over salespeople and waiters. The conversation about the new kind of kept women has long since been forgotten. "I'm so glad we could do this, darling," she says. "I miss you when I go so long without seeing you." I force a smile. "We worry so much about you."

I suddenly see my life as she must: single with nary a prospect on the horizon, barely able to pay my bills, trying to coax quotes out of third-rate celebrities, talking about articles that are probably never going to come to fruition. I decide right then that I'm going to make this prostitution story happen no matter what, even if it means parking myself at the Starbucks where Jessica is rumored to hang out until she shows up. Mom smiles brightly. "Our offer to pay for law school still stands."

I open the door. "Thanks, Mom," I say. "I'll keep that in mind."

"Please come home more." She cranes her neck so that she can still look at me as I step away from the car. "We don't see nearly enough of you."

"DECAF GRANDE LATTE, please," I say, feeling, as ever, secretly thrilled by the fact that I'm able to master Starbucksian language. It's the same sensation I get sometimes when I send text messages—like I'm some product of the twenty-first century and have mastered all of the requisite survival skills. The barista—who seems to have black earrings the size of pennies drilled into his ears—nods.

As I wait for my drink, I tell myself that even though it may not feel like it, what I'm doing right now is going to lead me to Jessica—and my story. In the early seventies, Gail Sheehy dressed up like a hooker and went out on the streets to research a piece on prostitution for *New York* magazine. While I'm not sure I could pull that kind of thing off, I somehow feel that I'm on the road to finding out.

Three decaf grande lattes later, I've made my way through most of a *New Yorker* article, have just put in an order for a fourth drink, and am beginning to doubt the wisdom of this plan. As I stand at the counter waiting for my drink, I'm eavesdropping on a guy and girl sitting at a nearby table; the girl is claiming she's never cheated on a boyfriend and the guy is reminding her she actually cheated on her boyfriend with him. I'm just deciding that I'm wasting my time here when suddenly, miraculously it seems, Jessica breezes in. After quickly reviewing the various approaches I'd been considering, I decide to abandon them all. I walk over to her.

"Hey, I'm Emma," I say, holding out my hand, as she finishes ordering her venti drip. "We met—or actually, we didn't meet but I saw you—at Steve and Celeste's baby shower."

Jessica crinkles her perfect little nose. "Right," she says. She examines me, the look on her face impossible to decipher. "I'm Jessica, how are you?"

"Good," I answer. Then I blurt out, "The truth is, I dated Matt and . . . I realize this must sound really weird, but I just wanted to know if you're seeing him now." I can't believe this is what I opted to say. But maybe it's okay—I want to establish a bond with her. Even a bond that makes me sound pitiable is, I figure, better than no bond at all. She'll probably tell me to leave the poor guy alone.

Instead, she laughs. "Seeing him?" she asks. "Um, that would be a no."

I smile. Her cavalier attitude about Matt unleashes something in me and I shock myself by saying, "He's kind of a prick, isn't he?" Although it's true, I'm surprised to hear these words come out of my mouth.

Jessica laughs again. "Yes," she says. "Kind of a prick is right. About one-third the size of a normal one, I'd say. What do you think?"

Now I laugh. I've never quite understood how to measure penis size—by which I mean that the ones I've seen have pretty much all seemed the same. I nonetheless feel myself relax at Jessica's comment, as if part of the wall of hurt I feel over Matt rejecting me just crumbled to the ground. I gaze at this woman who seems so indifferent to the guy I've been so obsessed with. "Maybe one-sixth," I say, imitating what I think a world-weary, cavalier girl would say in a situation like this.

Jessica smiles but motions her head toward the penny-sized-earring guy, who I suddenly notice is shrieking "Decaf grande latte" at the top of his lungs. I grab my drink from the counter and turn to her to keep talking but in the roughly five seconds that have passed, she's managed to escape. I see her out on Santa Monica, clicking open a convertible BMW before getting into it. I consider chasing after her like Jack on the tail of a celebrity but then I realize that there may actually be an easier way.

chapter 5

EMMA, BABY!" Antonio yelps as he swoops up to me outside a Laemmle 5 movie premiere, taking his space between me and the sixty-five-year-old woman from the *San Fernando Sunshine*. "Where's Jack?"

I shrug. "Either *Entertainment Weekly* didn't think this event was worth covering or someone from above just felt like cutting me a break tonight."

"Ahhhhhh!" he brays more than laughs as we watch someone from *Access Hollywood* interview Scarlett Johansson about fifty feet away. "You're something else, kid. Always have been."

"Actually, I have a question for you." I pause. "You know how you once told me you have friends in low places?" Antonio said this quite often, although I'd never been entirely sure what it meant—or certain I'd want to find out.

Antonio smiles. "Sure."

"Well, I want to do a story about prostitution in Hollywood—

but more about the girls who are sort of somewhere between hookers and kept women than actual prostitutes. Do you know what I mean?"

"Do I know what you mean?" Antonio looks unmistakably proud. "Are you kidding?" *San Fernando Sunshine*'s head swivels around and she beams at him; she's probably stone-cold deaf. He leans in closer to me. "Something new had to come along, right? The fucking governor of New York's getting busted, madams are publishing their little black books—the whole fucking business is getting messy as hell and the big league guys can't afford to get bogged down in some bullshit scandal." He pauses. "Am I right?"

Smiling, I wonder why it didn't occur to me to call Antonio from the get-go. "You're right."

"But these guys still gotta get their rocks off somehow, don't they? And their standards are getting higher. They don't want slutty-looking chicks whose brains are fried from drugs. They want sophisticated girls, smart-seeming girls, girls who can handle themselves just as well at an Ago business dinner as they can in the sack. It's like what they had in the sixteenth century, those court ladies or whatever?"

"Courtesans?" I ask. *Thank you, Brooke.*

"Yeah, exactly," Antonio says. "So it's an even trade: she'll go with the guy for as long as he wants her and in return, he'll help her 'maintain her lifestyle.' There's much less of a paper trail this way. Wives don't get suspicious of department store purchases or condo payments if they're snooping around the bills because most of these guys are major players, they put everything from presents for clients to rentals for actors they gotta fly in for shoots on their cards."

"Why would married guys be taking the girls to business dinners at Ago?" I ask.

"Who the fuck knows?" Antonio says. "Maybe the married

ones just keep 'em holed up at the Four Seasons. Or they bring one along and introduce her as a fucking assistant. These guys can get away with shit like that."

I nod as Scarlett Johansson makes her way down the line, followed by one of Robert Wagner's daughters—Courtney or Katie or something. Then I say, "I'm especially interested in finding this girl named Jessica. She—"

"Jessica Morrison? She's one of the very best."

I smile at him: somehow I'd felt sure he'd know her. "She's certainly beautiful."

"Smart as hell, too. But a little scary. You don't play this game as well as she does without being, on some level, a cold-hearted bitch—the thinks-her-shit-don't-stink type. A lot of the other girls are nice—real nice, the kind I'd have taken home to my mom, God rest her soul, you know?"

I nod and take a deep breath. "I want to meet them."

Antonio looks me in the eye. "Meaning?"

"I told you, I want to do a story."

He sighs. "Baby, I don't know. These gals don't look too kindly on reporter types." He sniffles loudly. "Did you see that piece in the *New York Times* a few months ago?" I nod; there had been an article about how prostitution was thriving in Hollywood. The story contained a bunch of anonymous quotes from girls who were sleeping with men for money but didn't say anything that wasn't fairly obvious—even to me. "Well," Antonio continues, "when that fucking cunt writer started poking around, asking them all this crap, it made 'em paranoid."

An idea starts forming in my head. "Then don't say I'm a reporter—just that I'm looking to get into their world. I'll tell them the truth later."

Antonio considers this. "I don't know, baby. I don't wanna be the guy who throws them under the bus."

"But you wouldn't be—all you'd be doing is making an introduction."

"That's true." He rubs his nose. "The guy who throws events where all the girls in town meet their clients is having his annual house party this weekend—Jessica'll be there, all of 'em will. I guess I could introduce you around."

My heart starts racing. "That would be great."

Antonio grins. "What the fuck, I like to live on the edge." He shrugs. "You get to know 'em, then you figure out how you wanna handle the fact that you're gonna write about them. 'Cause I'll be out of the picture by then, acting as surprised as they are that you, too, turned out to be a lying cunt—no offense." *San Fernando Sunshine* turns around and gives each of us a dirty look; clearly her hearing isn't entirely gone.

"That would be amazing."

"Baby, you save my ass every week. You think Antonio's not going to do you a solid?"

I smile. I'd forgotten how much Antonio liked to talk about himself in the third person. As Scarlett Johansson walks up to us, I answer, "Consider Emma most grateful."

SITTING ON MY BED with my laptop in front of me, I notice that my apartment looks like it's been pillaged. There are so many articles lining the floors that I can barely see the hardwood anymore, and half-finished bottles of Arrowhead line everything that can be conceived of as a ledge.

Picking up a story about kept women written by a woman who claimed to have had millions of dollars spent on her by various wealthy men and the most glamorous and fulfilling life she could have ever dreamed of, and then another piece about high-class prostitution in Hollywood, I try to figure out how to summarize where those two worlds meet.

I type the sentence, "These women are among the most powerful people in town." Then I delete it, lean back into my pillows, and think. Women who are paid—or compensated—for sex couldn't possibly be powerful. Once a woman has sex—even under normal circumstances—she actually loses whatever control she had up until that point. As my college roommate used to say, "Men can't see straight until they have sex, and women can't see straight after." It sounded antiquated and old-fashioned, but since I'd been living in Hollywood, it had always been the case for me: whenever I'd first start dating someone, he'd be dutiful, almost submissive, and endlessly interested in everything I had to say. But once I slept with him—whether it was after three dates or three months—I'd feel his interest start to wane and the power shift. Yet maybe that was only true for women who wanted some sort of emotional commitment from the men they slept with—those who hoped the men would want to date or even marry them. Girls selling sex wouldn't have such ulterior motives because what they were getting had already been negotiated upfront.

But how different, really, are these girls from the rest of us? Aren't all women, on some level, guilty of using their sexuality to get their needs met? We don't tend to think about it—in the same way that we don't say something smart in a job interview and then stop and consider the fact that we're using our intelligence to help our careers, our sexuality is just one of the tools in our arsenal. Clearly the stakes were higher when, say, a girl slept with a guy in exchange for having her rent paid than when she flirted to get free coffee, but isn't the decision to use what you have to get something you want the same?

Standing up and stretching, I remember reading the work of a 1930s feminist named Emma Goldman in a Skidmore women's studies class who said it was inevitable that all women would sell themselves, and it was only a question of whether they were bought by one man or many. And she had a point: from Jackie Onassis, who'd managed to snag both a president *and* a shipping magnate, to Hollywood trophy wives, there certainly were a lot of examples of women who seemed like they'd been bought by the highest bidder.

Maybe self-supporting women frown on those who sell sex in such a direct way because it's easier to simply label the whole concept as sinful rather than admit that on some level they did—or wanted to do—the same. Was the reason Rebecca and Brooke castigated Jessica that they wished they didn't feel such a need to prove themselves in the boys' world of deal-making—that they, too, wished they could end up with just a velvet imprint on the ass?

I write and write and write, describing how I want to bring this new kind of prostitute's life alive for the reader by pretending to be one myself. Looking up from my computer hours later—once I've emailed the completed pitch to Ethan—I realize that this is the first time I've been excited about work since I entered the working world.

chapter 6

CLAIRE REACHES PAST ME for the TiVo remote. "We need to see that again," she says. I nod as she rewinds the action so that we can witness two drunken *Real World*-ers get tossed in the back of a cop car one more time.

Obsessively watching *The Real World* has been a tradition for Claire and me since the show first came on the air and we do it with more zeal than a group of jocks in a sports bar cheering on the Super Bowl. Seeing the outrageously self-destructive people they cast—and predicting when and how each of their respective breakdowns will occur—is more than merely a spectator sport for us. I think it makes both of us feel better about our comparatively boring lives. And right now, with two months' worth of episodes to catch up on and a bowl of kettle corn between us, everything between us is—for the first time in a while—tension-free. If we keep our conversation limited solely to thoughts about *The Real World*, it actually seems possible that this state of affairs may even continue—at least for today.

"One more time?" I ask Claire after we've rewatched it.

"Of course." She grins, rewinds again, and then looks up suddenly. "Oh, hi, honey," she says, with a little start. Seemingly from out of nowhere, her husband Eric has appeared.

"Hello." He's standing in the doorway, looking surly as he runs his hand over his balding head. "Hi, Emma," he adds.

"Hi, Eric," I respond. We smile at each other, warily.

"Come sit down, sweetie," Claire says, patting the space next to her and pressing play on the TiVo remote. Eric rolls his eyes as if she's asking more of him than he can possibly bear but then, with a martyr-like sigh, takes a seat. This is a sort of game they play—she asks him to do something minor and he acts like it's a big deal—but the more I observe them acting this scenario out, the more I believe that it isn't so much a game as it is Eric simply expressing how he feels.

There's nothing actually wrong with Eric—if you don't mind a guy who considers a day at the golf course nirvana and whose idea of being nice is leaving an 11 percent tip. He's good to Claire—meaning he supports her and doesn't seem to be a cheater. I'm sure there are many women who believe this makes someone an ideal mate. I just find it difficult to believe that Claire is one of them.

To be fair, by the time Claire met Eric, she and I had already begun growing apart. When we were little, we'd plotted to live next door to each other on the same street we grew up on. But at some point when I was at college, this began to sound like one of the most depressing plans I could possibly imagine, and it was obvious that she saw my decision to find a place in Hollywood and work for *Substance*—and not, say, move back to the Palisades and forgo a career the way she had—as a sort of betrayal.

In the past few years, I'd started to realize that the world was essentially divided into those who believed you got married and then figured out how to do life and those who tried to figure it all out before attaching themselves to another person. Amazingly, all of my high school friends had turned out to be members of the first group, and when I saw how undeniably giddy they got over things like wedding dresses and honeymooning in Hawaii, I'd had to accept the fact that I was part of the second. "It's one day of your life!" I'd wanted to jump up and shout during a brunch in which three of the four girls present waxed rhapsodic over the joys of writing their own vows. The faith they had in the notion that they'd feel the same way about someone in a year—let alone twenty or fifty—was impressive, daunting, and deeply intimidating to me. But I couldn't help but notice that they all seemed to lose parts of themselves along the way.

"Christ, where do they find these people?" Eric asks, pointing to the TV, where three of the roommates—two girls and a guy—make out in a hot tub.

"I don't know." Claire suddenly sounds as disapproving as a PTA mom at a rave. She reaches out to grab Eric's hand. "They're ridiculous."

I want to remind Claire of the multitude of conversations we've had about the fact that our devotion to and obsession with this show is based on the fact that the people on it are *always* ridiculous and doing things we never would. But there's really no point. The fact is, Claire's personality does a complete one-eighty when her husband is around—the funny, opinionated girl who can laugh at outrageousness is replaced by a subservient, judgmental shrew who wouldn't dream of liking something as silly as *The Real World* or screaming and tossing kettle corn at the screen, the way she did five minutes before Eric walked in, when four of the roommates took a shower together. For a second, I want to ask her why Claire doesn't just act like who she really is in front of her husband. Then I start to wonder if maybe Claire's personality around Eric *is* who she really is and the one around me is false and that's when I get so thoroughly overwhelmed that all I can do is just sit back and hold my tongue by shoving kettle corn into my mouth.

Eric shakes his head as he watches and I have a sudden urge to be anywhere but here. Watching the cautious smile on Claire's face and the contemptuous way Eric is sitting with his arms crossed, I wonder if I'm witnessing the American dream—the enormous plasma screen, the husband who's paid for it. Is this what I should be hoping for instead of what I have?

The thought brings on an almost paralyzing sadness. I'm not happy with my life the way it is yet nothing about what's on display in front of me—the house and the mortgage, the closely controlled disapproval—looks appealing, either. But I'm trying to change my life, I remind myself. It occurs to me suddenly that maybe, just maybe, Ethan has responded to my pitch by now. While my phone wasn't showing any new e-mails, there's always the possibility that he called my home number. Hanging onto this distant hope, I stand up and announce that I have to make a call. Claire nods distractedly. I walk to their front door, sit down on the porch outside, and dial my voicemail, praying that Ethan's voice is waiting on the other end. Instead the computerized voice—which always manages to sound so cold when it has no news—informs me that I don't have any messages. I walk back into their living room and see Eric shaking his head at the TV. "Oh, Jesus," he says as another roommate jumps into the hot tub. "I can't take this another minute. Can we please watch something else?"

There's a pause, where I silently urge Claire to stand up to her husband and explain that she and I like *The Real World* no matter how ludicrous it is, adding that he wasn't even supposed to be here right now and that there's a perfectly good television in their upstairs bedroom that he can go watch if he's so disgusted by what's currently on the screen. Instead she says, "Yes—absolutely," and shoots me a look that seems to say, *Don't you dare cause any trouble right now.*

chapter 7

"THIS WAY," ANTONIO SAYS, leading me across a cavernous lawn in front of a four-story ultramodern house. We're passing a Zen garden where a couple is passionately making out—all but dry humping, ruining the lines that had probably been so carefully drawn in the sand by a gardener.

"Hey, Antonio!" The Zen garden girl, who's now kneeling in front of the guy, looks up and waves.

"Heya, baby," he responds, shaking his head with a smile. "Come on," he says as he grabs my arm and pulls me past a sauna and Jacuzzi filled with a slew of naked, smiling bodies.

The fact that I'm as Zen as the garden we just passed, considering the insanity on display, is actually quite surprising. Equally shocking is what I'm wearing—a tight dress I'd bought when I was in a risqué mood and never put on with knee-high boots I'd only worn before under jeans. I hadn't wanted to stand out as the lone conservative in this Dionysian paradise but with every glance I received, I felt more and more like I was running an ad campaign for myself.

As Antonio leads me past two girls who are arguing about who has dibs on "the guy from Paramount"—according to one, the guy was her "property" because she'd pointed him out originally, while the other claimed that was bullshit because she was the first one to say she wanted him—I try to prep myself to actually speak to some of these girls. Even though I still hadn't heard back from Ethan about my pitch, I'd decided to proceed as if I already had the assignment, figuring that the worst that could happen was that I'd be left with some interesting information.

Walking by the pool, we pass Antonio's friend Eva—a stripper he was either sleeping with or desperately trying to—who's being paid to swim naked all night alongside a Penthouse Pet who simply goes by "Foxy."

"I don't get it," I say to Antonio as Eva blows him a kiss. "She's hired to swim naked in a pool all night? What kind of a job is that?"

"A good one—that's what kind," Antonio answers, before wiping his nose and disappearing into the bathroom.

"I CAN'T BELIEVE this place," I marvel after Antonio has walked me through the four floors of tacky decadence—rooms filled with wall-to-wall carpeting and sleek furniture—and led me into a basement that houses a pool table, arcade games, and a karaoke machine. "The guy who lives here makes his money just by throwing parties?"

"Not just parties, baby—events where the girls all meet their clients."

"Still," I scream over music that's started blaring out of what seems to be the walls, "who knew those events could net such a profit?"

Antonio grins as he leads me back outside again. "Yeah, well, Jimmy's the fucking man." We're now standing next to an enormous outdoor buffet where two topless girls are serving prime rib, sushi, and fruit.

I have yet to see Jimmy—not to mention anyone I actually know—and I wonder where all these people have come from. While I'd figured that whatever party Antonio would take me to wouldn't exactly attract the Brooke and Rebecca crowd, it's still altogether bizarre to be in a sea of people I've never laid eyes on in my life. I almost feel like I've been deposited in a strange city for the night. Still, the environment is quintessentially L.A.: all the women are both devoid of body fat and in possession of enormous breasts they clearly hadn't grown naturally, and their clothing had been selected solely to highlight those two qualities. These girls don't, on the surface, look all that different from other women in L.A.—they're just a little shinier and their body parts are hoisted up a little higher. And while not every single one of them is attractive, it was clear that they'd all made personal preparation into something of an art form: hair extensions, extravagant jewelry, lower back tattoos, and tanned flesh accost me at every turn. The men, meanwhile, seem to be divided into two camps: either utterly boyish, their heads baseball cap–encased, their expressions eager, like they're a decade late for their fraternity's big party, or slick in expensive suits, their hair stiff with gel, their entire attitude bored and blasé, as if they've already seen all the world has to offer and haven't been terribly impressed.

"We got a few," Antonio says under his breath as he grabs my arm and leads me over to an outdoor fireplace. I'd been telling him in between his trips to the bathroom that as soon as he saw a girl he thought might be friendly, I wanted him to introduce me, insinuate that I wanted entrée into her world, make himself disappear, and trust me to find my own way home. I hadn't really expected this to work—Antonio is so ultraprotective that he likes me to call him when I get home from press lines just to let him know that I haven't been accosted by some random lunatic or crashed on the freeway. But suddenly he's steering me toward two girls—an exotic-looking brunette and a blonde with a pixie cut and impossibly long legs. While I feel like I want to throw up, I'm also excited. Waiting to interview a Lachey brother never felt like this.

"Hey, girls—this is Emma," Antonio says, giving me a tiny shove. He wipes his nose and scoots off.

The brunette watches Antonio go and then gives me a once-over. "What was all that about?" she asks coolly.

"Well . . ." I look down and then gather my courage. "I'm new." On the ride over, Antonio had promised me that this one word would be enough to open the gates to their world.

And apparently it was because the blonde—who, up close, has a rosy-cheeked, freshly scrubbed look to her—smiles at me. She seems far nicer than her face and body suggest she would be. Her friend gives me the one-up, one-down, and I suddenly feel embarrassingly conservative in the dress that had two minutes ago seemed risqué.

"Have you ever been to something like this before?" the blonde asks sweetly.

I consider a variety of potential responses before simply saying, "No."

It appears to be the right answer because suddenly she's patting the space next to her and gesturing for me to sit down. "I know what it's like to be the new girl," she says, introducing herself as Kristi. I immediately picture Kristi as an eight-year-old moving to a strange town and having to be introduced by a teacher as the "new girl"—assigning her, in this instant reverie, an army sergeant father and a little sister. Kristi's friend is now scowling at me like there's only a limited supply of oxygen in the area and she'd rather none of it be wasted on me. "Hang out with us if you want," Kristi continues and then glances at the brunette, who clearly wants no part of this whole "us" equation. "Oh," Kristi adds, "this is Amanda." Amanda's enormous brown eyes take me in as I smile exuberantly at her, her coldness causing me to try even harder to make her like me.

I wish that I'd concocted a good back story—one that involved my taking a bus here from Northern California or Oregon or some other place a lonely, desperate girl who longed to escape might come from. But I hadn't actually believed that Antonio—or I—would be able to pull this off. *Screw it,* I think, suddenly feeling superior to the *New York Times* reporter who'd made the girls so paranoid. *Eat your heart out, Gail Sheehy.* "So, are you working tonight?" I ask Kristi.

"No," she sighs. "I had a date but he canceled so I came here—only to see him working some B-movie actress in the Jacuzzi."

"I told her it's silly to get jealous when it's just a business arrangement," Amanda says, "but she doesn't always listen." I nod as Amanda looks me up and down. "So how do you know Antonio?" she asks.

The teacher of the one acting class I ever took—freshman year in high school—used to say that the key to convincing your audience was really believing what you were saying. "Oh, I don't," I respond.

"Then how'd you get on Jimmy's list?" Amanda asks.

I think about the men salivating at the buffet table boobs and Jessica and her alleged contracts. "Oh baby, I got ways," I say, sounding nothing like myself. I consider adding a wink or some kind of a sitting hip swivel but decide against it.

"Don't we all!" Kristi offers brightly.

Amanda doesn't seem to be done quizzing me. "So you're trying to get in?" she asks. Is "in" what they called it? I nod earnestly, telling myself that I truly believe what I'm saying. I do want in, after all—if "in" means out of the life I've been living. Amanda suddenly sits up straight and looks me in the eye. "Well, I don't know who you've met so far, but we're not like some of those other girls."

"I didn't think you were," I say.

Kristi nods emphatically. "We don't take money."

"I've been flown around the world, introduced to mothers, even brought to kids 'school events," Amanda says. I nod, opting not to ask how the kids felt about that.

"We know about wines and operas and ballet and all that," Kristi adds. "I love *La Bayadère*."

Amanda, who's facing Kristi but clearly talking to me, says, "We really have relationships with these guys—it's not just wham, bam, thank you, ma'am. When the family dog died, my client called *me* to console him—not his wife."

"We're not whores," Kristi adds. Her face is so innocent with her cute little ski-jump nose that the word "whore" seems altogether inappropriate coming out of her mouth. She looks at Amanda, who nods with approval.

"Sometimes girls will say that we're all the same," Amanda says. At that, Kristi snorts. Amanda continues, "But it's just what people tell themselves so they can justify what they do."

"I know what you mean," I respond after a pause. I can tell that this is what I have to say but I'm dying to know what, specifically, they get instead of money. Movie roles? Fur coats? Caviar? Amanda gives me the first smile of our acquaintance, and I decide to play up my ignorance. "Honestly, I don't know what I'm doing," I say. "You girls seem so . . . I don't know, calm and confident about the whole thing."

Kristi grins, displaying perfect teeth. I wonder if they were God-given or they'd been straightened through years of expensive orthodontia. Had Kristi's father—Sarge, in my mind—shelled out money for expensive toothwear only to have his daughter grow up to become a prostitute? Despite the fact that I'm still incredibly grateful that she's being so nice, something about how she smiles makes me uncomfortable; her lips turn up too suddenly, like they're following some external cue that has nothing to do with how she's feeling. "It gets better," she says. "The more you do it, the less bad it makes you feel."

I nod. "So are you an actress?" I ask. According to Antonio, most of these girls call themselves actresses—which isn't, come to think of it, an inaccurate description of what they do.

"Oh, no," Kristi says, her blue eyes crinkling with amusement. "I'm terrible at acting! Amanda is an actress," she adds, motioning her head in Amanda's direction. "She's gonna be a movie star. But I'm just a . . . a . . . nothing, I guess."

"Come on, that's not true." Amanda turns to face Kristi. "When I make it, you're gonna be my publicist."

Kristi grins, and it occurs to me that she would probably make a really good yes-woman Hollywood wife. "Oh, that's right."

"So how did you get into . . . this whole thing?" I ask Kristi, wondering if something terrible is going to happen to me for misrepresenting myself to such a nice girl. For a second, I imagine rumors that I'm a prostitute getting back to my family, and Mom and Dad trying to make sense of the news while Mahler blasts in the background.

Kristi shrugs. "The same way anyone does, I guess," she says. "I came out here from Ohio and tried working at production companies and as a receptionist, but I couldn't make ends meet on twenty grand a year, you know?" A dark cloud passes over her face but it's almost immediately swept away by one of her too-quick grins. She glances at Amanda and continues, "Amanda was already doing it, and she pointed out that I'd certainly slept with men for less good reasons." The sad look returns for a millisecond before her lips turn up once again. "And it's good. I mean, I meet really interesting people."

"We only have interesting clients," Amanda says. "Mostly Hollywood bigwigs who like glamorous girls."

Taking her in, I decide that she does, indeed, have a glamorous air to her. If she had walked down a press line as the latest starlet du jour, I wouldn't have been surprised. "You look like an actress," I say to Amanda, hoping my flattery will help me win her over.

"You think so?" she asks. A pause and then: "Are you?"

I shake my head. "No—I'm kind of like Kristi," I say, ironically doing the best acting job of my life. "I'm just a sort of nothing, too." I hope that I sound dispirited enough that she doesn't ask any more questions.

"Really?" Amanda's friendlier now. Then she suddenly hits Kristi's arm. "Oh, God. Guess who's headed in our direction?"

"Shit!" Kristi yelps and I'm surprised to hear a swear word escape from her pure-looking button mouth. "Too late to get away."

I look up, directly into the face of Jessica. Halle-fricking-lujah. A wave of gratitude for Antonio washes over me. I'm about to smile and reintroduce myself when I notice that she's too focused on Amanda to even notice me. "Hi, Mandy," she says, reaching down and plucking a cigarette from Amanda's pack without asking. "What's the latest?"

"It's Amanda," Amanda responds.

"Oh, Mandy, you're so sensitive," Jessica says, smiling at Kristi before glancing at me. "I know you. How?" she asks.

"Yes," I say, standing up. "I'm Emma. I ran into you at Starbucks. You were Matt's date at the baby shower."

She smiles and I notice a beauty mark just above her lip. "That's right." She glances past me to Amanda. "So are you pretty tight with Mandy?" she asks.

I look from Amanda to Jessica. "Actually," I say, "we just met." At least, I think, Amanda and Kristi are helping me to look somewhat credible in front of Jessica; I'm not just a decaf latte drinker who makes desperate-sounding approaches in Starbucks, but someone who associates with other women in her field. I want to explain to Jessica that I have no attachment to these girls and that I'd much rather talk to her, but now clearly isn't the time. I sit back down. "I'm new to this whole thing and, well, these girls are sharing some of their stories with me," I add.

A smirk gathers on Jessica's face. "Well, you're in good hands. Mandy's a pro. Have a good night, I'm off." She turns and saunters away.

"Christ," Amanda hisses as soon as Jessica's out of earshot. "I can't fucking stand her."

"What's her problem?" I ask.

"She's a psycho bitch," Amanda spits out. "She thinks she's smarter than everyone else."

"What does she do that's so bad?" I ask.

Amanda looks over at me and pats my head, like I'm a stray dog she suddenly realized is kind of cute. "You have so much to learn, Emma," she says. I think I'm more surprised by the fact that she heard and retained my name than that she's being nice.

"I know," I say. "I'm completely clueless." *Not a lie in the slightest,* I think with some satisfaction.

"Jessica Morrison is evil," Kristi offers.

"She calls me Mandy," Amanda adds, "because she knows it drives me crazy."

"And she steals clients," Kristi reminds her.

Amanda nods, "Plus, I think she shows up places where she knows we're going to be just to fuck with us."

"And she's a total snob," Kristi adds.

"She thinks she's hot shit—like she's the only girl in town."

"She always tries to make us feel uncomfortable."

"We hate her."

Despite the fact that I'm acting horrified, everything they're saying is making me all the more convinced that I need to interview Jessica. She's complicated, hated, infamous—the ideal central character for an article—while I'm sitting here with a wannabe actress and her yes-woman. But at the same time, I know that I'm incredibly lucky to be passing muster with these girls. As Amanda ashes her cigarette, she suddenly turns to me and announces, "If a producer client offers you a role, you've got to say no and tell him about me instead."

I nod, realizing that this girl is really bonkers. "Of course," I say.

She smiles, reaches into her purse, pulls out a card, and hands it to me. All it says is "Amanda" with an enormous heart around her name and a number. "Call me tomorrow," she says. "We'll go shopping."

I'm not sure if "shopping" is code for something else, but I nod and slide the card into my pocket excitedly. Then it occurs to me that maybe Jessica hasn't actually left the party, so I tell the girls it was nice meeting them and promise Amanda I'll call. I start making my way toward the front door—on my way noticing a woman wearing nothing but a lei and two couples making out—just in time to see Jessica hop into a town car outside. Damn it. Checking my watch, I see that it's already past two. Jimmy's house is only a couple blocks from Sunset so I decide to walk there to get a cab.

As I make my way down the hill, I feel victorious—entirely

certain, for the first time, that I'm capable of doing the article. The fact that I proved to myself that I can take risks in order to get a story is almost as exciting as the thought of Ethan actually assigning it to me. I had the ability to gain entry to a new world and then report back what it was like—and this could give me a name. *That's all I want,* I think as I get into the cab that will take me home. *A name.*

chapter 8

I HEAR SOMETHING RINGING. At first I think it's just in my head and then I realize the noise is too loud to be self-generated so it must be the alarm. I press the snooze button but the blaring continues. Encountering my phone, I suddenly realize that's the culprit. Mercifully, the noise stops but then almost immediately starts up again.

"What time is it?" I say in lieu of a greeting as I pick up. My eyes are still closed.

"Oh, I didn't wake you, did I?"

"Depends." I shift and stretch. "Who is this?"

"Ethan. Harrington? From *Substance*?"

On that, my eyes jolt open and I sit up in bed. "Ethan! No, of course not! I was just—"

He laughs. "Oh my God, you've got to be the world's worst liar. I'm sorry. I'm an idiot for calling you this early on a Sunday morning. But we were closing an issue all week so I just read your e-mail now. And I got so excited, I wanted to call you right away."

"Really?" Time seems to freeze.

"Really. You hit this pitch out of the park."

I get out of bed. "I did?"

"Absolutely. I just want you to do a little more research and then I'll get the editor in chief, Mark, to sign off on giving you the assignment. But that's essentially just a formality—I can't see how he'd say no to this."

"That's amazing. Because last night I—"

"There's just one more thing," he interrupts. "Your idea is great. But your approach isn't right." I feel my heart sink, wondering why the other shoe always has to drop. "Going undercover—trying to pretend you're one of these girls—isn't the way to go here."

Oh, God. "Why not?" I ask. I glance at Amanda's card, which I put on my desk when I came in last night.

"It's risky, for one. And look, these are less-than-stable people we're talking about, so the further you remain from them—the more objective you can be—the better off we all are. Writers on assignments like this can get so close to the topic that they become careless. You mentioned the Gail Sheehy *New York* piece in your pitch. Did you ever hear about what happened with that?"

"I did." It had turned out that the main prostitute she'd written about hadn't actually existed; Sheehy later claimed that it had been a composite character. My pulse increases as I try to imagine calling Amanda and explaining that I'd still love to go shopping with her but I'm actually a journalist so did she mind if I also tape-recorded her most personal thoughts about why she'd become a prostitute? "Well, I'd be really careful. I'd—"

"Trust me," Ethan says, suddenly stern, "you need to do a

straight reporting job here. Find these girls, explain you're doing a story, and then get them to cooperate."

"But I really think it would be far better if—"

"Look," Ethan snaps, "this isn't a debatable point." Softening slightly, he adds, "Once you have some material, send it to me and I'll talk to Mark about getting you the official assignment."

I feel suddenly ashamed of myself. Who do I think I am, trying to defy the one person who seems to be giving me a chance? I'm just going to have to find a way to come clean with Amanda and Kristi. "That sounds great, Ethan."

"I'm glad," he says. "Because if you do this right, it could be a cover story."

"Are you serious?"

"Sure. It has all the necessary elements. So go report the hell out of your piece. Find some solid sources. Wow them with your passion. And always be straightforward and honest. Remember, all a journalist really has is his integrity."

I gulp. "I'll keep that in mind."

"HEY, THERE," I say to Amanda when I see her gazing at a blue Fendi pocketbook in the purse department at Bloomingdale's. "That's nice," I add, nodding toward the bag.

"Do you think?" she asks, turning it over in her hand before putting it back on a rack. She walks over to a black quilted Chanel bag and picks it up.

"I do." I'd had an entire speech worked out in my head—about how I wasn't so much new to her world as I was interested in finding out about it—but I suddenly realize that there's no way I can deliver it. I see a craziness in her eyes that I'd somehow missed the other night and I feel certain that one wrong word on my part—let alone several hundred—could send her into some kind of a fit or breakdown. I tell myself that I'm just going to get to know her a little better and make sure she can handle the news before spilling the beans. Looking at the Chanel bag, I say, "Um, just so you know—I can't afford anything here." I figure this is a good way to establish the fact that I'm comfortable talking about money and she should be, too.

She nods as she wanders over to a Louis Vuitton bag and glances at the price tag. "Jesus—twelve hundred dollars," she says. Then she picks up a yellow suede pouchlike purse and looks at that tag. "This one's thirty-five hundred," she says. "It's Onatah." She puts the bag back in the pile it came from. "I haven't even heard of Onatah—have you?"

"No." Amanda's smiling now. Is she actually starting to like me? I try not to think about what will happen when she finds out the truth. She runs her fingers over a black bag covered in white, red, and turquoise *F*'s. "Fendi, I've heard of, so it makes more sense that they could charge . . ." She examines the price tag. "Two thousand for it. But Onatah? I'm sorry, but that sounds like some sort of fucked-up name a black girl might make up so she could stand out in Hollywood."

I laugh and glance at a table that holds a slew of Marc Jacobs bags, then pick up a white one with buckles on the side. "Marc Jacobs, as far as I'm concerned, can charge as much as he wants," I say. "Everything he makes is amazing." Lilly has two Marc Jacobs purses—both presents from her boyfriend, Felipe.

"Oh, I have this one—it's called the Ursula Elise," Amanda says, grabbing the bag from me.

I run my fingers over the luxurious leather. "It's gorgeous."

Amanda nods and then says, "Some of them I keep."

"What do you mean?"

She smiles. "It all started when Abdul, a Middle Eastern client of mine, gave me his Bloomingdale's credit card and explained that his family allotted a certain amount for him to charge each month on it as an allowance."

"What are you talking about?"

"I used to return bags at Barneys but they started to catch on," she says. She nods her head in the direction of an older saleswoman who's pulling a succession of bags out of an enormous suitcase and adds, "But Doris will always accept my returns without receipts, so long as she gets ten percent."

"Really?" I ask. The saleswoman—Doris—looks brisk and efficient, like a rule follower if ever there was one.

"You know how men always think we're obsessed with bags?" Amanda asks. I nod and shrug at the same time. She continues, "And, I mean, we are. That is, I am—although shoes more." Almost involuntarily, I glance down at her black suede boots, which are decorated with gold buckles. "Still, no matter how obsessed I get, I'm never going to want hundreds and hundreds of them! I mean, if I have more than twenty purses, I can't keep track anymore." As she picks up a pink satchel, I consider my own bag collection—a fake Prada, a Coach backpack my mother gave me for my birthday about a decade ago, and a few flea market finds. Amanda smiles. "But men don't seem to understand that." She pauses. "So rather than fight the situation, I just make sure to mention on every date how much I love the bags at Bloomingdale's." She starts walking toward the cash register, gesturing for me to follow her. "In a good month, I can make between ten and fifteen grand." She looks at Doris. "What's today's total?"

Doris looks up. "Eight thousand, five hundred," she says.

"Wow." I stare at the pile of bags, not quite able to ask Amanda why converting goods into cash is any different than simply accepting money in the first place.

"Can I get it in hundreds?" she asks Doris, and I can tell she's showing off for my benefit. Doris nods. "Be sure to subtract your handling fee," Amanda adds.

As I'm marveling at Amanda's practical efficiency—at the party, she'd seemed like she lived in a fantasy world and constantly needed people like Kristi to prop her up, but the girl clearly had survival skills.

Suddenly, seemingly out of nowhere, Jessica appears.

"Hey there, new girl," Jessica says to me, not even glancing at Amanda. "Mandy teaching you the tricks of the trade?"

I nod, my head spinning and my heart racing. There's no way I'm going to let her get away from me this time.

Sighing loudly, Amanda asks, "Emma, are you ready?"

"Actually, I need to talk to Jessica about something." I realize as I say this that it may well destroy the relationship I've started to have with Amanda, but I don't see any other option.

While Amanda looks surprised, Jessica doesn't. "I have something I need to talk to you about, too," Jessica says to me. I smile, certain that Jessica's only playing along to spite Amanda.

Amanda sighs and looks at me. "Well, if that's the case, then I guess we don't have much left to say to each other."

Looking into her eyes, I see that she's hurt. The last thing she needed was more evidence that Jessica had bested her again. "Actually," I find myself saying, "I wouldn't be so sure about that. Because I was telling a producer who works with Martin Scorsese about you this morning and he sounded really interested in meeting you for the movie he's casting." I'm utterly shocked by what's just come out of my mouth. Amanda eyes me.

"Really?" she asks. "What's his name? And why did you wait until now to say something?"

"I'll tell you later. I promise. I'll call you in a little bit." Amanda nods and glances from me to Jessica. I turn and start walking away with Jessica, whose deep green eyes are examining me so closely that I feel almost invaded. I plan to tell her what I said to Amanda and Kristi: that I want to learn the ropes. Once we're out of Amanda's earshot, I say, "So, Jessica—"

"I'm on to you," she interrupts.

"Excuse me?" I feel sweat on my lower back.

"Don't worry, I won't tell Mandy and her sycophant."

"Tell them what?" I ask, buying time. *How could she know anything?* I wonder, then immediately think, *Deny, just deny.*

"That you're not really one of us," she says, examining her fingernails. "That you're just doing research for a story."

"What are you talking about?"

She glances at me. "You don't have it in your eyes."

"Have what?"

"Desperation," she says. "That look that says you're willing to do anything." I gaze into her eyes, trying to see what she means, but when she stares right back at me, I get self-conscious and glance down. "Once I knew you were lying," she continues, "I wanted to find out why. So I asked around." Before I can respond, she asks, "Trying to work your way up the *Substance* food chain?"

My heart's bouncing all around my chest. What the hell made me think I could get away with this? "Yes," I say. "I'd really appreciate—"

"Appreciate what?" she asks. "My silence? Cooperation? Help?"

"All three," I say, feeling a sudden surge of confidence. "I want you to be the focus of my story."

She gives me the once-over, then crosses her arms and says, "Okay."

"Okay?" I repeat, shocked.

She nods. "Let me ask you something," she says. "Did you

read the *New York Times* piece last month? About the sex-for-money trade?"

"Yep. I didn't think it really said anything particularly interesting."

"Fuck, no," Jessica says. She hitches her bag higher on her shoulder. "And it made all of us sound pathetic. Amanda looks like Albert fucking Einstein compared to the girls quoted in that piece."

"I wouldn't do that, I'd—"

"I know," Jessica interrupts me. "You seem smart—savvy. I actually think you'd be able to show people that we're really not all that different from most women out there." She smiles and adds, "With my help, of course."

I'm vaguely aware of the fact that a compliment from her shouldn't make me feel this good, especially seeing as she doesn't know me at all. But, I tell myself, I'm not so much thrilled with her approval as I am excited by the fact that I can now proceed with the piece the way Ethan wants me to: with her as an on-the-record source. "Thank you," I say.

"You can't tell those other girls what you're doing, though," she says. "Let them think you're one of them."

"Actually, my editor wants me to come clean with everyone and—"

Jessica laughs. "Your editor? You're funny."

"What's that supposed to mean?"

"It means that no one gets anywhere by doing what they're supposed to. Sheep do what they're supposed to. Are you interested in being a sheep?" I shake my head. "That's what I thought." She looks at me. "So are you ready to hear my rules?"

"Go ahead."

"I don't want you printing the names of any of my clients. I'm not some sell-everyone-down-the-river type, trying to spill the contents of my little black book."

I think of Matt. "I wouldn't want to print their names, anyway," I say.

"And if you come with me places, people can't know that you're a magazine writer. If anyone asks, you're my friend, not a journalist. People in this world are idiotic and paranoid: they hear the word 'journalist' and immediately translate that to 'cop.'"

I think about Ethan, then about sheep. "Got it."

She smiles. "And you have to protect my identity in the piece. But I'm happy to talk to any fact-checker who wants to confirm any of my quotes before it runs."

I smile at her. "You've thought of everything, haven't you?"

"Let's just say that I know a few magazine editors." She suddenly laughs. "I've tossed out some freebies in my time."

chapter 9

"OH, LILLY, YOUR TARTS look absolutely marvelous," Mom says, eyeing the tiny pear pies my little sister whipped up this morning. And I have to admit, they appear to be pretty amazing; then again, that's Lilly.

For family dinners when Lilly is home from college, she always bakes some ridiculous dessert to accompany Mom's meals. And while we're eating, Mom talks obsessively about this while Dad, who's never had particularly great hearing, tends to stare off into space, occasionally checking into the conversation and offering up a non sequitur or two. It's thus up to Lilly and me to provide the entertainment, and since whatever Lilly has going on is always infinitely more fabulous than anything I can possibly come up with, dinner chez Swanson is almost always the Lilly Swanson Show.

"So how's everything with Felipe?" Mom asks Lilly as she

passes the spinach salad. Mom's golden retriever, Buddy, is at her feet, begging.

Lilly pushes a section of her hair out of her eyes and scoops salad onto her plate, surreptitiously tossing Buddy a sliver of chicken. "Great," she says, then asks, "Oh, is this the dressing I made for you last week?"

Mom smiles. "No, but did you get the recipe from the Chez Panisse cookbook?"

Lilly nods at Mom as she passes the salad bowl to me. "Don't tell me. You, too?"

"Great minds think alike," Mom says, shrugging. Lilly grins—her smile as bright and close-up-ready as always—as she reaches for the plate of salmon in front of her and serves herself a piece. "I gave Felipe the full Alice Waters treatment the night before he left," she says, placing the platter back on the table in front of her. "Wild nettle and beet green ravioli with ricotta and parmesan and then leg of lamb."

"With the mustard sauce?" Mom asks.

"Delish," Lilly says, nodding. Felipe is Lilly's boyfriend—she met him at Harvard last year—and when I say that he's Spanish royalty, I'm not actually lying or exaggerating. His father's cousin's grandfather was closely related to the King of Spain or something and he's fabulously wealthy and international but far too down-to-earth to actually elaborate on all this royalness. Mom is charmed silly by the guy—not because of his family, she's always quick to point out, but because he's literate and cultivated and also seems quite devoted to Lilly—and ever since their relationship started, I've been feeling like more and more of a failure in Mom's eyes for my inability to land a royal boyfriend, not to mention any boyfriend at all. I try to imagine my Whole Foods Birkenstocks-with-socks guy having a conversation with Felipe. About what, I couldn't imagine. Felipe didn't seem like the kind of guy who'd be too concerned about the dangers of aspartame.

"And how's work, Emma?" Mom asks.

I sit up a little straighter. "Actually, remember that story I told you I was writing? About the new kind of kept women?"

Mom looks distracted. "I'm not sure . . ." Her voice trails off.

"Well, I've made some serious progress," I say. I'm looking at her but talking to my entire family. "I found this fascinating girl who agreed to cooperate with me on a story." No one says anything. I want to tell them how I was able, on the drive over here, to convince Amanda that my fictional producer friend who works with Martin Scorsese had to suddenly leave to go on location for three months but was desperate to meet with her when he was back—and she'd believed me. While I was shocked by how easily the lie had flowed from my lips, uttering it had given me hope that maybe I was shrewd enough to pull this story off. I wasn't, as it turned out, a sheep. But I know that no one at the table cares about—or would even understand—this so I don't say anything else.

Dad suddenly looks up from his salad and asks Mom, "Did you tell her about Josie Lewis?"

"No." Mom shakes her head and then looks at me, blinking enthusiastically. "You remember Dave Lewis, Dad's college roommate? Well, his daughter got her business degree in just a few years and is already fielding job offers."

"Job offers in the *six figures*," Dad adds, "only a few years out of Harvard."

"And that's while raising *two kids*," says Mom.

I take a bite of my salmon—I've never liked fish, something Mom claims to forget every time I show up for dinner and there's yet another selection of something that once lived in saltwater. "That's nice for her," I say. I want to tell them I don't care about

Harvard degrees and people like Josie Lewis and jobs that pay in the six figures and women whose professional and personal lives are infinitely more impressive than mine, but I don't.

"I'm going to Seville next month so I can meet Felipe's parents," Lilly announces, mercifully changing the subject. "I'm a little freaked out."

"Sweetheart, what do you have to worry about? They're going to love you," Mom says. She doesn't add, "Everyone does," but she doesn't need to.

Dad looks up—his hearing troubles seem, more and more, to be selectively tuning out that which doesn't interest him—and grins. "Worried you're not going to be able to hold your own with the royal family?" he asks her. Dad smiles at me, as if to silently say, *Isn't it exciting how we all get to feel important thanks to Lilly?*

"What does Felipe say they're like?" I ask Lilly.

"Pretentious. Older. Judgmental." Lilly makes a face. "He's actually insisting on taking me to some Italian couture designer before we go to Spain so I can have what he's calling an entire trousseau—custom-designed dresses, suits, even *pajamas*—made. Apparently, that's the only kind of clothing his parents deem appropriate." Lilly grimaces, as if the concept of having her ridiculously wealthy royal boyfriend drown her in couture gowns is some great hardship, and Mom and Dad work overtime to pretend they're not impressed.

"Oh, and get this," Lilly continues. "His dad doesn't think women should work because it takes them away from time they could spend being devoted to their husbands and children." Lilly, who wants to go to law school and then into practice with Dad, punctuates this information with a gagging gesture.

"I'm not sure he's so wrong," Mom says and when I look at her, I notice that her eyes have a sudden sunken gloom. I don't know if I'm more surprised by the chink in her cheery façade or by what she's saying since it's so different from the "feminist values" speeches she typically delivers.

"That's ridiculous!" I say. Since I can't get a personal *or* professional life going, I'm not sure I'm even qualified to make this statement, but it seems to come out of me instinctively.

"What crap!" Lilly echoes.

Mom glances at Dad—now unbelievably riveted by the sports pages—and then down at her plate. "Having it all is harder than you think," she says, looking down. Mom doesn't usually admit to being anything other than gloriously happy—a testament, she always says, to her "inner glow." And clichés like "having it all" tend to make her cringe. Was she in the midst of some kind of a three-quarter-life crisis, questioning the choices she'd made or owning up to the fact that everything wasn't actually perfect?

"Plenty of people 'have it all,'" I say, determined to believe this myself. And then I think. "Like . . . Katie Couric. Well, her husband died but before that, right? Or Kelly Ripa?"

Mom smiles, seemingly willing her negative thoughts away. "Maybe you're right," she says. I doubt my mom even knows who Kelly Ripa is—her head is always occupied by paint strokes and Mahler, gardening trowels and Alice Waters meals. She smiles brightly and asks, "Now who wants one of Lilly's tarts?"

chapter 10

Jessica leans across the table at Dan Tana's so that I have a perfect view of her cleavage, which temporarily distracts me from the prices on the menu. The truth is, when we met at Starbucks and Jessica suggested we come here, I had assumed we'd never get in at seven on a Friday night. But before I had time to insist we go to the Koo Koo Roo across the street instead, the friendly maitre d' had greeted Jessica by name and immediately sat us at one of the booths. With a glance around as my eyes slowly adjust to the dark dining room—Harry Dean Stanton at one table, a *Lost* actor I once interviewed on a press line at another—I ask her how we were able to get the table while other people are still waiting in line.

"Oh, Craig takes care of me," she says, gesturing to the maitre d'. Then she calls over the waiter—who looks like he's about eighty and seems thoroughly indifferent to Jessica's cleavage—and orders two martinis. I'm about to object but then decide not to; Jessica's brazen confidence is daunting, and a drink will potentially help me feel like I'm the one in charge here. As the waiter walks away, she clears her throat. "So there was something I wanted to ask you," she says.

"Sure." I feel a flutter in my chest, not sure what's coming next.

"I was just curious . . . as a writer, what do you think of Fitzgerald?"

"The *Great Gatsby* writer?"

She nods and I shrug. "Um, he's good. I mean, I like him." I neglect to mention that *The Great Gatsby* is the only book of his I've actually read and that all I remember about it is that there were some eyes painted on a billboard somewhere. The *Lost* actor walks by and I hope this is enough of a distraction for Jessica to forget this whole American literature pop quiz thing.

"Did you ever hear what he said about his writing?" she asks. I shake my head as Jessica eyes me. "Every character he wrote, he claimed, always ended up being him."

"Really?" I ask. I'm not sure where she's going with this or why the conversation has just caused me to shudder involuntarily. The waiter delivers our drinks and I relish the speedy service and take a much-needed gulp of my martini before almost spitting it out when I realize how strong it is.

"Well, I think that's really interesting," she says, sipping her drink without, apparently, noticing its strength. "I guess he'd start out writing Amory Blaine or Nick Carraway or Dick Diver or whoever it was and in the end, no matter how many things he made up for them to do, he'd see they were all just extractions—or extensions—of him."

I watch her carefully, not sure if she's trying to tell me that I'm destined to become her or if she has one of those I-didn't-go-to-college chips on her shoulder and needs to constantly prove to everyone how knowledgeable she is. "Fitzgerald," I say, "wrote fiction."

She smiles. "Of course—I mean, as much as anyone who's trying to sort out his personal issues through his work writes fiction," she says, looking pensive. As I wonder just how many of her personal issues she's trying to sort out through her work, she takes a gulp of her drink and grins somewhat wickedly. "But how much do you love that nutjob he was married to?" She tosses her head back and laughs.

"Zelda?" I ask, not remotely sure what deep recess of my brain I managed to unearth this information from.

Jessica nods and sits up a little straighter. "Teach them to capitalize upon their natural resources and get their money's worth," she says, her voice dropping into a slight Southern lilt. "They are merely applying business ideas to being young." She grins. "Zelda wrote that. She was talking about flappers in the twenties, but she obviously knew what she was talking about. I mean, she may have gone batshit insane, but she did manage to marry one of the greatest writers of all time."

"Is that the way you see it? That you're just capitalizing on your natural resources?" I'm desperate to get the attention off how much more she seems to know about literature than I do. I vow to memorize a passage from a famous book—any book—so that I can impress people with it just as the waiter returns and Jessica orders Caesar salads and New York steaks for both of us. I'm so shocked by this—I have to imagine that the last time someone ordered for me was when I didn't know how to cut my own food—that I don't even know what to say so I simply let the moment pass without comment. "You're making being young your business?" I take my tape recorder out of my purse and place it on the table.

Jessica shrugs. "Well, I came out here from New York to be an actress." She grimaces. "What a cliché, right? I actually would have rather acted in New York but I came out here for a guy—cliché alert number two—and it didn't work out. I was depressed, and at least there was sun here, so I stayed."

I nod. "Go on."

"Well, I was in this apartment in Beverly Hills that I couldn't afford but was too much of a basket case to go looking for another place," she says, draining her martini. "And everywhere I went, I was getting hit on. I mean, the men here are just relentless, you know?" She looks at me expectantly and I nod, even though it's pretty much an annual event when I get hit on. "So it's about . . . um, maybe spring of 2001 and I'm at Barneys—where I have no business being, seeing as I'm completely broke and in debt, but Barneys just has a way of making you forget things like that, you know?" Stores where the average shirt costs three hundred dollars don't have a way of making me forget anything, but I nod and smile. "I'm trying on lipstick and this guy comes up to me—in the goddamn makeup department at Barneys!—and tells me that I have better lips than Angelina Jolie." As she says this, I suddenly notice that Jessica does, indeed, have those full, bee-stung lips people are always describing as "pillowy." "What he doesn't say," she continues, "but what we both know he's thinking, is 'great cock-sucking lips.'"

"Sure," I say, acting like I, too, use expressions like "cock-sucking lips" on a regular basis.

"And this guy's a real piece of work—not even making an effort to hide his wedding ring." Jessica pauses only to motion to the waiter to get her another drink. "He starts following me around the store—I spray on a couple perfumes and then go try on some Christian Louboutin shoes and he's there, on my tail, the whole time."

"Hmmm," I say, not sure what else to offer.

"Don't get me wrong—it wasn't some stalking situation," Jessica continues. "He was fucking hot—in a salt-and-pepper hair, I-make-a-couple-million-a-year-prebonus-and-have-a-massive-cock, arrogant ass kind of way. So I'm flirting with him, all the while thinking that I'm just amusing myself because I'd essentially sworn off married men years ago."

I'm not even sure how one starts an affair with a married man, let alone has enough of them for there to be a need to swear the behavior off, but I nevertheless fix her with a look meant to communicate that I relate. She continues, "And I keep trying on shoes and dishing back whatever flirty banter he's giving me. And then he says he has to return calls for a minute and would I excuse him." Jessica takes a gulp of her just-refreshed martini while I sip my first one. "Next thing I know, he's standing there in front of me and handing me this huge shopping bag." She pauses dramatically. "Filled with three pairs of the Louboutin boots." Jessica gives a little surprised laugh, as if she'd just seen the man's gift for the first time. "He'd spent almost four grand on a girl he didn't even know!" She smiles, clearly relishing the memory. " 'Now what would I do with three pairs of the same boots?' I asked him. They only came in black and brown and he'd gotten me two pairs of the black ones. He smiled and said, 'That's the first sign that you're going to be living a life of luxury—when you start acquiring not only what you need but also what you don't need.' Charming bastard." She smiles and shakes her head.

As the waiter delivers our salads, Jessica continues talking. "I kept them," she says. "Anyone would, right?" She doesn't wait for me to answer, which is a good thing because I'm not sure what I would say. She takes a bite and continues, "As we leave the store, he asks me if I'll drive him to his car, which is parked in one of those parking structures on Beverly Drive." I start eating my salad, hanging on her every word. "So we get into my beater of a car," she continues, "I drive him the block or two, and then, when we're at the structure, he asks me if I'll take him right to his car." She pauses for another bite. "Once we're there—he's on level P-three or -four or something—he tells me that he's always had this fantasy of fucking a girl on the hood of his sports car in a parking lot."

Taking a sip of my martini, I try not to look shocked.

Jessica drains her second drink. "So he pulled up my dress—I was wearing this Diane von Furstenberg wraparound I'd gotten at Wasteland secondhand—took out his cock, and fucked me right there, on the roof of his Porsche." She smiles dreamily and pops a bite of salad into her mouth, where she seems to savor it. "Usually," she says, "I need a lot of foreplay to come, but just being manhandled like that—having my panties practically torn off—got me incredibly hot. I don't know if it was that or just the idea that anyone could discover us, but I came harder and longer than I ever had."

"Did you ever see him again?" I ask. While I'm partially horrified by her story—and incredibly relieved that the waiter wasn't around for this part of it—I have to admit that I'm also turned on.

"See him again?" Jessica asks, laughing. She takes another bite of the salad. "Bernie's one of my best friends in the world."

"So why aren't the two of you together?" I ask, mystified that she was able to sleep with a powerful guy within a few minutes of meeting him and still consider him a friend.

"Well, for one, he's married to a little nervous Nellie he impregnated when they were both, like, twenty-four and in the William Morris trainee program."

"But how great a marriage is it if he's off, you know, meeting girls at Barneys?" I ask.

She shrugs. "Their marriage sucks, but so do most," she says. "Still, it's a nonissue. He's fine with Nervous Nellie, the happy homemaker, for the most part. And Christ, he'd drive me insane as a real honest-to-goodness boyfriend. I mean, I love him but the man is beyond narcissistic—he really just wants a woman to raise his kids and listen to him bitch about his clients. This way, everyone wins."

"Except his wife," I point out.

"Trust me, Wifey wins," Jessica says. "She loves the house in the hills, not to mention the one at Carbon Beach. She's on charity committees with all the other Hollywood wives, trying to save the environment with Bernie's money. And let's not forget that she's probably sick to death of her husband's cock." I smile uncomfortably; if I'm going to be around Jessica, I'm clearly going to have to stop flinching every time she says the word "cock." "I mean, who the hell wants to get laid by the same man for twenty years?" Jessica adds, shivering.

I wonder if Claire and all our other friends from high school who got married at the first possible second will be sick of sleeping with their husbands after twenty years—or if, perhaps, they already are. Then again, Claire seems to expend so much mental energy convincing herself that Eric is wonderful, she probably wholeheartedly believes she's never going to want another guy again. Can she keep a self-delusion like that going for the rest of her life? While it's impossible to imagine either of them cheating—Eric's passion seems to be limited to his golf games and Claire just doesn't have it in her—it's almost as difficult to conceive of them having sex with each other. Theirs seems just like a partnership—the coming together of two entities to share a bed, plasma screen TV, and last name—with their baser impulses, if they had any, rendered almost irrelevant.

"From the beginning," Jessica continues, "Bernie was clear with me that he couldn't give me anything, you know, real. Right after the whole car hood thing, he told me he was married with kids, as if it wasn't completely obvious before he even opened his mouth. 'But I like you,' he said, 'and want to see you again.'" The waiter delivers our steaks and Jessica immediately cuts into hers. "He just said, 'Beverly Hills Hotel. This Friday. I'm supposed to be on set with a client in New York this weekend, but I'd rather play hooky with you.'" Jessica takes a bite and gestures for another martini. "So whenever we weren't fucking or eating that weekend, we were talking. I told him about my situation—the bastard I'd moved to L.A. for, the debt, the rent I couldn't pay. And when he went home on Sunday night, he had already taken care of my rent for the next six months." As she puts a sliver of meat in her mouth, I try to imagine what it might be like to have rent concerns for the next half a year evaporate in an instant. "And he's been setting me up with other clients ever since."

"Are you serious?"

"Well, Bernie knew a lot of men like him—wealthy and sexually unsatisfied, but not interested in the drama of having an affair or fucking one of the by-the-hour or by-the-night girls who consider having a GED some great educational achievement." She smiles. "And he saw it as a real opportunity for me. As he put it, I should first figure out what I wanted, then find the people who could give it to me." She takes a gulp of her just-delivered drink. "So, whether it's my credit card bill or my car payment or my rent, I explain what I want and then find out what, exactly, I'm going to have to do to get it. Is it a week of regular sex, plus spending the night? A full weekend of anal? Hours of 69 with his wife while he watches and jerks off? Playing live-in girlfriend for a month? Or just a night of something 'special'?"

"'Special'?"

"Oh, you know. Maybe there's a guy who likes to have his face shoved into the toilet before he's chained to the sink faucet. Or he wants to stick his head in my ass until he comes or have me piss in his mouth. Or . . ." I must look completely appalled because she laughs when she sees my face and continues, "Get this: I have a guy with a perfectly normal-sized penis who likes to have me tease him by calling his cock small—literally mock its size—and then bring in a big black guy for me to blow in front of him. When the black guy comes all over my tits, I have to make the guy—my client—lick the come up and then suck on the black guy's cock himself." She shakes her head and laughs again. "Turns out there's a whole subsection of humanity that's into that kind of thing—the 'forced bi 'guys. I swear. You can look it up online."

"Right," I say, gulping my martini, now grateful for its strength. "Sure." I want to ask if Matt is one of her "special" clients but don't. After downing a final fortifying sip, I say, "So then, once you work out the trade, they sign something?"

"Exactly. Bernie drew up a document for me—he used to be a lawyer. And he's quite a businessman."

"But how enforceable are your contracts?" I ask.

"Well, they're really just evidence to show wives and girlfriends if the guys don't fulfill their end of the bargain. But luckily, it's been a nonissue: in nearly four years, no one has ever reneged." She hits the table. "Knock on wood."

"And what's your arrangement with Bernie?" I ask. "Does he take a percentage?"

"Not a financial one—the guy's got more money than he knows what to do with—but trust me, he's compensated." She smiles.

"And has business always been good?"

"Always," she says. "Something about me seems to inspire men to part with large wads of cash." She flutters her eyelashes dramatically. "What can I say? I'm like my soul sister, Blanche DuBois: always depending on the kindness of strangers." She laughs.

"What about the single guys who use you?" I ask. "Successful men in this town can have sex with whoever they want. Why would they need you?" I tell myself that I'm asking for professional and not personal reasons.

"Look, Hollywood men just want a hassle-free life," Jessica says. "They live in this dream land where they went from answering some asshole's phone for a few years to making a million or one point five a year, and they're coddled like babies. Perfect-looking women offer them blow jobs on a regular basis. And while the girls all act like they think these guys are so marvelous, the guys know that there's no such thing as a free blow job. The girls want careers or, even worse, to claim them. *They're* actually the ones trying to take advantage of the men. Would they like these guys if they were plumbers or electricians? Did they give them the time of day when they were prom-queening it around Georgia or wherever? Fuck, no." Jessica leans back and shakes her head. "Believe me, I want far less from the single guys than the so-called regular girls out here do. These guys are eventually going to pick one of them to marry: usually they take the most submissive-seeming ones they can find, girls who are nothing like me. They don't need to find the hottest—surgery and trainers can make any woman hot and, besides, hotter wives may be more likely to cheat. Down the line, when these guys are bored stiff and realize they want a girl who actually has something to say—a person who challenges them—they find me." She smiles. "And they can do all sorts of things to me that would make your average D-girl run for the hills." She laughs. "Or from them, as the case may be."

I stare at her, nodding. I hadn't really questioned how much of my attraction to Matt McCarthy had to do with the fact that he was a successful agent with a second house in Palm Springs. I just knew that he was sought-after, the kind of guy a girl like me would be lucky to date. I try to imagine Matt showing up at my door as an Arrowhead deliveryman or someone there to install my cable but the image is impossible to conjure up. I suddenly wish that money *had* been all I'd wanted from him—that would have been clear, whereas what I always seem to be longing for from men is so vague and messy and desperate. I feel certain that Jessica's never sat in her bedroom, curled up in a small ball, pining for Matt—or someone like him. She just shows up as herself, silently announcing that they can take it or leave it.

"So what's the deal with you and Amanda?" I ask. "Why don't you get along?"

Jessica laughs. "She and that little ass-kisser of hers just bug me. They think that if they put on enough airs, they'll be able to do what I do. But taking a wine class at the Learning Annex doesn't make you sophisticated."

"Do you have the same clientele?" I ask.

Jessica shrugs. "Not really."

"So you never stole any clients from them?"

Jessica, annoyed, blows a wisp of hair out of her face. "Christ, they told you that?" I nod. "And you bought it?" she asks.

I consider the question; while I want to believe Jessica, it's too easy to picture her calmly appropriating Amanda's clients just because she could. "No," I ultimately say.

Jessica smiles and, as the waiter deposits the check in front of us, reaches down her dress and pops her breasts up with the kind of casual absentmindedness another girl might display while reaching for her lipstick. "Good," she says. She pulls the check over to her side of the table.

"You're not going to pay," I say, reaching for the bill.

"Don't be ridiculous." Jessica swats my hand away. She pulls out a black Amex. "I know what magazine reporters make."

"But you're the one who's giving me all this information and—"

"Look, I'm playing by some of your rules," Jessica says, motioning to my tape recorder. She hands her credit card to the waiter without even glancing at the total. Giving me a thin smile, she adds, "So you're going to have to play by some of mine."

chapter 11

I'M PULLING INTO the parking lot across the street from *Substance* when my phone rings and I see on caller ID that it's Claire. "Hi, there," I say. We haven't spoken since our aborted *Real World*–watching experience, when I ended up leaving just a few minutes after Eric thoroughly poisoned the experience.

"How are you?" she asks sweetly.

"Good," I say. "You?"

"You're never going to believe this," she says dramatically.

"What?" I have a brief fantasy that she's going to inform me that she's suddenly realized Eric is a douchebag.

"Eric's brother, Andrew, is dating—and looks like he's going to marry—a woman who's related to the director of admissions at Crossroads!" When Claire's in one of her my-life's-so-great-and-here's-how moods, her two favorite topics are couples that are going to commit to matrimony at any moment and those who can help with admissions at the school we went to and didn't like all that much.

"You told me," I say, not reminding her that this is actually the third time I've heard about this blessed near-union. I wonder if the energy Claire puts into trying to make everything sound so great constricts the flow of oxygen to her brain and causes memory loss.

"Well, it's just a major relief," Claire continues, "because it's getting harder to get in there all the time. You remember Gina Solomon, right? A legacy for, like, three generations and her son won't be considered until 2013!"

I finally ask Claire the question that's been on my mind since the first time she mentioned this. "Claire, since you're not pregnant yet, doesn't it seem a little premature to be worried about where your kid—kids—will go to school?" She doesn't say anything. "Oh, come on," I say, feeling bad. "Don't be like that. Look, I'm just stressed. I'm about to go in and meet with an editor about this feature story I'm going to be writing." She doesn't respond. "Did you hear me?" I ask. "I may well be doing a real article—not just party coverage." There's complete silence on the other end. "Are you there?" I ask.

"I am." She sounds like she's pouting.

"Then say something."

"I want to, but I'm not sure you're going to like it."

"Well, if you put it that way, I bet you're right."

She pauses and then spits out, "I think you need to get out of Hollywood."

"What's that supposed to mean?" The silent rule Claire and I have always abided by is that we don't outwardly criticize each other's choices.

"I think you focus so much on work to distract yourself from being lonely. You pursue this totally impractical writing career so you don't have to think about the fact that you haven't had a boyfriend in years."

"Jesus, Claire," I snap. "You sound like my mother."

"Your mother has a point, you know. Life isn't only about working. Nobody ever gets to the end of her life and says, 'Well, I just really wish I'd worked harder.'" Good God. Why do married people have to trot out the same tired clichés and constantly insist that they've made the right—or actually only—choice? If straight people talked that way about gay relationships, they'd rightfully be labeled homophobic, but somehow those who buy wholeheartedly into the notion that a wedding ring is the key to everlasting bliss feel perfectly justified in making single people feel like they're doing something wrong.

"Well, I'll think about that," I say.

"I just want to see you happy, Emma," Claire says. "You deserve that."

And that's when I lose it. "I *am* happy, Claire! Don't you understand? I—AM—HAPPY!" I yell this so loud that my throat immediately aches. Suddenly, tears are running down my face and I add, more quietly this time, "I am happy." Claire doesn't respond.

"SORRY I'M LATE," I say to Ethan as I walk into his office. With a start, I realize that Mark, the magazine's editor in chief—who I know only from the biannual editorial meetings he presides over and not from any actual personal interactions—is standing next to Ethan's desk. I smile somewhat manically, desperately hoping I don't look like what I am—that is, someone who just spent ten minutes crying in her car.

"Thanks for coming in," Ethan responds.

"No problem," I answer with what I hope is a carefree smile. After I'd e-mailed Ethan a transcript of the Jessica dinner, as well as my notes from Jimmy's party, he'd written me back to say he wanted me to come in to talk about the assignment. But I hadn't expected the big guy—who was so revered by the bureau that he was actually known as "the big guy" by most of the staff—to be present.

"So, I'm just going to give it to you straight here," Mark says. "When Ethan first said he wanted to give a party reporter a chance on a feature, I told him it was out of the question. But since he was fairly insistent, I started to take him seriously." He leans against the wall and folds his arms. "And then he forwarded me what you sent him." Breaking into an enormous smile, he says, "It's great, Emma. Racy, gritty, disturbing—just the kind of only-in-L.A. feature I like to see coming out of this bureau." Surprised, and suddenly anxiety-stricken, I choke out a laugh. "But doing a feature story—a potential cover story—for *Substance* is no easy task," he continues. "And if we're going to tackle this topic, we have to do it right."

"I can do it right," I say, sounding like I actually believe it.

Mark tilts his head in Ethan's direction. "That's what Ethan says. But I just want to make sure you know what you're getting into here. Everything, absolutely everything, has to be done on the up-and-up." I nod, burying a gulp. "You're going to need to go back to these girls and find out a lot more. Is this whole pseudo-sophistication thing a crock? Do they *ever* just take money? Also, Jessica at one point derides the other girls for having GEDs. When did she drop out of school? And what are her relationships with her clients really like? That kind of thing."

Forcing my face into a calm smile, I say, "Of course." A tremor shoots through my body.

"The more specific you can get them to be, the better," he

says. "The whole car hood incident that Jessica describes is perfect." The thought of Mark reading about how hard Jessica came makes me suddenly wonder about his home life. Had my transcript given him new ideas about how to liven up his sex life? Possibly contemplating the same thing, Mark suddenly looks uncomfortable and shifts his focus down to my feet.

"Because it was the one time where she didn't seem like she was in complete control," Ethan adds. I nod.

"Of course, we'll need transcripts and tapes of all your interviews for fact-checking," Mark says.

I nod and gulp at the same time. "Makes sense." The fact is, I don't have answers to any of the questions he's just posed, and Amanda and Kristi still think I'm one of them. Even more alarming, Jessica hasn't returned a message I left her three days ago asking if we could schedule another interview. I was, potentially, screwed. But explaining all of this to Mark and Ethan certainly isn't a way to make them feel confident in me. And once I hear back from Jessica, I feel certain she'll help me work out everything else. *It will be fine,* I think as I grin like I have no worries whatsoever.

Mark consults a dry-erase board on Ethan's office wall, which lists stories with due dates next to them. "The thing is, September will be our biggest issue this year—it has double the ad pages of August—so I'd like to run it then." He looks at me. "Do you think it's possible to get copy in on the fifteenth? I'd love to have it a few weeks early if we're going to make it the cover."

Glancing at the calendar next to the dry-erase board, I see that the fifteenth is just over two weeks away. My panic over that is drowned out by excitement at hearing that it's the cover story. To my shock, I don't respond to that news. "Sounds perfect," I purr, trying to channel the way I believe Jessica would respond to a client. "Shouldn't be a problem."

"That's what I like to hear," Mark says. "And remember, if you screw up, it's on this guy." He points to Ethan.

"Ha!" The word seems to catch in my throat.

"We can only pay you a thousand dollars," Mark says, "but if this story is as strong as I think it's going to be, we'll bump you up to the regular word rate for future work."

I nod. I'd probably, honestly, pay him to let me do the piece. "No problem."

"Also, I'll let Lauren know that she shouldn't give you as many events to cover over the next couple of weeks," Mark says.

"Great." I smile. "You guys don't have anything to worry about." Announcing this out loud, I figure, may help make it true. But if that's the case, why is my left eye suddenly twitching uncontrollably?

I CALL KRISTI after I leave, thinking that I better get as much information as I can from her now that Jessica has gone MIA. "Hi, Emma!" she squeals. "How are you feeling?"

"Much better—thanks," I answer. She and Amanda had invited me to a party the other night but when she'd said that it would be "lucrative," I'd realized that if I went, I might have to do more than just *act* like one of them. So I'd told her that I had one of my migraines—thinking that saying "one of my" would allow me to use the excuse again to get out of future similar-sounding events. "Practically reborn."

"Great!" she chirps. "You should come meet me at the Luxe Hotel."

I envision scores of men standing around in suits, piles of cocaine, and Kristi naked in the middle of the room. "I wish I could," I say, marveling at the fact that lying is starting to come so naturally to me that I don't even have to plan it: alternate realities are simply forming and flowing out of my mouth before they're even fully realized. "I have a stomach virus—it came on the minute the migraine left, of course."

"Aw, that's too bad," she responds. "Because I wanted you to either talk me into or out of buying this white gold Versace bracelet. I'm on the verge of going dialing for dollars and I can't decide if it's worth the trouble."

"Dialing for dollars?" I adjust the headset of my cell phone.

"Oh, you know—when you see something you want and just call up clients until you make enough money to get it."

"I thought you didn't take money."

Kristi pauses for about half a second. "If you saw this bracelet, you'd understand," she says.

"A Versace bracelet, you said?" I turn right onto Fountain.

"Mmmm-hmmm," she answers dreamily. "It would go perfectly with this new necklace I got and would probably attract all kinds of new clients."

"Well, that's a big decision," I say, picking up speed. "I can't let you make it alone."

"What about your stomach?"

I switch into a faster lane. "Nothing that a little shopping can't cure."

"ISN'T IT GORGEOUS?" Kristi asks, holding out her dainty, tanned arm. A sparkly bracelet dangles from her tiny wrist.

"It is," I say. I've never been much of a jewelry person but I can tell expensive when I see it. I glance at the swarthy, grinning man standing proudly behind the necklaces, bracelets, and rings on display in the hotel's indoor terrace and smile.

"This is Giovanni," Kristi says. "He brings back the best stuff from Italy and sells it wholesale once a month."

"I make only tiny profit," Giovanni says in a strong Italian accent. He holds his thumb and index finger together to indicate "tiny" before stepping into the hallway and leaving me alone in the room with Kristi.

"So how much is it?" I ask her.

Kristi smiles. "Three thousand five hundred," she says, quickly adding, "but it retails for over five thousand."

"How much do you have?"

"Well, I had over ten thousand dollars last week but then I wiped out my entire savings account last Friday." She pulls her scarf aside to reveal a necklace sparkling with so many diamonds that it's literally blinding. "On this."

"Wow."

"Fourteen thousand dollars worth of wow," she whispers, hanging her head.

"What?" I ask, stunned. "Are you serious?"

She shrugs. "You've got to spend money to make money," she says. "Hence . . ." She holds out her cell.

"So you're thinking of calling around?" I ask. "Going dialing for dollars?" I say the expression quickly in an effort to make it sound like it's something I've heard before today.

Pursing her lips in concentration, Kristi nods. "I already have Brian, a TV producer in the Valley. He says he'll see me at three o'clock today but I give him a good rate since he's literally my oldest client. So I need two or three more and no one, absolutely no one, is around right now. My two female clients haven't even called me back, so Amanda let me try a couple of hers." Her eyes narrow and she looks almost panicked. "I just have to have the bracelet." She sounds slightly hysterical now.

"I know," I respond, not sure what else to say. I point to her cell. "Have you been leaving people messages?"

She nods and seems to calm down. "Look," she says, "I know the bracelet's not going to make everything okay." She locks eyes with me and I'm astounded by how empty and blue they look. "But right now, it feels like it will."

I nod. There's something both sad and familiar about the way she's clinging to this bracelet for dear life and I realize that she's reminding me of me when I was wholly convinced that everything would be perfect if only I could have Matt back. I point to a pair of nearby lounge chairs set up on the sunny side of the hotel's veranda. "Why don't we sit down and wait for some people to call you back?" I ask.

Kristi nods and takes a deep breath. "Good idea," she says. She's subservient now to the point where she seems almost incapable of taking care of herself.

Leading her outside, I feel a terrible pang of guilt. *This girl is lost and I'm taking advantage of her,* I think. That's immediately followed by the thought that an ambitious journalist wouldn't let her conscience stop her from getting the story. "So how did you meet this Brian guy?" I ask.

"Craigslist," she says as she arranges herself on the chair, one of her too-quick smiles suddenly dancing across her face.

"You put up an ad or answered one?"

"Answered one," Kristi says, the bracelet suddenly a distant—or at least not pertinent—memory. "It said that he was looking for a host for an MTV show. I was working as a receptionist at Disney at the time so I sent my picture in, thinking what did I have to lose?" She smiles. "A week later, I get a call from this girl who says she works for Brian telling me that while I didn't get the hosting job, he did have something he wanted to offer me. 'He likes your look,' she said. 'And he's always really generous with the women in his life.'"

"So it was just a front then, right? There was no show?"

Kristi shrugs. "Who knows? I never asked."

"And you did it? You just said, 'Okay'?" I'm doing everything in my power not to sound judgmental.

Stretching languidly, Kristi watches a uniform-clad maid pass by. "Well, Amanda had just gotten back from a trip to Bermuda on some guy's yacht. There were servants—cooks and cleaning ladies and even a beauty person, who gave Amanda pedicures and massages—onboard." Her eyes grow wide at the prospect. "This was just some guy she'd met at a club! They hadn't had sex yet when he had his driver drop off a wad of cash and instruct her to get seven bathing suits, each one for a different day, and be ready to take a private plane the next day at noon. Isn't that crazy?"

"It is," I say.

"When they got back, he told her that since she didn't really have any skills and there was no guarantee that the acting thing was going to work out, she should just keep selling the one thing she had."

"That's awful," I say, before I can help myself.

Kristi glances at me, surprised. "Oh, it wasn't. He paid her really well, and wasn't dangerous or too freaky or anything. And by then she'd figured out it wasn't that hard to pretend the guy was someone else entirely." She laughs. "You just have to be careful—I guess she came really close to calling out her ex-boyfriend's name one time." She picks at a cuticle.

I nod, thinking about how Jessica had said that I didn't have the look in my eyes that said I'd be willing to do anything. Gazing at Kristi, I decide that she doesn't, either. I suddenly blurt out, "I don't know, Kristi. You just seem so . . . sweet. Like someone who should be teaching kindergarten and not being with guys who put up fake Craigslist ads." Kristi looks at me and blinks.

Her eyes immediately fill with tears but she doesn't say anything, and I suddenly regret my words. I notice with relief that her cell is flashing. "Hey, someone's calling you," I say weakly.

She glances at the device excitedly, immediately back in her manic, must-buy-bracelet mode. "Todd?" she says into the phone as she picks it up. "How are you?" She laughs. "Feel like getting together?" She laughs again. "Sounds perfect."

Standing up, I motion to Kristi that I have to go. She nods at me, thoroughly distracted, solely focused on the financial negotiation she's making and how it will lead her to the jewelry she believes will make her forget how she got the money to pay for it.

chapter 12

"CATHERINE!" JACK SCREECHES at Catherine Zeta-Jones, spraying my cheek with his spittle in the process. We're standing on a press line outside a Catherine Zeta-Jones and Jim Carrey movie premiere. "Caaaaaatherine!"

I wipe my cheek with my sleeve as I look back at him. "I don't think she's stopping," I say.

"She has to!" he exclaims. He gives me a shove. "Get her!"

I yell her name halfheartedly, and she either ignores me or doesn't hear. I turn to Jack. "Look, you win some, you lose some. I don't think *Entertainment Weekly* will go under just because it's lacking a Catherine Zeta-Jones quote."

Jack stares at me as if my priorities are seriously askew. "But I wanted to ask her about life with Michael!"

As I shake my head, I see Ethan making his way into the theater with a woman—presumably his wife. We wave at each other before I glance down the press line: *San Fernando Sunshine* is chatting enthusiastically with the stylist Phillip Bloch, while Jim Carrey is being interviewed by *Access Hollywood*. No sign of Antonio, who hadn't returned any of the messages I'd left for him in the past couple of days.

Then Jim Carrey starts making his way toward us. "Look, it's the guest of honor," I say to Jack, trying to psych myself up. Jack ignores me and I concentrate on feigning excitement. "Jim!" I yell at him, doing my best Jack impersonation. "Over here! *Substance* magazine?"

Jim approaches our area but Jack steps in front of me to get to him. "John, can I just tell you how much I loved *The Majestic*?" Jack says passionately. "It's really a sacrilege that it didn't do better."

Can I just tell you how much I loved The Majestic? *It's really a sacrilege that it didn't do better*? I want Jim to brush Jack out of the way and call him a transparent sycophant who's trying to tread all over the interview he was just about to give to *Substance* magazine but instead the movie star breaks into a loud laugh. "I like you!" he says to Jack, turning to the publicist by his side and exclaiming, "I like him!"

I sigh and look on as Jack interviews Jim about the film and his personal life, nabbing a series of good quotes in the process. I reach my tape recorder out. "Jim, um, Mr. Carrey—can you spare a moment for *Substance* magazine?"

"Sorry," the publicist says, not looking the slightest bit apologetic. She points to the movie theater, where the lights are flashing on and off. "He has to go inside. No more interviews." She steers Jim and a slew of his hangers-on away from the press line and into the theater. I sigh and toss my tape recorder into my purse.

"It's been a pleasure, Jack," I mutter under my breath.

"Totally!" Jack screams. I'm about to respond when I see that he's talking into a cell phone earpiece. "And then he said, 'I like you!'" Jack squeals. "And then he said to his publicist, 'I like him!'"

I shake my head, wishing an earthquake could suddenly erupt and take only Jack out. My phone starts ringing and I answer it without even glancing at caller ID, thinking, *Please let this be something good.* Anxiety about my prostitution story, combined with my utter failure to do my real job, seemed to be conspiring to fling me into a massive depression.

"Em?" It's Claire, sounding friendly. "Bad time?"

"Depends on how you look at it," I say, walking to the parking lot next to the theater and handing in my ticket. "It *is* a bad time, though not necessarily a bad time to talk. Bad joke. Bad time. What can I say? How are you, Claire?"

Claire laughs. "Wow, you're fried. You sound like how you used to during Crossroads finals."

That makes me miss her. "Watch out, you're going to make me nostalgic," I say. "What's going on?"

"Look, I'm sorry about our last conversation."

Surprised, I say, "Me, too."

She takes a deep breath. "And I have a great guy I want you to meet."

I stiffen. The last "great guy" Claire wanted me to meet was a three-hundred-pound accountant friend of Eric's with hair plugs. "I thought we weren't doing any more setups, Claire."

"I just really think you'd like him," she says. She pauses. "If you could get past the age thing."

"How old?"

Claire pauses. "Fifty-seven," she says.

"Fifty-seven?" I screech so loudly that it actually hurts my throat. "That's basically *sixty*! Are you out of your mind?"

"He's very sweet. He'd dote on you."

"Are we really in such a desperate place that we're resorting to people from our parents 'generation?" I ask.

"I just don't want you to be alone," she says. "And I think you're too picky. No one's ever going to meet your expectations."

"Look, I appreciate your concern, but the answer is no." Just then, I notice my friend Steve and his wife Celeste pulling into the lot and getting out of their car. "And the next time you think of a wonderfully fantastic guy who just happens to be obese or twenty-five years older or who has no legs or some other defect that makes you think he might actually like me, the answer will still be no." I take a deep breath. "And I'm not hanging up on you because I don't think it's cool to do that, but I have to go. Okay?"

"I don't know what's gotten into you," Claire responds.

Feeling too exhausted to fight, I say, "Me, neither," and close the phone, just in time to greet Steve and Celeste. "Going to the premiere?" I ask them in what I hope is a cheerful voice.

Celeste nods as Steve says, "Hey, why don't you come with us? We have an extra ticket."

The thought of sailing past Jack inside the theater is immensely appealing but I know I need to be figuring out how to save my prostitution story and not trying to one-up someone who was always going to be several steps ahead. "I can't, but thank you," I smile. "And have fun."

Steve nods as he puts his arm around Celeste and they walk across the street to the theater. As the valet parker drives my car up, my phone starts ringing again. Assuming it's Claire calling back for let's-set-Emma-up-with-a-senior-citizen-part-two, I answer with, "I just don't want to talk right now, Claire. Please."

"Emma?" It's a girl's voice, but not Claire's.

"Yes?" I say hesitantly.

"It's Jessica."

I get into my car, relief flooding through me. "Oh my God! Jessica! Thanks so much for calling me back. How have you been? Where have you been?" Suddenly it seems possible that my *Substance* story will work and I'll actually be able to make some changes to my life, that I won't be a lonely press-liner until the end of time after all. For some reason, I think of Kristi's faith in the white gold bracelet.

"What are you doing?" she asks. "Are you busy?"

"Not at all. Why do you ask?"

"Come pick me up," she says. "We're going to a client's house. You can interview me there."

Rather than asking for any details, I accept the fact that at this point I'd go to a Tupperware convention in Barstow with her if she asked me.

HIP-HOP MUSIC BLASTS through the speakers of the mansion as Jessica leads me down a hallway. "This is where Adrian's 'baby mama' sleeps," she says, bringing me into a massive bedroom with a four-poster bed so high off the ground that it has a mini staircase leading up to it. "And this is his sneakers room—a very tangible example of obsessive lunacy." We're standing in a closet that's bigger than my entire apartment, and it's filled entirely with sneakers—Air Jordans, Nike Air Force Ones, old-school Adidas tennis shoes, and Puma high tops, a smorgasbord of styles and colors, some in glass cases, more displayed on the floor and others on specially designed sneaker shelves. Jessica shakes her head ever so slightly and then starts walking downstairs.

I follow her into a room that seems to contain only sunken couches topped with enormous, stuffed pillows, a massive stereo system, and a rocking chair. A group of middle-aged black men decked out in all kinds of jewelry are propped all around. One of them, an enormous guy wearing several diamond necklaces, immediately approaches Jessica and puts his arms around her. "Hey, Jessie baby," he coos. "You gonna be nice to me tonight?"

Jessica removes each of his arms and gives him a thin smile. "Nice try, Sean. But you know how that goes." The man—Sean—then gives me a once-over.

"How about you, baby? You as cruel as Jessie?"

I feel my heart begin to do an anxious dance but before I can answer, Jessica shakes her head. "Hands off, Sean," she says. "She's not working tonight." She pulls me over to a couch on the other side of the room as I wonder why I'm not more offended that I've just been mistaken for a hooker.

"Look," Jessica says, lighting a cigarette once we're out of earshot of Sean and the other men gathered in various pockets around the room. "All of this"—she gestures toward a guy with a video camera, another busying himself with a stereo, and a couple men sharing a spliff—"is a big display for Adrian's ego. It may look like it's fun—or something like it—but we all know where our bread is buttered."

"So everyone here is on your client's payroll?"

Jessica exhales a clean line of smoke. "Well, not literally," she says. "Some are, and some just smell money and power so they hang around hoping for a leg up on whatever it is they've convinced themselves will make them happy."

I watch Jessica wink at the guy with the video camera and give a thin, smiling, nervous-looking woman just entering the room a wave. "Baby mama," Jessica whispers under her breath. I nod as if I think it's perfectly normal for a guy to have the mother of his children and his prostitute in the same room, let alone waving and smiling at each other.

Just then, Adrian—a black guy with diamonds pinned to, it

seems, every orifice of his body, from his ears to his nose to his jacket coat—enters the room. Jessica had told me I'd recognize him once I saw him and she's right: as a rap producer who started out in a hip-hop band in the '90s, Adrian has been in enough magazine stories and on enough TV specials for his face to be undeniably familiar. "Ahhhh!" he screams, seemingly pleased by the group gathered. "Now *that's* what I'm talkin' about!"

"Hi, baby!" Jessica chirps and Adrian makes his way past his cronies—one of whom is trying to hand him a spliff—past his baby mama, and over to our couch. "This is Emma," Jessica announces and Adrian kisses Jessica on the top of her head and then looks at me appreciatively.

"How ya doing?" he asks, not waiting for a reply before taking out his cell phone and immediately punching numbers into it.

"You want a Bellini, baby?" Jessica asks.

"That I do," he says without looking up from his phone. Jessica nods at Sean—who, along with everyone else, is now hovering around Adrian—and Sean presses an intercom button and announces, "Bellinis for everyone." It reminds me of that Dr. Seuss story where one cat makes his second-in-command carry his tail so that it doesn't drag on the ground, and then the second-in-command makes the third-in-command carry his tail and so on, until every last cat in town has another carrying his tail—except for the very last one, who finally gets fed up and quits.

Adrian walks over to the stereo and his mini entourage follows him. "You ever had a Bellini?" Jessica asks me. I shake my head. "It's champagne and peach schnapps—my signature drink in college and also, coincidentally, Adrian's favorite." She lights a cigarette.

"So, where did you go to college?" I ask her, making every attempt to hide how surprised I am to hear her mention school at all. Someone turns up the music—old school hip hop.

"In Connecticut," she says. "I'm from New York, so I just stuck close to home."

"Where in Connecticut?" I ask.

"Yale," she says, making a face. "Or, as I liked to call it back then, jail."

For a second, I assume she's joking and start to laugh. And then I realize she's entirely serious. Because my parents have yet to recover from the fact that I was rejected from Harvard—despite the family members who both attended and donated money—Jessica's blasé attitude about having gotten into its main rival seems almost unfathomable.

"Did you graduate?" I ask.

"Sure," she says. "When you're a scholarship kid, you don't have any option but to kick ass. Class of 2003." *Great—smarter and younger than me, too,* I think.

A fleet of girls in bright pink uniforms suddenly enters the room carrying trays holding champagne flutes filled with pink liquid and two of them walk over to Adrian and his hangers-on while another makes her way over to us. Nobody brings a drink to Adrian's baby mama, who's now sitting alone on the rocking chair. Taking two glasses from the pink-uniformed girl and handing one to me, Jessica sits back with her drink and sighs contentedly.

"Sorry for not being around this past week," she says. "When I'm tending to Bernie's needs, everything else seems to get swept aside."

"No problem." I sip my drink.

Adrian seems to be yelling at some member of his entourage—for, from what I can hear, liking a kind of tennis shoe that Adrian hates. During a tirade against the guy—which everyone else pretends isn't happening—Adrian orders the man videotaping everything to shut the "motherfucking" camera off.

"What's the video camera for, anyway?" I ask.

Jessica rolls her eyes. "Adrian's under the impression that everything he does will end up having great historical value someday." She lowers her voice. "In his deluded mind, I think he imagines that rap will be studied in school and the students will someday be utterly captivated by footage of what the great Adrian Bisson did during his down time." She laughs.

"Yo, Jessie!" Adrian suddenly yells from across the room.

"What's that, babe?" she responds, smiling at him so sweetly that you'd never believe she'd just been calling him delusional.

"Got some private business to discuss with you!"

"Be back in a few," Jessica says to me. "Anyone tries anything with you, just make sure you tell them you're not working tonight, you hear?"

"Got it," I respond as Jessica stands, does a curtsy in Adrian's direction, and follows him up the staircase. I gaze around the room with this vague sense that I should probably be a bit more unnerved than I am. The fact is, I'm sitting in a not-particularly-sane-seeming rap producer's house with a slew of his surely shady yes-people, and most of them probably think I'm a hooker. But instead, I feel oddly calm—almost powerful—and I wonder if that's because some of Jessica's confidence is beginning to rub off on me. Sean lumbers over but as he starts to sit down, I give him a quick shake of the head and he turns around, immediately apologetic, and shuffles back toward the stereo like a dog that's been shooed away. I laugh. Was fending people off really that easy? I pick up my drink and walk toward the other side of the room, where French doors lead to a patio. No one seems to be paying any attention to me so I wander outside and am immediately confronted with a well-lit greenhouse and an array of fruit trees—nearly ripe plums, apples, and oranges accost me at every turn. I walk around the grounds, passing by an infinity pool and guest house with a home gym attached to it before realizing that I've wandered quite far and should probably be making my way back.

Returning to the room, I find everyone in much the same positions they were in when I left—entourage around the stereo, videographer with video camera down on the ground, baby mama still sitting by herself. Nobody seems to have noticed either my absence or return. I sit back down on a couch just as Jessica and Adrian reappear and Adrian immediately launches back into a verbal assault on the guy he was fighting with about sneakers. Jessica joins me, her glass now filled to the brim.

"So how did it go?" I ask as she lights a cigarette.

"Fine," she says, blowing out a smoke ring and lowering her voice. "Adrian's into the rape thing, you know? Where he pretends I'm some chick he met at a party who wasn't into him and then he followed me home and had his way with me—that kind of scenario." She rolls her eyes as she gulps her drink.

"What?" I ask, stunned. My serenity of just a few moments ago is long gone.

"Oh, come on, you've never heard people talk about their rape fantasies?" she asks. When I don't respond, she continues, "Trust me, a lot of guys have them—Christ, I'm sure you've been fucked by men who were pretending you were some helpless victim."

"I don't think—"

"What about you?" she asks, raising an eyebrow.

"What *about* me?"

"Oh, come on. The fantasy's far more common among women. You know that twinge of guilt you feel whenever you spread your legs because you're conditioned to believe that you're bad for surrendering to your baser impulses? If you pretend the guy is raping you, you're off the hook. And you've got to admit, there's something pretty hot about the notion of getting off on sex you're being forced to have."

I nod, wondering if an appropriate response to such a statement even exists. "Do you think it's easier for you to go along with that kind of thing because you used to be an actress?" I ask.

Jessica inhales on her cigarette and stares off into space. "God, I don't know." She exhales a plume of smoke as I feel relieved that I actually succeeded in changing the subject. "I really let that whole actress thing go a long time ago." She smiles weakly and at first I think she looks embarrassed but then realize she actually appears somewhat sad.

"How come?"

"Well, I came out here with my theater degree, thinking I was the shit—that, you know, Meryl Streep and Paul Newman careers were just what all the Yalies deserved," she says, downing the rest of her drink and motioning to Sean that she'd like another. "I did some theater in New York—off-Broadway but still, Ben Brantley went out of his way to praise me once in the *Times*." She crosses her legs as Sean walks over to us, fills Jessica's glass, and then retreats. "I didn't have a clue how Hollywood worked—I mean, I knew it was competitive but I thought, I guess, that if you were good, you'd get hired." I nod. "The CAAs and ICMs weren't interested in me, but I figured that was okay—that I just needed to get in a good acting class out here and sign with whatever agency would have me," she says. "But all the acting classes were overrun with phonies or Scientologists or people trying to get on reality shows."

"What made you want to be an actress in the first place?" I ask. I've always been so grateful I didn't want that—I may well be a glutton for punishment but I've long been clear about the fact that my self-esteem wouldn't have been able to withstand all those auditions and rejections.

"I'm sure this sounds pathetic, but acting like someone else is pretty much the only way I ever felt comfortable," she says as she crushes her cigarette into the ashtray. She laughs. "Acting seemed easier and cheaper than going to therapy to try to get comfortable or figure out why I was so uncomfortable." A pensive smile crosses her lips. "When I got into the theater program at Yale, my mom, who raised me—her only child—was happier than I'd ever seen her." She shakes her head, seemingly willing her vulnerability away. "That was back when I actually gave a shit about pleasing her. So there are surely some twisted psychological reasons why I wanted to be an actress, not to mention the obvious escapist fantasies—this I-don't-have-to-really-deal-with-my-own-shit, I-can-just-pretend-I'm-someone-else thing." She sips her drink and continues, "But at the auditions that I went on, I met with casting directors and producers who were either gay men or women who really needed to get laid and hated anyone who looked like she could." She sighs. "I was waiting tables at this place on Beverly, making, like, a couple hundred dollars a week and constantly auditioning for, like, one-line parts on *Two and Half Men*. That I wasn't getting." She leans back on the couch. "And then, I started meeting those other kinds of producers—the you-scratch-my-back, I'll-scratch-yours kind of guys. They essentially treated me like they could already buy me. They'd say shit like, 'If you want to make it in this town, you've got to learn to be *very* generous,' and wink. So that's happening and I'm watching these absolute bimbos land jobs that I'd have killed for and realizing that whatever the acting game is out here, it's not something I want to join." She lights another cigarette. "Of course, I'm probably making myself sound far more noble than I am. The fact is, what I'm doing now is a hell of a lot more lucrative and I like having nice things."

As we watch Adrian bark some order at the mother of his children, I ask, "Do you have any qualms about what you do? Do you ever go, 'Wait a minute, this is wrong'?"

Jessica shrugs. "It's only wrong if you make sex into something more than it is. The way I see it, we're making a trade. I'm pretty and the guy's rich—we each have something the other values. What's so bad about an even exchange?" I nod slowly, wondering if I make sex into more than it is. After a pause, Jessica asks, "Look, how much do you make? Forty grand a year? Fifty?"

"Somewhere around there," I mutter.

"Well, that doesn't go very far, does it?" I shake my head. "Mommy and Daddy pay your rent?"

"No, they don't. They actually—"

"Then I bet there are a whole lot of things you can't have. Either that or your credit cards must be maxed to the limit."

"Sure, I have credit card bills and yes there are things I can't afford, but—"

"Can you imagine what it would be like to have anything you want?" Jessica asks, looking me directly in the eye. I don't say anything. "If you could, you wouldn't have any qualms, either." She laughs. "See, all you lack is imagination."

I smile uncomfortably as Sean wanders over to us again. "You're done," he announces to Jessica. "Free to go."

"Great," Jessica says, gulping down the rest of her drink and turning to me. "You ready?"

I watch Sean's retreating back. "That's it?" I ask, surprised. "We just leave?"

"Sure," Jessica says, standing up and motioning for me to follow her. As we cross the room, she lowers her voice slightly and adds, "Adrian's business manager pays my Amex every month and in exchange, I'm pretty much always on call. Whenever I get a text from Sean that Adrian wants me—it could be three nights in a row, every week, or once a month—I come over." She leads me up the stairs. "I stay as long as he wants me to, do whatever he asks, and then leave."

"But should we say good-bye to anyone? Tell them we're going?"

"Nah," Jessica says as we walk outside. "They don't give a shit."

We get in my car. "So what does the baby mama think? That he really has business to discuss with you?"

"Who knows?" Jessica takes a cigarette out and pushes the lighter in and I don't say anything, even though no one's ever smoked in my car before. "The main requirement for her job is not to think." As I ease the car out of Adrian's driveway and security gate, Jessica's phone starts buzzing and she answers it on speakerphone.

"Hi, it's me," I hear Matt McCarthy say and I jump at the sound of his voice. "Where the hell are you?" he asks. "Why haven't you been returning my calls?" He sounds different than I've ever heard him—hyped up, almost aggressive.

"I'm here now," she says. "You've got me. So, what do you want?"

"Shit, am I on speaker?" Matt asks, insecurity leaking out of his voice. I can't help but relish witnessing him sound so pathetic. "You know I hate that."

"Yep," she says, not taking him off speaker.

"What are you doing? Can we get together?" he asks, his trademark cockiness a bit more apparent now.

"I don't know," Jessica says. "You've already used up all of your June time."

"So take one off of next month's."

Jessica rolls her eyes at me. "Okay," she says. "How about Casa Del Mar? A half hour?" I glance at her, surprised. Casa Del Mar is out in Santa Monica and we're on our way back to West Hollywood. "Go sit at the bar and wait for me," she adds.

"Wait, you're breaking up," he responds. "Take me off speaker so I can hear you better."

She sighs, presses a button, and then puts her phone to her ear. Enunciating each word condescendingly, she repeats, "I said, go sit at the bar and wait for me. Is that clear enough for you?" She hangs up without waiting for an answer.

"Should I get on the 10?" I ask, vacillating between feelings of vicarious pleasure and intense jealousy. "So I can get you to Santa Monica?"

She takes a drag and exhales. "Oh, no. I'm not really going."

I smile. "You mean, you just told Matt to go wait for you in a hotel bar but you have no intention of actually being there yourself?" I ask. Jessica nods. "And he'll put up with that?"

Jessica eyes me. "Look, you dated the guy. Right?"

I shift uncomfortably. Except for the day I approached her at Starbucks, she and I had never discussed Matt. "Yeah—for about a month, anyway."

She examines me closely. "Wow, he really got to you, didn't he?" I don't say anything and she laughs. "It's too bad you didn't know me back then. Because I could have told you how easy he is to master." She grins. "McCarthy's a classic martyr. The only thing that guy responds to is indifference and rejection."

chapter 13

THE SUN'S GLARE seems absolutely unbearable as I make my way through Melrose afternoon traffic on my way home from yoga. It was the first time I'd been since I started working on the prostitution story and, based on how my muscles are aching, I may have overtaxed myself. The more I think about it, though, the more the pain seems to be based primarily in my head. Putting my hand on my throbbing temple, I speculate that by telling Kristi and Amanda I get migraines, I've actually managed to bring one on.

Sighing, I wonder how and when I'm actually going to come clean with them. "Hey girls, I was just lying to you to find out some information for my article" simply isn't a sentence I can imagine making its way out of my mouth. Yet I know I have to tell them the truth if I want to use anything they've said in the story. I suddenly wonder what made me so convinced that I could tackle this piece. I was someone who gathered quotes from people like Flavor Flav on press lines. How on earth did I think I'd be able to handle a feature story—a cover story—while I'm lying to some of my sources *and* to my editor about how I'm getting the information?

"Hey!" A guy on a bicycle suddenly knocks on my window while I'm sitting at a red light, causing me to jump.

"What the hell?" I yell. The guy, who's wearing a massive bike helmet and a pair of wraparound sunglasses, is looking at me expectantly, like he's waiting for me to offer him a sincere apology for driving too close to him. Then it crosses my mind that he may be one of those policemen on bicycles who's just not wearing his uniform so I smile and roll down the passenger side window.

"Excuse me, miss," he says. He appears to be laughing and clearly isn't a cop. "But you were driving like a bat out of hell."

"Look," I say, annoyed. "I'm sorry, but—"

"Whoa," he says, holding up his right hand. "Emma, right?" I nod. He points at himself. "Danny, from Whole Foods? The guy who probably saved you from any number of brain tumors?"

"Oh, yeah," I respond, thoroughly surprised and the slightest bit unnerved. "How are you?"

He removes his helmet and smiles. "Potentially calmer than you."

Torn between feeling slightly aroused by the sight of the veins popping out of his arm and annoyed by the fact that he seems to be judging my driving and stress level, I sigh. "Look, I just have a lot on my mind and—"

"Hold it right there," Danny says, seemingly oblivious to my cantankerous tone. "You sound like someone who could use a calming beverage."

Despite myself, I start to soften. I don't think I've ever heard someone use the words "calming" and "beverage" together in my life. “Is that so?” I ask. The person in the car behind me lays his hand on the horn. I look up: the light’s green.

I gesture toward the road. “I should probably go.”

“Nonsense,” he says, casually giving the honking driver a “hold on a minute” hand signal. He points to a nearby space and says, “Park and take a load off. Let me buy you a tea.”

I smile for the first time all day and surprise myself by pulling into the space while Danny locks his bike to a nearby post. As I get out of the car, Danny asks, “So what was it that had you gripping the wheel like it was some sort of a flotation device and you were drowning at sea?”

“Work, life, stress—the usual,” I say. He smiles soothingly and leads me into a café that’s filled with glowing Southern Californians who look like they subsist solely on wheat germ, soy, and positive affirmations. Some are being massaged in vertical massage chairs while others are gathered in a small group in the back, holding hands and repeating some sort of mantra. I gesture to a rotund Asian lady digging her elbow into the back of a petite woman with short hair. “I could probably use a little of that.”

Danny shakes his head. “Look, technically speaking, there’s nothing wrong with massage. But people use it as a Band-Aid solution to chronic pain.”

I laugh. “Wow. And here I thought a massage was sort of like a puppy or rainbow—you know, something benign and relatively controversy-free. What have you got against it?”

“Nothing, really.” Danny folds his arms. “It’s just that it can’t do much for a misaligned spine.” He orders two teas as I smile, surprised and amused by his sudden seriousness. “What are you—a chiropractor?” I ask.

“Not yet—but I will be soon,” he says, sliding money across the counter.

I laugh. "Oh, I was kidding."

Danny picks up his mug of tea, gestures for me to do the same, and leads me to an outdoor porch. "Well, I'm not," he says. "I go to Cleveland College over on Highland—do you know it?" I shake my head as we sit down in wicker chairs that are propped next to a fountain. "What did you think?" he asks, smiling. "That I wanted to spend my whole life directing people toward gluten-free desserts?"

I feel myself blush. "No, of course not. It's just . . ." I smile. "I can't remember the last time I met someone in L.A. who wasn't a writer, actor, aspiring writer, or aspiring actor." I try to force my mom's thoughts about chiropractors—"tacky charlatans"—out of my head.

"You're funny," he says. He blows on his tea before taking a sip. "You want to know something else you probably won't hear much around here? I love being in school. When I was a kid and even in college, I could never really focus in class because I couldn't seem to understand why I was being taught calculus or physics or Spanish or whatever it was when I probably wasn't going to ever use any of it. And that's one of my major regrets. Do you know what I mean?"

I nod as I take a sip of tea. "I feel the same way, actually. I spent most of my time in school stressing about what I was going to do when I got out; it was only once I did that I realized I'd somehow missed the chance to learn just for the sake of learning."

"Exactly." Danny nods. "So to be studying something now that I care about, and know I'm going to use, feels great." He sips his tea. "Like I've finally grown up, or something." He smiles, the gap between his teeth on full display.

I watch the mantra-chanters wander out onto the porch and think about how much more interesting Danny is than he seemed at first. Everyone I know announces their career goals the first second you're in their presence and he hadn't let on that he was anything more than a guy who worked at Whole Foods when we met, despite hearing all about my career. Then again, maybe aspiring chiropractors learn to keep that kind of thing to themselves. I decide to change the subject entirely. "So why are you risking life and limb by biking in a city where the drivers are so renowned for being crazy that pedestrians don't even exist?" I ask.

"And why are you driving around looking like the world's problems rest on your shoulders?" His voice sounds like a wink.

I smile. "Haven't you ever heard that it's rude to answer a question with a question?"

Danny shakes his head. "Nope. That particular rule of etiquette must not have made it out to New Jersey." I watch him drink his tea as I think about how Lilly calls New Jersey the "armpit of America." Then he adds, "So seriously, what's on your mind?"

"I'll answer your question if you answer mine," I say.

"Deal." He takes another sip. "I was biking on the mean streets of L.A. because I don't like contributing to environmental problems when I can avoid it—you know, the whole Al Gore–carbon footprint thing. But I'm not some annoying do-gooder, I swear. Honestly, it's great excercise, and between work and school, it's hard to find time to get to the gym. Your turn."

"Your bike is your mode of transportation?"

He nods. "Yep. I mean, I have a car and use it sometimes. But my roommate—who doesn't have a car—works in the Valley so I let him drive it most of the time."

"You have a roommate?" I ask, silently ordering the judgmental voice in my head to be quiet. "A housemate or a roommate?" I picture Danny sharing a one-bedroom—or a studio!—with another guy, their twin beds side by side in a tiny, dilapidated shack of some kind.

"Housemate, I guess you'd call it," he says. "We have a big place with a yard that's pretty awesome." *He's an adult who shares a house with a carless guy and uses words like "awesome,"* I think. Danny looks at me. "So, what about you?" he asks. "I believe you owe me some answers."

Glancing at a girl sitting below the fountain reading a book on transcendental meditation, I think that this nice guy whose biggest concerns are about his carbon footprints and biking to chiropractor class could never understand my complicated problems. "I don't really know how to break it down," I say.

"Try." He smiles encouragingly.

"Well, I guess I've always assumed that I was a good, honest person—better than most," I start. "But lately I haven't been. I've become so deceptive, in fact, that I don't even seem to realize when I'm lying." I stop, surprised by my sudden honesty. Maybe the uber-Zen meditators and chanters and inner child affirmers were helping to bring out my higher self.

"Lying about what?" He rests his index finger on his face and stares at me with curiosity.

I look at his trusting green eyes. "Everything," I say, unable to keep meeting his gaze. "Who I am, what I am, what I do."

"Why?"

I glance at the meditators and then back at Danny. "Because I don't believe I'm going to get what I need unless I lie," I say, shocking myself again with how easily I'm able to identify and articulate the truth. Either the tea contained sodium pentathol or Danny's straightforwardness was highly contagious.

"Why wouldn't you get what you need?" he asks, appearing genuinely curious. "Don't you have everything you need?"

"What do you mean?"

He leans forward. "I used to really believe I needed all this stuff:

the right car, the perfect girlfriend, different parents." I glance at him, startled. It seems impossible to imagine him being anything other than giddily content. "But then I realized that all these external things were never going to make me happy. Nothing out there"—he points to the street—"is going to do it for me. It's the whole Joseph Campbell secure-way-is-the-insecure-way thing."

"Joseph Campbell?" I can never manage to keep straight if he's the guy who wrote *Heart of Darkness* or the one who talks about heroes and their journeys. I figure my chances are fifty-fifty. "The hero's journey?" I ask.

Danny nods. "Yeah, but his best quotes are about the importance of following your bliss." He sips his tea. "Basically—and I'm seriously paraphrasing here—he said that if your goal is money, you can lose money and then you're screwed. But if your goal is bliss, then you'll always have that—whether you've got money or not. And to me, bliss has a lot to do with just appreciating what I have and seeing that I'm exactly where I'm meant to be."

I nod and my heart starts racing the way it does whenever I hear something that I know is important. I've never been motivated by money—at least not solely. But am I motivated by bliss? I'm not even sure I'd recognize that. What is bliss to me, anyway? Success? Validation? Validation in the form of a successful boyfriend? I feel torn between admiring Danny's clarity and good values and being jealous that I don't share them. "That makes sense," I say. "I'm just not there." I meet his gaze. "You're probably a much better person than I am."

He shakes his head. "That's ridiculous. Don't you know there's no such thing as someone being 'better than' or 'worse than' another person—that that's just a way for people to compare themselves to each other and feel superior or miserable?" I think of Rebecca and Brooke and the other Hollywood people I know. "Maybe," Danny says, smiling, "you didn't get *that* etiquette lesson."

"I guess not." I smile. "I seem to have missed a few."

"Aw, you're much too hard on yourself," Danny says. He looks at me with so much compassion that for a second, I feel like I'm going to cry. Then I hear my cell phone ringing from inside my purse and think, *Saved by the bell.* I see on caller ID that it's Jessica and, thrilled to be hearing from her only a day after our visit to Adrian's, I pick up immediately. "Hey," I say.

"Can you meet me at Fred Segal in ten minutes?" she asks.

I glance at my watch, then at Danny. "Okay."

"Find me in shoes, right near the bag store," she says and I smile, wondering if Jessica's planning to show me her version of exchanging goods for cash. "I'll be somewhere between Marc Jacobs and Michael Kors."

"If I didn't know they were both gay, I might say that sounds a little dirty," I say.

She laughs. "Aw, you made a sex joke!" she yelps. "There may be hope for you after all."

"HERE," JESSICA SAYS, holding out the Ursula Elise Marc Jacobs bag as I walk up to her in Fred Segal Shoes.

"What is this?" I ask.

Jessica grins. "A present," she says. "You told Amanda you thought it was gorgeous, didn't you?"

I nod, feeling slightly unnerved. Had she been spying on us that day at Bloomingdale's? "Yes, but—"

"I absolutely insist," Jessica says, continuing to stand there and hold it out.

"That's really nice of you, but I can't take it," I say. Accepting gifts from sources is a serious no-no in journalism; supposedly the former fashion director at *Substance* was fired for *borrowing* diamonds from a jeweler to wear to an event.

Jessica's face darkens. "Oh, really?" she says, her voice suddenly icy. "Well, then, how about this? How about I won't talk to you anymore for your article *unless* you take it?"

"You can't be serious," I say.

"Oh, I am," she says, looking at me coldly.

"Why do you care?" I ask, adding what I hope is a casual little laugh.

Jessica just stares at me, and I suddenly notice anger in her eyes. "If someone gives you a present, it's impolite to refuse," she says, as if she's Miss Manners' most exceptional protégé. I see from her tone and stance that she's not going to budge on this point and although that seems absolutely insane, I figure she might be having some kind of a manic mood swing and I can always insist on giving it back to her when she's in a normal frame of mind again. I smile and hold out my hand. "Thanks very much," I say, as Jessica hands the bag over to me. "I didn't mean to sound ungrateful."

Jessica grins and I'm amazed by how relieved I am to be back in her good graces. "You're welcome," she says. "Now, let's go have coffee." Following Jessica to the counter of the restaurant inside the store, I tuck the bag under my arm and feel a surprising rush of pleasure over holding something so beautiful. "Ohhh, check *her* out," Jessica says, tilting her head in the direction of a somewhat familiar-looking petite brunette with dainty features dressed in a Chanel suit. I watch the woman, who's obnoxiously berating someone on her cell phone, walk by as Jessica orders our coffee.

"Do you know her?" I ask.

Jessica nods, one eyebrow raised. "Serena?" she asks. "Yes and no. She's from some white trash town in Northern California, and when she got here—this was way before my time, back when everyone just did straight-up prostitution—she immediately became the number one girl for Lori, the madam who started running Heidi's business after she got busted." We sit down at a table and Jessica takes an enormous gulp of coffee. I sip mine and when it nearly lacerates my tongue, I wonder if Jessica's mouth is somehow immune to heat. "Serena was some catalogue model, I guess, and Lori started helping her get seventy-five and eighty grand a weekend," Jessica says.

"Seventy-five or eighty grand a weekend?" I ask, dumbfounded.

"I know, can you believe that shit?" Jessica asks. "Playmates, Penthouse Pets, porn stars, and catalogue models can make bank because they're considered, on some level, famous. Or at least they're the kind of girls that these guys once fantasized about fucking." She shakes her head. "Sometimes, the clients get so excited to be with those girls that they can't even get it up. So they pay almost six figures to have some whore console them over their softie." She shakes her head. "Anyway, Lori had it in for Serena. She was always stiffing her on payments and sending her on these jobs that were really dangerous—like to go see Arab guys who were on terrorist watch lists. Basically just constantly fucking her over."

"But Serena looks like she's doing okay now," I say. Strolling through Fred Segal in her Chanel suit, yelling at someone on her cell phone, she'd actually seemed far more like a Hollywood producer than a high-class hooker.

"Yeah," Jessica half says and half snorts. "Lo and behold, one of those clients that Lori was sending Serena to went and fucking proposed to her." Jessica rolls her eyes. "Lori may have won the battle but Serena won the fucking war." She grimaces and I can't tell if she's envious of Serena, judging her, or both.

"Did they get married?" I ask.

Jessica nods. "Oh, yeah," she says. "She's Mrs. James Carlson, the ultimate kept woman."

My jaw drops to somewhere below, I think, my coffee cup. James Carlson is a producer with probably the best track record in town—he's made about ten hit movies and has won at least two Oscars. I suddenly remember interviewing James and his wife, Serena, on a press line. "*She* was a prostitute? Are you sure?"

Jessica nods. "Oh, yeah."

"Is this common knowledge? Could I prove it?" I ask.

Jessica laughs. "Prove it? That's a good one." She shrugs. "Come on, you know how it is around here: it doesn't really matter what you did yesterday. Who gives a shit that Angelina Jolie used to wear blood around her neck, cut herself, and wreck marriages? Nobody. Today, she's considered Mother fucking Teresa. It's all about what you've got going on today, and today Serena Carlson is doing mighty well."

I shake my head, trying to brainstorm a way to work the Serena information into my story as a blind item. "She must give a lot of you hope," I say.

"Is that what you think?" Jessica asks, her face suddenly pink with anger and her nostrils flaring. "That I should look up to that tramp?"

"No," I object, wishing I could rewind time just about five seconds. I hadn't even been thinking when I spoke. "That isn't what I meant. I just—"

"Look, Serena is *still* a prostitute—more so than ever before, actually," Jessica says. "She just has one boss and he happens to be her pimp and money manager, too. And if you think that's something I should hope for—handing my power over to one man—then you haven't listened to one fucking word I've told you."

I take a deep breath, hating the fact that I've pissed Jessica off and willing to say or do almost anything to calm her down. "Look, I don't think you'd want her life," I say. "But I bet that people like Amanda or Kristi would." Jessica nods, her features now calm, and I feel ashamed of myself for being such a wimp. If I were ballsier, I'd tell Jessica that I think she sounds blatantly jealous of Serena. But I'm not ballsy, certainly not compared to Jessica, so instead I use the fact that my phone is beeping with a calendar reminder to distract her from the conversation altogether.

"Oh, Christ," I say when I look at it. "I'm supposed to cover an awards show tonight and I completely spaced. I haven't even checked in with the publicist yet." Stress begins coursing through my system as I realize that it's after five and the press will be lining up any minute. "I'm probably already late and—"

"Hang on a second," Jessica says, holding up her hand. "You're not going to get anything done if you continue to exist at that level of anxiety. Breathe." I take a long, deep breath, exhale, and feel calmer, but that's at least partially due to the fact that Jessica seems to have entirely forgotten about her anger. "Now, what were you saying?"

"Just that I have to cover an awards show for *Substance*."

Jessica nods. "Sounds like fun."

"It does. But it isn't. Not at all. When you're covering, you're not invited. You're only there, in fact, to harass and disturb the people who are invited. And while you're necessary—without you, there wouldn't be any quotes to go with the pictures of the celebrities that the people organizing the event want to run in your magazine—you're also a complete nuisance. It's actually incredibly humiliating."

Jessica eyes me. "I think that really depends on your attitude."

"Trust me, attitude doesn't matter. The whole thing is just a lot better in theory than it is in practice."

"I don't know." Jessica leans back in her chair and looks at me. "Attitude is everything. Take me, for instance. I could go around berating myself, deciding that I'm nothing but a scheming, soulless, slutty cheap whore." I nod slowly, surprised to hear her talk about herself in such a way, even though I know she's only doing it to make a point. "Or," she says, "I can choose to have a different attitude and say that I'm young and beautiful and using the natural gifts I've been blessed with to get the things in life that I want. That," she says, smiling, "is attitude."

I down the rest of my coffee. "Look, you have a point," I say. "But you just don't understand—covering events is a nightmare. The editor, Lauren, is never happy with the quotes I get."

"Fuck her."

"And I'm just not aggressive enough for the press lines—I never seem to be able to do what I'm supposed to while everyone else—"

"You stand on those press lines?" Jessica asks, cutting me off, her little nose wrinkling with distaste.

"They're horrible, I know, but I have to because—"

"Who says you have to?"

"I need to interview all the celebrities there and I'm usually not allowed inside the events because—"

"We'll see about that."

"Jessica, you don't understand. This is just the way it is."

"Do you have the number of the person organizing tonight's event?"

I nod. "I have to call her and check in."

Jessica pulls a phone out of her purse. "What's the number?"

"Oh, I don't think you should—"

Jessica snaps her fingers somewhat impatiently. "Emma,

give me the number," she says. "You need to have a little more faith."

I glance down at my phone, see the publicist's contact information listed in the event reminder, and suddenly feel a great sense of comfort over the fact that someone else has temporarily taken control of my life. I read Jessica the number. "Her name is Nancy," I say, as Jessica dials.

Jessica nods and almost immediately says, "Hello, Nancy?" into the phone. I lean in to try to hear the other side of the conversation. "How are you? I'm calling on behalf of Emma Swanson from *Substance* magazine. I understand you'd like her to cover your event tonight?"

"It's not that she'd *like me* to, it's that I have to—" I start to say.

Jessica puts a finger in her ear to tune me out. "I can understand why, since *Substance* was, the last time circulation numbers were released, one of the most successful publications in America."

I want to grab the phone out of her hand, certain that this Nancy woman is asking her what the hell she's talking about and I'm going to end up getting in trouble. Jessica ignores me as I motion for her to hand me the phone and says, "Unfortunately, Emma won't be able to stand on the press line. So you're going to have to find her a seat inside the event."

Oh, God. I'm dead, I think. I reach over for the phone again but Jessica swats my hand away. "It would probably be best if you put her at a table with the most important celebrities you have coming," Jessica says, and I bury my head in my hands. "That is, if you want the best coverage."

On that, I stand up. If Jessica continues with this, Nancy will call Lauren and I'll lose my contract with the magazine. Jessica ignores me so I sit down again.

"Mmmm, I'm afraid not," Jessica says into the phone. "Do you have something a little more . . . appropriate?" Jessica listens to Nancy and then breaks into a satisfied grin. "Now, that sounds much better," she says. "And there's just one more thing." She pauses. "Oh, that's exactly what I was going to ask—thanks for reading my mind." She hangs up and smiles coyly at me.

"What happened?" I ask. "What did she say?"

"You'll be sitting with *Miami Herald* columnist Lesley Abravanel, Cathy Griffin from *L.A. Confidential,* Tyra Banks, Renee Zellweger, the stars of *Grey's Anatomy,* and Timothy Watson."

"Are you serious?" I ask, stunned. Timothy Watson went from starring in a Sundance hit last year to suddenly being hailed as the Next Big Thing; Lauren, in fact, had told me that *Substance* had been trying to get him for a cover story and his publicist had turned the magazine down.

She shrugs and gives a sly smile. "She hopes you like the gift bag—it's worth over a thousand dollars."

"But Jessica, what you were saying about *Substance* . . . it's nowhere near one of the most successful publications in America."

"You think *she* knows that?"

"Yes! She's an event coordinator. Of course she does."

"Look, if you say something with confidence, people simply believe you."

"I guess so." What she's just accomplished suddenly seems to dawn on me. "It's just amazing . . . I mean, the people who organize events treat me like crap. They don't invite me inside, let alone to sit with celebrities and take the gift bags. They—"

"They treat you like shit because you allow them to," Jessica says calmly. Her eyes flicker over my face. "Face it, you're one of those too-nice people."

"Believe me, I'm not that nice," I say, thinking about how I've deceived Ethan, Amanda, and Kristi, and how much I judge Danny.

She smiles. "I didn't say 'nice.' I said, 'one of those too-nice people.'"

"What's the difference?"

"You probably talk to those kids with petitions who stand on the street asking if you can spare a minute to save planet earth."

"I don't stop every time. But they're hard to ignore. What am I supposed to say? 'No, I don't care about planet earth'?"

Jessica shakes her head. "Emma, those people are on the clock—they're just silly fools that some company hired to stand there and bug the shit out of strangers by guilting them. They could give a fuck about planet earth."

"Are you sure?" I ask. "I always assume they're people who really care about the right things. And I figure, since their values are so much better than mine, the least I can do is hear them out."

Jessica looks at me and says, "You know, nobody makes you feel inferior without your own consent."

That hits me hard. How many times a day do I allow people to make me feel bad? "God, that's brilliant."

Jessica shrugs. "Eleanor Roosevelt said it. I'm just quoting. But it's true: if you let some jackass on the street convince you that your not stopping to talk to him makes you a terrible person, then you'll feel like shit. If you act like people are doing you such a favor by allowing you to go to their parties to give them press, that's how they'll treat you. It's just a fact."

I feel, rather suddenly, elated—the thought that I can gain more confidence simply by thinking about things differently feels amazing, as does the fact that I allowed Jessica to take a risk with my career and it actually worked. If I told Jessica that what she had done could have caused me to lose my contract with the magazine, she'd probably have shrugged and said it sounded like the job sucked anyway. And she would have been right.

Jessica glances at her watch and then at me. "But we should get going—Nancy's expecting us at the Beverly Hills Hotel in an hour so we have just enough time to swing by your place and then mine without being late."

I stand up. "Us?" I ask.

"Of course," Jessica smiles. "You only have one more week to work on your story so you should take as much time with me as possible." She raises an eyebrow. "Plus, you didn't think I was going to do all that work for nothing, did you?"

chapter 14

WHO THE HELL is throwing this awards show, anyway?" Jessica asks as we sit down.

"I don't know," I hear a guy say. When I look up, I see that the voice belongs to tonight's star attraction, Timothy Watson, and I feel immediately gripped with the same tension I always have around celebrities—knowing we're going to engage in a metaphorical wrestling match where I'll try to get something interesting out of him while he'll attempt to say as little as possible. "All these things blend together after a while," he continues. "The Movieline Awards. The Young Hollywood Awards. The MTV and VH1 and whatever-the-hell-else-somebody-thinks-of awards."

A tall skinny guy sitting with Timothy picks up the bottle of red wine in the middle of the table and fills two glasses. "I'll drink to that," he says, and he and Timothy clink glasses and sip.

"As long as there's booze, I guess it doesn't really matter what the event is," Jessica says, reaching her empty wineglass over. Timothy fills her cup, as I just sit in a sort of stunned silence. I'm so used to interviewing celebrities when they have their full-on PR face on—listening to them spout off quotes that are both magazine-perfect and utterly boring—that it seems altogether foreign to hear one of them say something that isn't forced and fake.

"Listen to this," Timothy says, leaning in. "They told me ahead of time that I'm getting this big award, just to make sure I showed up. What kind of bullshit is that?" He tilts his head toward his tall, skinny friend and laughs. "But whatever. This guy would have me go to the opening of an envelope if he could."

The skinny guy laughs and mumbles something about how it's all part of building a public image just as Jessica gestures toward me and says, "Hey, can she get you to say that on tape?" She looks at Timothy. "For *Substance* magazine?"

Timothy's casual expression suddenly morphs into a panicked one. "Oh, Christ. You're one of *them*?" he asks me.

I nod, feeling the casual, happy exchange we—or rather, they—were just having evaporate before my eyes. "Yes, but—"

"Well, why didn't you say so?" Timothy asks, looking pissed.

The guy with Timothy holds out his hand. "I'm Will Griffiths, Tim's manager," he says. He glances from me to Timothy, his eyes concerned. "Let me go get Tim's publicist, Leslie."

"Oh, why don't you all calm the fuck down?" Jessica says. "Emma doesn't actually bite."

Timothy laughs while Will looks over at Jessica nervously. "Well, all quotes need to be approved by Leslie," he says apologetically, starting to rise before Timothy glances at him and he sits back down. I stay put, marveling at the fact that I've become the focus of a conversation I haven't even really participated in yet.

"Look, she's not going to make you look bad," Jessica says

and I realize that I have a far better publicist than Timothy—or anyone else. "In fact, she won't quote you unless you sound fan-fucking-tastic." She looks at me. "Right?"

"Right," I answer weakly. The best quotes are usually ones where the celebrities don't sound fan-fucking-tastic. But what am I supposed to say? *No, I want to make you look bad?* "Absolutely," I add.

"In that case," Timothy says, now smiling again, "let's start the interview."

I dig my tape recorder out of my purse and lean toward him with it. "What does tonight mean to you?" I ask, smiling, feeling oddly close to him after having followed him through a gamut of emotions—first cheerful, then uncomfortable, then forgiving, and now seemingly content.

He smiles. "Everything," he says, giving me a fake smile. I can tell I'm in for a doozy of a silly, publicist-approved sound bite. "It's a huge honor." He winks and adds, "That's my quote."

"CHEERS." I CLINK GLASSES with Will and take a sip from my glass, marveling at how fun the night was turning out to be. Although I used to have a semi-strict policy about not drinking at the events I'm covering, the Timothy Watson thing stressed me out enough that I'd immediately downed a few glasses of wine. And then something even more unusual happened: I suddenly didn't care that he was a big celebrity giving me canned quotes and I was nothing more than a human tape recorder. I just relaxed. By the time the *Herald* columnist, *L.A. Confidential* writer, cast of *Grey's Anatomy,* Tyra Banks, and Renee Zellweger showed up, I was buzzed to the point that I didn't mind if anyone noticed that a lowly press line reporter was in their midst. When Jack walked up to the table sometime during the main course to ask

Renee Zellweger if he could interview her and saw me chatting away with Timothy Watson, I felt sheer joy watching his eyes almost pop out of his head. And I decided at that moment that if alcohol had helped create this turn of events, then I needed to drink more often.

Will points to the stage. "Could this event get any more random?" he laughs and gestures to the podium, where Robert Duvall is delivering a speech about the importance of tango.

"Come on," I answer. "You know the tango speech is a staple of every awards show." As Will cracks up, it occurs to me that he's oddly attractive. *Oh, no more alcohol for me,* I think, remembering that at the beginning of the evening, I'd found him positively reptilian.

Just then, Jessica leans over to me. "Want to pee?" she asks. I nod, and she grabs my hand and leads me out of the dining room and to a seemingly endless line outside the women's bathroom. "Screw this," Jessica says, yanking me past the women and over to the lineless men's room. Normally I'd be embarrassed or concerned, positive that someone I know would see me. But right now, I'm a little too tipsy to care. Jessica stomps into the men's bathroom, holding her hands over the side of her eyes as blinders. "Coming through, not peeking, just taking care of a basic bodily function!" she trills as a surprised-looking guy turns from the urinal in shock. He quickly zips up and runs out.

"Yikes—I feel bad for him," I say to Jessica once we're in a bathroom stall.

Jessica yanks down her underwear and squats over the toilet seat without bothering to close the door. "You should," she says. "He was about the size of a crayon." For some reason, this absolutely cracks me up. *I haven't,* I think as I laugh, *had this much fun in ages—years, maybe.* After I go, Jessica tugs me out of the bathroom with her, past the shocked-looking women standing in the still-endless line, and over to the front of the hotel. "Nicotine withdrawal," Jessica announces, pointing to a group of people in formal wear—clearly fellow escapees from the event—standing outside smoking.

Pulling a Marlboro Red from her pack, Jessica walks directly into the group. "Anybody have a light?" she asks. The men all glance at her appreciatively while the women look annoyed. After one of the men lights her cigarette, Jessica thanks him and turns away.

"Come on," she says, gesturing for me to follow her toward a bench with a black cushion on it. As we sit down, I watch Jessica inhale and exhale cool, clean lines of smoke. And suddenly, for the first time in my life, I want a cigarette.

"Hey, can I have one of those?" I ask Jessica, pointing to her pack. She nods, hands me a cigarette, and pulls an engraved Zippo from her purse.

"If you have a lighter, why did you ask for a light?" I ask as she gives me one. I inhale an enormous plume of smoke, which catches in my throat and causes me to break into a massive coughing fit.

"I just wanted to see if the guys were cute," she says in a matter-of-fact tone, thankfully oblivious to the humiliating way I'm essentially hacking up a lung. I inhale on my cigarette again and manage to exhale without collapsing into a succession of coughs. "Smoking is the greatest way to meet men," Jessica continues. "I think I like that more than I do the nicotine." She blows out a smoke ring and shrugs. "Unfortunately, those guys looked better as a group than they did on their own."

I giggle. I always have that exact thought about men in L.A.—that when you look at a crowd of them, you'd swear they were all gorgeous, but without the others none of them seemed individually attractive. I laugh again—so hard this time that I wonder if the cigarette has somehow made me drunker—but when I look up and see Rebecca and Brooke walking toward us, I suddenly stiffen.

"Well, hello there," Brooke says, slobbering spittle onto my cheek. "Did you work the press line tonight?"

"Actually," I say, trying to hold her gaze despite the fact that I'm having trouble focusing my eyes on anything, "I covered the event from inside."

Rebecca steps up next to Brooke and holds out her hand to Jessica. "I don't believe we've met. But I certainly have seen you around."

Jessica flicks her eyes over Rebecca but ignores the outstretched hand. "Really?" she asks. "Because I've never noticed you."

Brooke looks from me to Jessica, seemingly trying to understand what we're doing together, while Rebecca forces a smile. "Well, you've always been quite preoccupied," Rebecca says. She kicks Brooke, who immediately turns to Jessica.

"So, Jessica," Brooke says, clearly grasping for something to talk to her about. "Who made your dress?" Jessica doesn't answer.

Rebecca leans in toward me. "What are you doing?" she hisses.

I smile innocently. "Just taking a smoke break." I feel suddenly intensely grateful for the fact that I'm drunk.

"You don't smoke," Rebecca whispers as I hear Brooke continue to try to engage Jessica in a conversation. "And you know what I mean."

"Actually, I don't," I lie. While I could quietly explain to Rebecca that I'm only sitting with Jessica because of my story, I'm somehow enjoying confusing and overwhelming her.

Rebecca shakes her head and says, under her breath, "Don't you know that if you lie down with dogs, you're destined to become one yourself?"

Before I can respond, Jessica blows smoke in Rebecca's face.

"Actually, the expression is 'If you lie down with dogs, you're going to get fleas,'" Jessica says. "I don't usually correct people but you seem like the kind of person who uses clichés a lot so I thought you should know."

Rebecca plasters a smile onto her face and starts blinking rapidly, while Brooke looks at me. "Emma, why don't you come with us?" she asks. "We can give you a ride home."

I glance from Jessica to Brooke, then drop my cigarette on the ground and grind it out with my foot. "That's okay," I respond, surprising myself. "I'm fine right here."

Rebecca sighs loudly and shakes her head. "Well, have fun," she says, suddenly turning and walking away. Brooke follows.

"Please tell me you're not one of them," Jessica says after a pause.

"I'm not. At least I don't think so." I pause. "Well, what do you mean?"

"I mean one of the single, soulless, aging, bitter women who walk around this town gossiping about everybody else as a way to escape the sad emptiness of their lives." I notice that her voice sounds shaky.

"Look, you shouldn't let what Rebecca said bother you. You're right about her life being empty, she—"

Jessica lights another cigarette from the one she's holding, and I notice her hands are shaking. "Look, I don't care," she says. "You think I give a shit what that Botoxed cow with the Mystic Tan says about me?"

I want to tell Jessica that she doesn't have to put up a tough exterior for me. "I just—"

"Now, come on," Jessica says, suddenly standing. "Let's go back and get the other quotes you need." She pulls me up, and we start walking inside. Then her cell phone rings and she immediately lets go of me, cooing into her headset, "Hi, Bernie."

"Come on," I say, tugging on her arm the way she's been tugging on mine, and trying to pull her back toward the dining room. She shakes my hand off and I feel oddly stung by the gesture. My drunkenness turns just the slightest bit belligerent as I stomp into the dining room without her; when I get there, however, I see that it's empty and realize with surprise that the event is over and everyone is making—or has made—their way out. I walk back to the hotel's entrance, where Jessica is now moving briskly toward me.

"Looks like things have wrapped up," I say.

She nods. "That's good because I have to go."

"Have to go? What are you talking about? You drove me here, remember?"

Jessica looks surprised. "Oh, that's right. Sorry, Emma, but when I told Bernie where I was, he said he was right around the corner and he'd meet me here." She shrugs and smiles. "So I'm going up to the penthouse suite." She glances at her watch, suddenly appearing to be in a major hurry.

"Really?" I ask.

Now she looks annoyed. "Oh, God. No guilt trips, please," she says. "Just find another ride home or take a cab."

I feel hurt, abandoned, and angry but tell myself that I'm probably overreacting. "Okay," I say.

"Good," Jessica says, quickly turning and flitting off. Feeling my head start to spin a little, I make my way up to the hotel's front desk.

"Where can I find a cab?" I ask the man standing there. He smiles and points to a crowd of people gathered outside. "They're all waiting?" I ask and he nods. Just then, I notice that my tape recorder isn't in my purse and I realize I must have left it in the dining room but I feel too dizzy to go look for it now. I look at the people waiting for cabs, feeling completely alone. Stranded.

And drunk. *And stupid,* I think. Stupid for thinking that Jessica was my friend and conveniently forgetting that she was actually a source—a prostitute!—I was interviewing for a story. The cigarette I smoked earlier seems to have worked its way through my system and conspired with the alcohol already there to make me utterly nauseous. I search for a place to sit down.

"YOU DON'T LOOK so good," Danny says, shaking my shoulder. "Or let me rephrase: you look great. But you also look like you don't feel so good."

I smile and laugh, thoroughly confused, then glance around and realize with horror that he's waking me up from where I've been passed out on a bench outside the Beverly Hills Hotel. Nothing seems clear and I think my glasses must need cleaning before I remember that I'm not wearing them. "Wait, what's going on?" I ask him.

"I'm not entirely sure," he responds. "The concierge here called Whole Foods asking if they could get a delivery of wild nettle rice, cage-free eggs, and soy milk for an organic foods–obsessed insistent hotel guest. It's not the kind of thing we normally do but we were overstaffed so my manager sent me."

I laugh, which somehow turns into a hiccup. "Wild nettle rice and cage-free eggs?" I ask. "What on earth could a hotel guest do with those things?"

"God knows." He smiles as he shakes his head. "You learn not to ask such questions. Speaking of which, what the hell happened to you?"

I sigh. "It's a long story." I hiccup again.

"Well, it looks like you could use a ride home. Why don't you tell it to me on the way?"

I gaze at him gratefully, trying to remember when we had

tea. Was it today? Yesterday? A month ago? "I can't believe you're here," I say. "It's a really bizarre coincidence." I hiccup again.

He shrugs as he leads me to a truck parked in the loading zone. "Well, you know what they say: coincidences are God's way of remaining anonymous."

I nod, freaked out by his use of the word "God" as a proper noun and wondering if he's some sort of Jesus freak. I forget to worry about that once we're driving as I suddenly notice that his head is heart-shaped. *His mom must adore him,* I think, wondering why on earth that thought would occur to me now. As he drives, he glances over at me. "Now, I'm taking it you weren't roofied so there's no one I need to beat up."

"Nope." I hiccup. "I did this without anyone's help."

Danny smiles. "Has anyone told you that you're cute when you're drunk?" I hiccup in response and we both laugh. "Don't get me wrong—I think you're better *not* drunk. But you manage to make drunkenness look oddly adorable."

Hiccupping, I think, *This guy thinks I'm so much better than I really am.* And then: *He must not be that great himself.* I hiccup again.

"You know," Danny offers, "I have a way of getting rid of those."

I gaze at the car in front of us, a flashy red sporty thing, and feel another wave of dizziness come on. "I'm not drinking a glass of water upside down or anything like that," I say, hiccuping yet again.

"Don't be silly," he says. "Just close your eyes." I do that and realize it brings on full-on nausea. "Hey, keep 'em shut," he says when I start to open them. "This won't work otherwise."

So I close my eyes again and listen as Danny tells me to picture and describe my hiccups to him (kernels of popcorn), then to envision a box (the kind the UPS guy brings) and imagine myself taking all of the kernels of popcorn, stuffing them in the box, and shutting it tight. I do that and just as I'm about to inform him that I think I got the very last stubborn, jumpy popcorn piece, an overwhelming wave of nausea hits. "Danny," I say, opening my eyes. "I think I'm going to—"

"Got it," he says. "Pulling over."

"Oh no," I moan as a wave of sickness hits. By this time, Danny has parked on the side of the road, and I immediately fling my door open, collapse, and start throwing up—emptying what feels like parts of my stomach lining on the ground, praying that no one inside one of the houses happens to be looking out the window or taking a nighttime walk. Eventually, my stomach finishes its horrific evacuation process and I stand up, relieved beyond any measure I can describe that I'm done. But before I have time to relish that feeling, I realize with sudden sobriety where I am—which is by the side of the road with a Whole Foods employee I barely know. *This is not the vision I had for my life,* I think, feeling somewhat guilty for the thought. Danny, who's standing about twenty feet away, turns toward me. "Feeling better?" He smiles.

"Yes and no," I say. "Physically, yes. But mentally, I'm just so sorry—"

Danny walks over. "Please, no apologizing. I'm the one who made you close your eyes in a car when you already didn't feel well."

"I just—"

"I said no apologizing," he says, managing to sound both stern and light-hearted. He walks closer to me.

"I'm disgusting right now," I say, gesturing that he should probably keep his distance.

"Well, at least your hiccups are gone," he says and we both laugh.

chapter 15

"OH, MAN," I SAY, opening my eyes and immediately feeling like a three-hundred-pound person is lounging on my forehead. My mouth is so dry that the words barely escape from my mouth. I sit up—way too fast. Overwhelmed by the head rush, I lie back down and then try getting up again, this time at a far more appropriate pace—that of, say, a caterpillar.

"Oh, man," I say again, dragging myself to my kitchen, where I want to put my mouth under my Arrowhead dispenser faucet. Instead, I settle for grabbing a glass, filling it with water, draining it, then immediately replenishing the cup again.

Making my way over to my couch, I cringe as I recall Danny helping me inside last night. I need, I think, to go by Whole Foods and thank him. And I had to make some other changes, too. Reflecting on my interaction with Rebecca and Brooke, I now see that it was ridiculous for me to be abandoning every cultural value I've ever had and suddenly befriending prostitutes instead of the kind of people I've been around my whole life. And this wasn't, I decide, a snobby decision: the fact is, everyone had warned me about Jessica before I met her, and while I'd tried to be open-minded about her, she'd proven herself to be selfish. I need to concentrate, I now see, on distancing myself from her personally while still being able to use her for the story. As I'm deciding this, the phone rings, sounding louder—and thus more painful to my head—than ever before. Thankfully, it's within arm's reach. I garble a hello.

"Good, you made it home!" Jessica says. "For a minute I was worried about you, but then I thought, why be concerned about Emma? She's a trouper."

"Hi, Jessica," I say, my cool tone making me realize that I'm a lot more hurt by her behavior than I'm admitting to myself. I make a conscious effort to mask my bruised feelings. "How are you? How was your night with Bernie?" I ask. My voice sounds cheerier now.

"Don't be pissed at me," she says, her cell phone reception cutting in and out. "I thought maybe without me around, you might get lucky."

"Lucky? Please. All I got was sick."

"Good! That means you got most of it out of your system and aren't too hung over today."

"Hardly," I croak. "I can't even move."

"That's what I thought you might say," Jessica says—her cell reception all screwy again—just as my doorbell rings. I decide it's not worth standing up to find out who's there. "What are you doing? Get it!" I hear Jessica say into the phone and also, at that moment, in person—as I suddenly realize that she's outside my apartment. I drag myself to the front door and open it to see her in a yellow sundress, the very picture of nonhungover health.

"Why are you here?" I ask, looking at her and slowly realizing that means I can hang up the phone.

"To save you from being hungover."

"It's a little late for that," I say, just as Jessica calls out, "Hey, Irving!"

I glance past her and see a Lincoln Town Car parked in my driveway. A burly black driver emerges from it and ambles over, handing her an enormous thermos. "Do you need cups?" he asks.

Jessica shakes her head. "Just give us about ten minutes," she says to him.

"What are you doing?" I ask her as the driver goes back to the car.

"You'll see. Can I come in?"

"I don't know," I say, not moving.

"Please, Emma. Let me take care of you to make up for what I did last night."

With the words "Let me take care of you," I feel myself soften. "Don't worry about it," I say, continuing to hold the door where it is.

She opens her eyes just a bit wider, making her appear uncharacteristically genuine. "Are you really not going to let me inside?" She smiles. "When we both know you'd probably offer a Hare Krishna walking door to door a cup of tea?"

Despite myself, I laugh and take a step back. Jessica saunters past me, leaving a fresh, summery scent in her wake. She walks into my kitchen. "Sit down!" she shouts as I hear her opening a cupboard.

"I already have!" I yell from the couch, which kills my cigarette-charred throat. "So how was your night?" I ask, with great effort.

"Great!" she yells from the kitchen. "I still haven't gone to sleep." She comes into the living room holding two Bloody Marys. "Here you go," she says, handing one to me. "Just what the doctor ordered."

I shake my head as I accept the glass. "Are you kidding? I'll puke again," I say, putting the drink on the floor.

"That's what you think, but you're wrong. Take it from someone who's had a lifetime's worth of experiences in dealing with hangovers: the best cure for them is more alcohol." She sips and gestures for me to do the same.

Looking at her bright eyes and clear skin, I ask, "Why do you look so . . ." It takes me a few second to come up with the right word. " . . . refreshed?"

Jessica laughs. "You've got me." She shrugs. "I've just always had this sort of Dorian Gray thing going: the more degenerate and exhausting my night, the better I look the next day." She laughs as she picks my Bloody Mary off the floor. "Now, bottoms up."

"I don't know." I remember how the football players who lived on the floor below me at Skidmore always used to chant, "Hair of the dog!" and chug beers on Sunday after partying all night on Saturday. I had considered them borderline insane.

She reaches into her purse and pulls out a plastic bag filled with pills. "Here," she says, handing me two. "Advil, for the pain." I put the Advil in my mouth, and then realize I have nothing to take it with but the Bloody Mary unless I want to get up, so I gulp the drink to wash them down. It doesn't actually taste that bad, and I have the odd feeling that the tomato juice is restoring some important minerals I may have depleted last night. As if she's reading my mind, Jessica gestures for me to open my hand and then drops two vitamins into it, saying, "Vitamin B, which replenishes something crucial having to do with alcohol, though I can never remember what." I put the two vitamins in my mouth and take another sip of the Bloody Mary. "And St. John's wort," she says, handing me two more pills. "Because let's not forget that alcohol is a depressant, and part of every hangover is emotional and not physical." I swallow those, too.

"Thanks," I say. "But I'm not going anywhere. I still can't move." I hate the fact that Jessica's kindness to me in my weakened state is making me start to forgive her. *Remember, she abandoned you last night,* I tell myself as I take another sip of my Bloody Mary.

"That's too bad," she says. "Because I invited two other working girls I know—Lindsay and Courtney—to meet us for brunch at the Little Door. They don't really operate the way I do—they're more straight-up hookers—but if you want to, you could probably use whatever they say as background material for your story, or even quote them as off-the-record sources."

Jessica had said she'd find me some other girls to interview, but with the story due in less than a week, I'd basically assumed this was never going to happen. "Can't we do it another time—tomorrow, maybe?"

She applies lip gloss. "I have Bernie's car and driver for the day—an altogether rare experience, but both he and Wifey had to leave town," she says, as if we can only have this experience when we're being chauffeured.

I look at her, and then at my glass, which I'm surprised to note is half drained. And I have to admit that I *do* feel better—the throbbing headache seems to be gone and the feeling that I might as well lie in bed all day has also seemingly evaporated. I still don't want to cave in to her entirely, though.

"It was shitty—what you did last night."

"I know," she says, looking me in the eye and appearing genuinely sorry. "Sometimes I can be a real selfish bitch. I'm working on it, though."

Standing up and smiling, I ask, "Working on being more of a selfish bitch or less of one?"

She laughs and starts leading me toward my bedroom. "Whichever will get you to throw on a dress and come with me," she says.

"MY MADAM IS a complete loon but I gotta admit, she delivers," Lindsay says as she gazes at her reflection in a compact mirror and fluffs her white-blond hair.

"I swear, I don't know why you put up with her shit," says Courtney, a petite, wavy-haired brunette. "Not a day goes by that I don't thank my lucky stars I'm not dealing with her anymore."

We're drinking Bloody Marys and eating brunch at one of the Little Door's outdoor tables and Lindsay and Courtney are basically talking to Jessica like I'm not even here. In most situations, this would make me uncomfortable, but after Jessica announced that I was her friend, Lindsay and Courtney both shrugged and immediately started ignoring me so I'm able to sit here nursing my hangover while gathering background material for my piece.

"How can you hate someone you've never met?" Lindsay asks Courtney. She puts the compact down and sips her coffee.

"Wait a minute," I say to Courtney, immediately abandoning my plans to just keep quiet and let them talk. "You've never met your madam? I thought you said you worked with her for years."

Courtney laughs. "I know, isn't that a kick?"

"But how is that possible?" I ask.

"You know what they say," Lindsay shrugs. "A madam today is only as good as her modem."

Courtney laughs. "Ha! I've never heard that. But it's true."

"So you guys just e-mail each other?" I ask. "Isn't that risky?"

"Who knows?" Lindsay asks. "I mean, if they can review escorts on The Erotic Review dot com, how much worse can it be for her to send me an e-mail asking me to meet a client in Dubai and telling me she'll wire me twenty grand?"

"She gets you twenty grand?" Courtney asks.

Lindsay nods. "Sometimes more."

"Look, making that much would be nice," Jessica says, pointing her fork at Lindsay. "But I still can't understand why anyone would want to give a percentage of that kind of money to a psycho woman who's hiding behind a computer."

"It's worth it," Lindsay says, finally putting her compact mirror away. "I mean, she only goes completely schizo—yelling and saying she won't work with me anymore—every few weeks." Lindsay's not really her name and Courtney isn't Courtney's either—Jessica had explained this to me during the ride over, and while I understood wanting to change your name for this kind of work, I don't get why they can't use their real names the rest of the time. This isn't, however, the time to ask—Jessica had also mentioned that the girls, while "the best of the bunch" of the working girls she knew, were former porn stars who had "the self-awareness of a couple of fleas." She'd added, "But anything for you, Em," in a voice that showed just how much she was still trying to work her way back into my favor and I couldn't help but be flattered that she'd shortened my name seemingly unconsciously.

"I have this sweetheart of a guy who just likes to bathe me and whisper, 'I'm cleansing you of your sins,'" Lindsay says. "Then he pats me dry and puts me in these pajamas that have footsies on them." She shrugs. "I think he has some sicko little girl thing going on."

"The worst are the ones who want to punish you because they

know you'd never give them a chance if they weren't paying," Courtney says. "Like this one guy, Craig, in Toronto." She looks at Lindsay. "Have you . . . ?"

"Have I ever," Lindsay says, her blue shadowed eyes flaring. "I call him Craig the Cock."

Courtney nods at Lindsay and then looks at Jessica. "He's this gross guy—like practically a dwarf! Or whatever. And he orders you for the weekend and then, like, spends every minute telling you how ugly you are."

"Did he call you fat?" Lindsay asks Courtney.

Courtney nods. "Call me fat? He would pinch my ass and tell me I needed to go on a diet."

"And he'd make you go to the mall with him—"

"And, like, hold his hand," Courtney interrupts.

"And tell him how hot he was," Lindsay adds.

"Ewwww!" Courtney shrieks at the memory. "What a cock. I like that name, Craig the Cock."

"But he pays well," Lindsay says, looking at Jessica.

"I know—I'd get thirty grand out of him," Courtney adds. "And he flies you there first-class."

"If you're trying to make me jealous, it's not working," Jessica says. She lights a cigarette. I'm about to tell her that you can't smoke out here but before I can, she continues, "I get to act as my own madam, keeping everything I get and hand-selecting all my clients." She taps ashes into her untouched water glass. "The only problem, of course, is that my boss is kind of a bitch."

Lindsay, Courtney, and I all laugh. "I swear, Jessica, you could make so much more if you worked for Taryn," Lindsay says.

"So I can have some midget pinch my cellulite?" Jessica asks, smiling. "No, thanks."

"But you could, like, buy a house—or something," Lindsay says.

Jessica glances at Lindsay and Courtney. "Have either of you bought houses?"

Lindsay shakes her head. Courtney doesn't answer. Jessica looks from Lindsay to me. "Easy come, easy go," she says. "I swear, I've never met one girl in this business who could handle her finances for shit."

"I handle my finances," Lindsay pouts.

"It's guilt money, don't you understand?" Jessica says, her eyes suddenly squinting with sadness. "You feel like shit over how you get it so you treat it like it's toxic and needs to be disposed of as quickly as possible." Jessica drains her Bloody Mary and wipes her lip. Noticing her sudden shame makes me want to reach out and hug her, and I realize that the line I'd been so intent on drawing between reporter and source has definitely been eradicated, and there probably isn't any going back now. I know this is inappropriate—that journalists are always warned to keep sources at a distance so as to remain objective, that Ethan would surely have a conniption fit if he could take my emotional temperature right now—but sitting here at the Little Door, sipping my Bloody Mary, I reason that I simply like her too much to care.

"She always gets really heady," Courtney says to me.

I glance at Jessica, whose face has been restored to her trademark smirk. "That's why I take goods instead of cash." She laughs. "I'm not going to have an impulse to get rid of my apartment or my car."

The waitress approaches the table. "I'm sorry but you can't smoke in here," she says to Jessica.

"I know." Jessica shrugs, tossing the nearly finished cigarette in her water glass. "But I'm just really bad at abiding by the law."

Lindsay and Courtney crack up and I wonder if Jessica only lit up so she could use her witty comeback.

chapter 16

I'M CONCENTRATING ON not feeling drunk as I e-mail Lauren the quotes I can remember getting from Timothy Watson, the *Grey's Anatomy* castmates, and everyone else at the awards show. Jessica had told me that I didn't need to worry about having lost my tape recorder, that everyone had surely been too wasted to recall what they said, and that I could probably make up whatever I wanted. I'm nevertheless making an ample—if ineffective—effort to comb my memory banks for actual quotations. If I'm screwing up, I decide, it's Lauren's fault for sending me to cover an awards show when my prostitution story's due in a week and Mark had specifically instructed her to cut down on assigning me events to cover.

Pulling out my outline for the piece, I realize that the Lindsay and Courtney conversation I observed earlier today balances perfectly with my Kristi and Amanda tidbits—even though I have yet to figure out how, exactly, I'm going to handle explaining to Amanda and Kristi that I'm using them as source material. My phone rings and I pick it up but before I even have a chance to say hello, I hear my mother scream, "Oh, sweetheart! Did you hear?"

"Hear what?" I ask.

"He proposed!" she yells.

Even though I'm entirely certain who she's talking about, I resent the fact that Mom assumes this news is so monumental that names aren't necessary. "Who?" I ask.

"Felipe!" she says, sounding slightly exasperated. "Lilly is going to be a princess! Or something. Not," she adds quickly, "that that's what's important."

"Wow," I say, fervently wishing that I could feel that flush of joy people are supposed to experience when something wonderful happens to someone they know instead of the aching, bitter jealousy that seems to be gripping my heart. "That's really great," I say. My voice sounds dead.

"Of course, we knew about it," she says. "Weeks ago, Felipe asked Dad's permission. I didn't say anything to you because why get people's hopes up until we *knew* knew? And Lilly was completely surprised. Of course, he did it in grand style: they were at Two Bunch Palms, getting a watsu—you know, that underwater, back-to-the-womb treatment they give you in the pool—and while the therapist was cradling her, Felipe got down below her in the pool and slipped the ring on her finger."

"Somebody actually charges people good money to cradle them in a pool so they can pretend they're going back to the womb?"

Mom sighs. "Honey, that's not the point. Your little sister's getting married. Aren't you just the slightest bit excited?"

I consider her question. Determining that the answer is no, I nevertheless try to feign enthusiasm. "When are they going to do it?" I ask. "I mean, are they waiting until after they graduate?" I suddenly imagine the wedding—and me, dateless, or with Danny from Whole Foods by my side.

"I don't think they've worked any of that out yet," Mom says. "They're too busy just blissing out." She pauses. "I'm surprised Lilly didn't call and tell you herself," she adds.

Mom must, on a certain level, understand that Lilly wouldn't have called me—she knows that we've barely talked on the phone in tears and that we're too different, too far away from each other, for us to have ever had the kind of relationship that sisters should. I simply couldn't relate to the way she never seemed to have any problems and she clearly didn't think of me as someone worthy of her attention. By the time she was in high school, we'd stopped even trying to pretend we could be friends. But Mom is in one of her let's-pretend-we're-a-close-family moods and I know from experience there's no point in trying to break through that. "Maybe she tried," I say. "I've been really busy and not always getting my phone."

My other line beeps in and I see from caller ID that it's Jessica. "Mom," I say. "I have to go."

"We need to start planning the engagement party," she says, ignoring me. Whenever I tell my mom I have to get off the phone, she tends to continue talking until whatever reason I had for saying good-bye has passed.

This time, I don't let her. "I'll talk to you soon," I say firmly.

"But don't you want to hear when—"

"Good-bye, Mom," I say, clicking over to the other line. "Hello?"

"Drink your way through it—whatever it is," Jessica says.

I laugh. "How did you know I was upset?"

"Your voice tells all. So is it romance or finance?"

I laugh again. "The former—or, more accurately, the lack of

the former in my life," I say. I pause for dramatic emphasis. "My little sister got engaged."

"So?"

"My sister who's ten years younger than me," I say. "Who's always been perfect." Jessica doesn't say anything. "She's going to be Spanish royalty," I add. Still nothing from Jessica. "Did you hear me?"

"I heard," she says calmly. She pauses. "What does that have to do with you?"

"What do you mean? It has everything to do with me! It shows what an utter failure I am—I mean, I can't even get a guy to date me for more than a month, and here she's still in college and already has princes proposing to her."

"Who says you and your sister are in some sort of competition?"

"Look, you're an only child, Jessica," I say. "You don't get what it's like to be the sister of someone so extraordinary. Ever since she was little, our parents have been comparing me to her and I've never even come close to measuring—"

"Yeah, well, your parents sound pretty screwed up."

I immediately feel like I have to leap to their defense. "They mean well," I say.

"My guess is that they're like all those other parents out there: desperate for their progeny to fill the world with babies they're too immature and clueless to know how to parent because they subconsciously believe it will reinforce their having done the same thing."

I consider how surprisingly accurate this theory sounds as I notice a cigarette sitting on my coffee table. It must have fallen out of Jessica's pack when she came by to pick me up the other morning. Reaching for it, I remember that I have matches under my kitchen sink. Sliding my cordless phone between my shoulder and ear, I walk into the kitchen and open the cupboard.

"Look, my parents aren't that bad," I say, lighting the cigarette and inhaling deeply. When I blow the smoke out, I note with satisfaction that I don't even have to stifle the urge to cough. "And what are they supposed to do? Not compare me to Lilly? Pretend she isn't perfect?"

Jessica sighs. "Christ, you let everyone treat you like shit."

"That's not true," I protest. "The fact is, I *am* inferior to Lilly. She's aced every test she's ever taken and men have fallen at her feet from the moment she could walk on them. She—"

"So what?" Jessica asks. "Does that mean that they can't fall at yours, too?"

"Trust me, they don't," I say, suddenly smashing the cigarette out and cursing myself for having somehow succumbed to the temptation to smoke.

"Haven't you been listening to anything I've said? We show people how they can treat us. If you act like they *should be* falling at your feet, they will. And just because one person has something, that doesn't mean it's impossible for her sister to have the same thing. Don't you know there's enough for everyone to get theirs eventually?"

"I guess," I say halfheartedly.

"I think you're addicted to manufacturing misery. In primitive times, we'd be sad if our husbands were clawed to death by bears or our babies starved. Now that we don't need to focus on survival, some of us make up shit to feel bad about to keep ourselves occupied. Like deciding that your life sucks because you're inferior to your sister." As I consider that, Jessica adds, "Look, what are you doing right now?"

"Now?" Jessica had dropped me off from our Little Door brunch only a few hours ago. "I'm recovering from last night and today."

"Be ready in ten. I have Irving the driver through tomorrow."

"Jessica, I can't go anywhere right now."

"Oh, right. Because you need to sit home and mourn the fact that you'll never measure up to your sister."

"Plus my deadline for the piece is next week."

"And one night out is going to stop you from meeting it? Please."

"I—"

"Wear something hot," she says, and hangs up.

"HONESTLY, JESSICA, I feel like I'm dying," I say, as Irving starts up the car. A headache I'd been working hard to ignore has now reached its previously hinted-at apex, and my stomach is cramped and making alienesque noises. "I don't know if I'm still hungover from last night or if it's a fresh one from today."

"Buckle up, soldier," she says, patting my leg as she glances at me. "You look good, and that's really all that matters."

I sigh and smooth down the sexy tank dress I'd found stuffed in the back of my closet. Although on a certain level I feel like I've been run over by a truck and should just curl up in a fetal position for a good, say, fifteen hours, I have to admit that all the jealous misery I was just mired in has somehow transferred into a sort of manic excitement and I seem to be getting an endorphin rush from going out again after drinking last night and today.

"Drive around the block a few times," Jessica instructs Irving as we pull alongside a club on Sunset. I glance at her quizzically as Irving turns onto Fairfax but Jessica just smiles and takes a vial out of her purse. And even though I can guess what's inside, I'm somehow still surprised when she takes a compact out of her purse and starts pouring cocaine onto the mirrored side of it. She glances at me. "You said you felt like shit," she says as she cuts the powder with a credit card.

Now, I've always been entirely clear about my point of view on coke: it's a dangerous, highly addictive drug that makes people maniacally self-obsessed and usually completely annoying. I wrote a goddamn paper about the dangers of it for a health class I took in college to fulfill my science requirement. But somehow, watching Jessica shape the powder into tiny little lines with her American Express card, that feeling of revulsion I've had every other time I've heard about or seen someone do it is absent.

"It feels good to be bad," I say, the words coming out of my mouth before I have a chance to think about how silly they sound. My heart starts beating faster as I suddenly remember someone in high school telling me about a basketball player who died after trying coke for the first time. Then, as I watch Jessica snort the two lines, I recall hearing that more people perish crossing the street than they do from taking drugs.

"Voilà!" she says after another line. "Instant Prozac." She pours more coke onto the mirror. "So?" she asks, raising one of her eyebrows at me.

What has being so good ever gotten me? I think as I watch Jessica wipe her nose. "Maybe," I say. I stare at the mirror, wondering if she knows I've never done this before.

"Look, no worries," Jessica says unconvincingly. "It just leaves more for me." She leans down yet again, ingests the powder, and looks up in what seems like record time. Then she fixes her eyes on me. "I just don't want to hear any bitching tonight about how exhausted or miserable you are." I nod, enjoying the illusion that for once, no matter how tenuous and ridiculous it is, I hold the power between us. "And I don't see how one or two little lines are going to hurt you."

I look at her, and then up at Irving, who's doing an outstanding job of appearing to be wholly unaware of the illicit activities taking place in the backseat of the car. "Can I use your dollar bill?" I ask. She smiles and nods.

"HEY," JESSICA SAYS, tugging on the shirtsleeve of a curly-haired guy walking by. "My friend thinks you're cute." She nods her head in my direction and he gives me an enormous grin.

Even though I'm looking into the face of a man I don't find remotely attractive, I find myself nodding and smiling crazily, wondering why no one ever told me how amazing cocaine was. Obviously I assumed it had to make people pretty happy or they wouldn't put up with all that went along with it, but I hadn't expected to feel, quite literally, like I just found a way to exhale after holding my breath my entire life.

"Really?" he asks, leaning in and looking me in the eye. "Well, I think *she* is."

The fact that he finds me cute doesn't seem surprising—for the first time in my life, it seems possible that I may even be as attractive as my little sister. "I'm Emma," I say to him.

"Graham," he says, shaking my hand. He motions to a group of guys at a corner booth. "We're sitting over there. What should I get us to drink?"

I glance at my almost-drained martini. "How about—"

"Cristal," Jessica says, cutting me off. "We'll come over in a minute." Then she grabs my hand and tugs me toward the bathroom. And while I'm slightly annoyed with her for taking charge as usual and leading me around and putting words into my mouth like she's a ventriloquist and I'm her dummy, I really feel too ecstatic from the cocaine flowing through my system to even bother getting worked up about it. "Why did you tell that guy a bald-faced lie?" I ask. "I don't find him cute at all."

Jessica takes the vial out and pours coke onto her compact

mirror. "Because he's sitting with a guy who you will think is hot," she says, cutting the lines. "It was a purely strategic move."

"So while I thought we were sitting at the bar talking, you were actually scanning the bar for appropriate men and planning how we could meet them?"

She smiles as she hands me the mirror. "What can I say?" She shrugs. "I'm a multitasker."

I take the rolled-up dollar bill she hands me, lean over the mirror, and snort, feeling the coke go up my nose and down through my throat. "I had no idea cocaine was like this," I say, not sure how to describe the feeling it's giving me. "I mean, I just want to use a superlative to describe absolutely everything."

Jessica laughs. "It's pure," she says proudly. "Most people in L.A. do the stuff that's under a hundred bucks a gram and cut with all kinds of shit—baby laxatives, God knows what else." She shakes some more coke onto her mirror and snorts it. "You're talking to a woman with over twenty pairs of Manolo Blahnik shoes. I'm a big advocate of you-get-what-you-pay-for."

I laugh as she puts her vial back in her purse. "So here's the deal," she says. "That guy is going to make you look sought after—and thus more appealing—in front of the hot one. Since, of course, you wouldn't fuck the first one blindfolded and on a hundred hits of ecstasy, you'll blow him off—and the more you reject him, the harder he's going to work to win you back, which will in turn make you appear even more worth having to his gorgeous friend." I nod as Jessica continues. "Most people are happy to believe you like them but the second you act like you don't, they think you're even more worth having because your sudden indifference makes them believe you're superior to them. And we all know there's nothing more alluring than someone who's just out of reach."

"Christ," I sigh. Even though Jessica's observations are, on a certain level, common sense, I'm astounded—as usual—by how well thought out it all is. "You should be a shrink."

Jessica smiles as she wipes her nose. "I know! I actually minored in psychology at Yale. But why sit and listen to people's boring problems all day when you can fuck with them instead?"

"HOW ARE YOU?" Jessica asks as she shakes each of the guys' hands. "I'm Jessica." She tilts her head in the direction of an empty seat that happens to be next to a stunning, dark-haired guy with an enormous, toothy grin and motions for me to sit down. *Right again, Jessica,* I think as I introduce myself to the guy, who says his name is Nick.

"And where are you from, Nick?" I ask, the drug coating me in confidence. Usually, I'd just assume a guy like him would never be interested in me so I wouldn't even bother trying to flirt.

"New York," he says as he fixes me with an intent gaze.

"The city or state?" I ask, amazed at how eye contact can make even the most benign words seem utterly tantalizing.

"Manhattan." He smiles and I want to crawl into his gray-green eyes and take a swim. "And while I've always considered myself a died-in-the-wool New Yorker, as an independent producer," he continues, "I need to accept the fact that the business is really out here."

As he starts to explain that his most recent movie won the audience favorite award at Sundance, that he has Colin Farrell and Vince Vaughn attached to his next project, and that he'll buy a place out here when it goes into production, I start to imagine myself as Nick's date at the movie's premiere. I'm fantasizing about the two of us joking around with Colin Farrell and Vince Vaughn while Jack begs Colin or Vince for a quote when

Graham leans over and looks at me. "Hey, don't be moving in, man," he says to Nick. "I found her first."

Nick glances from Graham to me with a slightly miffed expression on his face and I realize that he actually seems a bit jealous. More points for Jessica. Then Nick and I make eye contact again.

"Oh, please don't fight over me," I say, smiling flirtatiously while staring intently at Nick. I keep expecting him—or me—to look away, but neither of us does. "Or actually, please do—just don't let it get physical." Graham and Nick both laugh and I relish how valuable I suddenly feel. Graham leans back in his seat and Nick and I continue to banter. As he laughs hysterically at something I say, a tremendous feeling of pride starts to wash over me. I've always longed to be a Type A personality but usually feel too anxiety-prone and scared to get out of my Type B mentality. Yet suddenly I'm the very definition of a brazen woman who goes after what she wants—*like Jessica,* I think. Nick rests his hand right next to my thigh and the closeness feels delicious.

"So how does a girl like you survive out here?" Nick asks as he sips his drink.

"What do you mean?" I ask. I feel the cocaine dripping down the back of my throat and think that if I could bottle and legalize the combination of coke and Nick and sell it on eBay, I'd probably be a gazillionaire.

"I don't know." He glances around the club. "It just seems like there's something wrong with the men out here. Show them a gorgeous, independent woman with a brain and they run for the nearest bimbo with breast implants, a fake ass, and probably even a surgically revirginized pussy."

I laugh. "You're preaching to the choir. It must be something in the water."

Nick smiles, shifting his hand away from my leg and making

me crave its closeness again. "Except that the guys I'm talking about all drink Evian."

I laugh. "Please, Evian is too déclassé for some of them." Remembering a date I had with a producer Steve set me up with, I say, "I once went out with a guy who insisted we leave the restaurant because they didn't have Volvic or Fiji."

Nick shakes his head. "If I have to actually hang out with guys who spend their time out with beautiful women worrying about the bottled water, I might not survive here." He smiles at me, displaying delicious dimples. "I'll tell you what," he says. "Let me take you out—sometime this week. It will be a tap-water-only evening. What do you say?"

"I'd love to," I respond, thrilled. He pulls his phone out and I give him my number just as Jessica leans over. "Hate to break up the moment," she says. "But I have to meet with you in my office." I smile at Nick as I follow Jessica to the bathroom.

"LOOK WHO'S HERE," Jessica says, pulling me out of the bathroom after we've done a few more lines and I've yammered on about how adorable and attentive Nick is. I follow Jessica's gaze and see that Matt McCarthy is sitting at the bar.

"What the hell?" My heart is racing so fast that, for a second, I worry that the sight of Matt, combined with all the cocaine and my experience with Nick, will actually conspire to give me a heart attack like the one that took out the basketball player. "What's he doing here?"

Jessica shrugs and winks in a way that makes me certain she knows more than she's letting on. But before I have time to find out, Matt walks over to us.

"Hey, Jess," he says, giving her a kiss on the cheek, and then he turns to me. "You look fantastic."

"Thank you," I respond as he takes my hand and leads me over to his space at the bar. I smile at him, confused. *Why isn't he doing his typical pretending-not-to-know-or-see-me thing?* I think. *What the hell is going on?* Matt pats the stool next to him. "Take a seat."

"But we're—" I point toward where Nick and Graham and the other guys are gathered but Jessica, who's followed us over to the bar, simply says, "You stay here. I'll tell them that you ran into someone you know." Then she flits over to Nick's table. I glance from Matt to Nick, overwhelmed, in the midst of a quality problem if ever there was one. Do I pick the one I've been obsessed with for the better part of the year, I wonder, or the most gorgeous stranger I've ever flirted with? Then I realize that Jessica seems to have this whole situation figured out so I should probably just do exactly what she's telling me. Which, right at this minute, means being face to face with Matt. Looking at him now, I realize that in all the time I've spent thinking about him, I've remembered his face incorrectly—that his nose is a little bigger and his eyes farther apart than they've been in my mind.

"So how are you?" he asks, staring at me with a kind of appreciation that's altogether new.

"Great." At the moment, this feels wholly accurate.

Matt gulps his drink. "I didn't know you were friends with Jess until I was talking to her earlier tonight and she mentioned it." I smile as I study his face, attempting to understand the meaning behind his words. Did she tell him I'm doing a story on her? Is he worried that I'm going to write about him in it? Or does he think that I'm joining her ranks? Whatever it is, he looks, more than anything, impressed. So all I had to do to get his attention was befriend the girl he compensates to sleep with him. "She loves you," Matt adds.

I smile. "How long have you known her?"

"Years," he says, almost dreamily, while I pat myself on the back for not judging the fact that Jessica sells her body or that Matt is one of the men who buys it. *I really have broken from the shackles of my upbringing,* I think.

"It's interesting," Matt says. "When I was talking to Jessica and she started saying how great you were, I began to think that maybe I'd ended things between us prematurely."

"Really?" I ask, wondering if lives do, indeed, change in an instant. It always seems to happen for other people—one day they're coming up with some computer code, the next they're the billionaire head of the next big Internet company—but in my life, change has always come so slowly and after what feels like a ridiculous amount of effort and pain. Then again, the more time I spend with Jessica, the more I feel this constant glimmer of hopefulness—like exciting possibilities lurk around every corner. I glance over at Nick—who's looking back at me with a slightly jealous gleam in his eyes—and then at Matt. "Really?" I repeat.

"You're just so down-to-earth," Matt responds. "And with all the wack-job women in this town, that's a highly rare quality." He sips his drink and adds, "I'd love to try this—us—again." I blink and grin and nod and continue to soak up the attention he's giving me like a dying daisy would the bright sun until Jessica wanders over, announces to Matt that "girls need their beauty sleep," and motions for me that it's time to go. And I have to hand it to her for her timing because I'd just been thinking that the equilibrium of this surreal night couldn't hold much longer. As we walk out the door, I fervently hope that the feeling I have right now of being wanted won't ever end and know at the same time that of course it will.

chapter 17

"THIS ONE LOOKS FINE," I say to the guy at Fairfax Nursery. I'm pointing at a flowery thing growing out of a pot, which is the only way I know how to describe it since I've always been terrible at identifying types of flowers—that and types of dogs. I never understand how words like "hydrangea" and "border collie" flow off people's lips with such confidence and comfort. I'm not sure if I have a mental block about this type of information because gardening and dogs are both things that Mom and Lilly bond over or if I just wasn't paying attention when these particular life lessons were taught.

The guy, a wizened old hippie, smiles. "Ah, African violets," he says. "A sound choice." I nod hurriedly as he stares at me. "You look like a pink ice cream sandwich—delicious enough to eat," he says. He's motioning to my pink sweat pants. I'm not sure I understand what's happening with me lately. Granted, he's a kind of creepy-seeming, practically ancient guy who looks like he's taken too much acid at too many Dead shows, but suddenly, out of nowhere, men appear to be enamored of me. I seem to have been accidentally doused in some of Jessica's allure.

"How much do I owe you?" I ask, not sure how else to respond.

"For you, beautiful girl, it's on the house," he says.

"Don't be silly."

"Oh, I'm never silly," he assures me. "Consider it incentive to make you come back soon."

I smile. "Well, thank you," I say as I walk to my car, sounding very much the way Lilly always has when she's politely accepted the flowers, gifts, drinks, and free desserts that men have drowned her in her entire life. As I start driving, I get a flash of how it felt to be fawned over by Matt and Nick last night and suddenly wonder if I've somehow stepped into an alternate universe where I only get what I want. Didn't that happen to someone on *The Twilight Zone* once? Then I remind myself that I'm on my way to thank Danny for the ride home the other night and apologize for turning the experience into an *Exorcist* flashback, and realize that only getting what I want would require deleting everything embarrassing that took place beforehand.

Walking into Whole Foods, I spy Danny talking earnestly to a woman with long gray hair in the produce aisle. *He looks so sweet and innocent,* I think, remembering with sudden shame the cocaine I did last night, *and I'm the opposite.* Then I remind myself that sweet and innocent is boring so I shake the feeling off and approach him.

"What's up, Emma?" he says, enveloping me in a hug. The fact that our relationship has progressed to the point that we now hug seems surprising at first but I guess once you've watched someone evacuate her stomach onto the side of the road, you get to skip several steps on the path to intimacy. Feeling uncomfortable, I extricate myself from his grasp and hand him the plant.

"I wanted to give this to you—to say how sorry I am about the other night. And to thank you for being such a life saver." I look up at him and notice that he's giggling. "What?" I ask, immediately thinking he's laughing at me.

"Hang on, I'll show you," he says, then rushes off. He returns a second later holding out a plant that looks just like the one I gave him but in a ceramic pot. He hands it to me.

"Oh, you have one already," I say, confused. "Oops."

"No, this is for *you*," he says.

"But—"

"I thought you might beat yourself up over what happened. And I figured you'd come around here at some point with your tail between your legs, so I wanted to have something for you to show you that you shouldn't feel bad."

I can't help but laugh. "And you randomly chose an African violet, too?"

"Yep, but it wasn't random at all," he says. "When I was helping you into your place the other night, I noticed that you had a lot of windows facing west, and since African violets need at least ten hours of bright light a day to blossom, I knew it would grow well there. Plus, they don't need a lot of watering—once a month should do it—so I figured if you weren't a plant person, and I was kind of feeling like maybe you weren't, this would be hard to kill."

Smiling, I think, *I bet he knows all the different dog breeds, too.* "What are you—some kind of a gardening expert?"

He laughs. "If managing to keep plants alive qualifies me as an expert, then yes." He glances at the store's bakery, then gives me one of his gap-toothed smiles. "Hey, do you have time for a cup of coffee? I can regale you with stories about watering ferns and you can finally tell me what you were doing passed out in front of the Beverly Hills Hotel." I sigh, torn. He's so damn sweet but the last thing I feel like talking about is what happened with Jessica the other night at the awards show. Then he adds, "Come on, you know you want coffee—Laura from baked goods will completely hook us up." He's grinning impishly.

"Why not?" I find myself saying. I glance around the store, marveling at how Danny seems to have turned Whole Foods into his own personal oasis. "You really have everything you need here, don't you?" I ask as he leads me over to the bakery. "A cup of coffee when you need an extra bounce in your step, a serving of samples when you're feeling peckish?"

Danny laughs. "I sure do." He points to the aisle lined with organic moisturizers and environmentally pure creams. "You should see when I get the ladies who work in that section to rub herbal ointments into my temples. It's like being at a spa."

I smile. "Your boss doesn't mind you treating work like it's a spa?" I ask.

"Not really," Danny says. He waves at the woman behind the counter—Laura, presumably—and fills two to-go cups with coffee. "Not to brag, but he loves me."

I smile. "Let me guess. Because you bring him African violets every day?"

Danny laughs. "Please. That I reserve for girls I like." As soon as the phrase is out of his mouth, he looks as embarrassed as I suddenly feel. The sentence just sits there in the air and I silently urge him to say something else to put space between it and us, but he doesn't.

"Well, thanks again for the other night," I finally mumble as I stir Sugar In The Raw into my cup. "I may well have spent the night on that bench if you hadn't showed up."

"Nonsense," he responds. "I'm sure the Beverly Hills Hotel

wouldn't have stood for that." He pauses. "You'd actually probably be in the Beverly Hills jail for public drunkenness."

"God." I try to imagine such a scenario—and can't. "Now I feel even more grateful." Just then, my cell phone beeps a calendar reminder and when I glance at it, annoyance shoots through me. "Oh, no."

"What?"

"I completely forgot about this goddamn tea party I'm supposed to be at." Claire had sent out an Evite weeks ago inviting a few of us over for tea and I'd RSVP'd, put the event in my phone calendar, and essentially forgotten all about it. Of course, I'd *wanted* to forget about it—the four other people invited were Crossroads friends I'd succeeded in losing touch with over the years as they became marriage-and-baby-obsessed yentas—but I'd still said I would go. Why the hell hadn't I made up an excuse?

He laughs. "A *goddamn* tea party? Isn't that an oxymoron?"

"The tea part is fine." I smile. "The 'goddamn' is in reference to the fact that I'll be surrounded by a group of increasingly distant friends—perfectly capable and responsible women who seem to have forgotten how to utter sentences that don't contain words like 'trimester' and 'play date.'"

Danny smiles. "Just remember: chamomile makes new mothers a lot less annoying. It's a proven fact."

"Ha." I look at my watch. If traffic isn't too much of a nightmare, I can probably swing home to change and make it there within a half hour. "Sorry to run out on you. Another time?"

"Absolutely," he says as I grab the African violet and scurry out to my car.

I start driving to my apartment, cursing Claire the entire way, and, once home, throw open my closet and try to figure out if I have anything remotely tea party–esque to wear. Spying a tight black dress Jessica left over here the other day, I put it on—*Sorry, Claire,* I think, *you're not getting a shower out of me*—along with flats. Piling makeup in a bag, I manage to get out the door and into my car in just a few minutes.

As I drive on the 10 and apply eyeliner—and barely miss colliding with a crazy-looking woman in a Dodge minivan who opts to merge into my lane at the worst possible moment—I realize that I'm going to be only about twenty minutes late. *If this were a Hollywood event,* I think, *I'd essentially be considered early.*

I SEE CLAIRE careening out of her house as I pull up. "Emma!" she screeches, running over to me. She's wearing some Ralph Lauren–looking dress that's all lace and shoulder pads, and her makeup is so well-applied, I immediately know she had it professionally done for the occasion. I smile at her and apologize for being late.

"Don't worry about it," she says, hooking her arm in mine and leading me onto her porch and through her front door. "We've come to expect that from you." Even though I immediately want to sock her in the face, I throw on a fake grin as she walks me into the living room.

Our high school friends Gina, Cindy, and Melissa are standing there, a collection of knee-length skirts and hairspray. I feel about fifteen years younger than everyone else in the room. "Hi girls!" I chirp. My voice actually sounds convincingly enthusiastic.

"You look good," Gina says.

"You, too," I say, even though she doesn't. Her skin seems to be orange and streaked—like she bathed in pumpkin soup before hitting a tanning booth. I try to remember if she's always been this suburban and pinched—before realizing that I can't recall the last time I saw any of them. Was it at Melissa's wedding last summer? A larger-than-ever Cindy gives me a hug while Melissa's eyes linger on the top of my cleavage-displaying dress.

"Oh my God, we heard about Lilly!" Cindy squeals. "Is the prince gorgeous?"

"He's not quite a prince," I respond. "His father's cousin's grandfather was the King of Spain. Or something."

"Still, that's so cool," Cindy says. "If anyone would grow up to be a princess, it's Lilly." I try to smile at her, reminding myself that Cindy, as a successful money manager with a husband and two kids, in no way deserves my derision.

"So how are you?" Melissa asks, turning her hand over and over in what appears to be an attempt to show off some massive ring. Either that or the girl has developed an extreme wrist twitch that might require immediate medical attention. "Have you met anyone yet?"

I shake my head and consider how they'd respond if I told them about doing coke at the Hollywood club last night. The idea of outrageous rebellion, to these girls, was coming home late to the babysitter or not flossing your teeth one night. Rather suddenly, I can't resist asking Cindy if she's pregnant again. "No," Cindy says, looking stricken, glancing down at her protruding belly and placing a half-eaten cookie down on the table next to her. "Just still trying to get the Dakota baby weight off."

Gina puts her arm around Cindy. "You look great," Gina says, facing me and adding, "People in Hollywood are so screwed up when it comes to weight that they gain about ten pounds when they're pregnant, then lose it the minute their babies are born."

I force a smile, thinking that I should probably feel bad for getting that fat dig in at Cindy, but Gina's "people in Hollywood" comment only made me wish I'd said something to irk her as well. Like Claire, Gina had quit working when she got married and seemed intent on promoting full-time dependence on a man as an ideal way of living. As I look around the room, I marvel at the fact that these had once been my best friends.

Claire hands me an empty teacup. "Earl Grey, chamomile, or green tea?" she asks brightly.

"I don't care," I say and Claire's face falls. She'd clearly been quite proud of her three options. "Actually, green tea has caffeine, right?" Claire nods. "Give me some of that, please." Claire, thrilled, picks up a ceramic pot and fills my cup.

"Cucumber sandwich?" she asks. I nod, so Claire hands me a tea plate and points to a display of sandwiches and sweets that I can tell also fills her with pride. I put a cucumber sandwich and creamy, puffy-looking thing on my plate.

"Sit down, sit down," Claire says. "I want you all to be comfortable and sated for my announcement." Cindy claps her hands and Melissa and Gina exchange knowing looks. Had I missed the fact that this was an "announcement" tea party? It figures. Claire never does anything just because anymore. Since no one else seems to be eating—Gina and Melissa probably gobbled down about ten cookies apiece before I got here and I seem to have scared Cindy away from the food table for at least the rest of the afternoon—I realize that Claire is talking to me, so I sit in one of her sleek, modern metallic chairs. Trying to plaster on a smile, I'm suddenly filled with dread over whatever she's going to say and wishing like hell I'd just called and canceled at the last minute.

"It happened," she says and Cindy and Gina both squeal. "I'm pregnant!"

Melissa, looking like she's about to burst into tears, runs over to Claire and takes her in her arms and Cindy and Gina pile onto the hug. Claire gazes out at me from the middle and I smile at her. "Congratulations, Claire," I say. I make an effort to silence the thought that she's in an unhappy marriage and has convinced herself that pregnancy will solve, rather than exacerbate, her relationship issues. "That's great." I remind myself that if Claire sees this as a happy event, then it's not up to me to decide it isn't.

Claire releases herself from the group's grasp and walks over to me. She reaches out a hand. "I'm so glad you could be here for this," she says.

"Me, too," I lie, and then take a breath. "Do you know what kind it's going to be?"

"What *kind*? You're cute," Claire says. She glances at the other girls and they all share a chuckle. "We're sort of thinking we don't want to know. It's such a blessing either way, what does it really matter?"

"Right," I say. It hits me with sudden despondency that I can't even keep a plant alive—Danny's African violet is probably dying in the car at this very moment—and I'm standing among a group of women who are creating and raising *people*.

"I have to go, Claire," I say, surprising myself probably as much as her. "I'm on deadline." I get some pleasure out of saying the word "deadline" because it sounds so official—so unlike a word that a person living in the Palisades and getting her makeup done for her four high school friends would ever use.

Claire, looking hurt, says, "So what do you think your mom's going to say?"

"What do you mean?" I ask.

"Remember how she bet my mom that you would have kids before me?" Claire asks. I have a vague recollection of the four of us discussing this when Claire and I were teenagers.

"I think she'll survive the news," I say. This comes out sounding harsher than I intended, so I smile. "I mean, we were kids ourselves when we talked about that."

Claire continues to look serious and overly genuine, like we're discussing the future of humanity and not some throwaway silly conversation from over a decade ago. "I just know how much she wants you to have this, too," Claire says, gesturing, it seems, not only to her stomach but also to the tea party, plasma TV, and entire house. I'm rather suddenly filled with vitriol. How the hell does Claire know what my mom wants? "And I hope my happiness doesn't make her feel worse," Claire adds, looking at me with a cheer-up-things-will-get-better smile that makes me suddenly explode.

"Is that what you think, Claire? I mean, is your mom sad that she and your dad spent so much on your private schools when all you do is set Eric's tee times?" This comes out of my mouth before I know what's happening, as if a flap inside my brain that's meant to stop thoughts from becoming statements has suddenly crumbled. Claire flinches and I find myself raising my voice. "Those Kaplan SAT classes so you could get into the best college? The trips to Switzerland to give you a taste of what the U.N. was like? All the crap they enrolled you in so you could get somewhere in life? Do you think they're disappointed that you don't seem to aspire to do anything more than plan fucking tea parties?"

"There's no more noble a job than raising children," Claire responds, her lower lip quivering.

"Look, you're not the first woman alive to get knocked up," I say, standing up. Cindy stares at me while Gina pretends to talk to Melissa but simultaneously holds her hand over her eyes as if I'm an evil force that will blind her if she actually looks over. "So save the superiority trip for someone who will actually buy into it." I pick up my purse and start walking toward the door, pausing just before I leave. "If I go now, I figure that will give you more than enough time to trash me." With that, I walk out the door.

chapter 18

"I HAVE A SURPRISE for you," Jessica says, her voice alive and alert.

I realize suddenly that I'm on the phone and must have been asleep when I answered it. Glancing at my bedside clock, I note that it says 8:03 but I can't seem to figure out if it's a.m. or p.m. Since Jessica wouldn't dream of being up at eight in the morning, I deduce that it's night. And then I remember chain-smoking my way back from Claire's, arriving home, and crawling into bed with sudden exhaustion.

Before dozing off, I'd thought about what had happened at Claire's before deciding instead to focus on more pleasant topics, like the night before with Matt and Nick. But Nick was probably never going to call me after I completely blew him off for Matt, and according to Jessica, Matt only responded to women who treated him badly. These thoughts, combined with the memory of the verbal lashing I'd given my former best friend, seemed agonizingly tragic. Mercifully, I must have fallen asleep before spiraling into depression.

"I'm exhausted," I croak out. God, my throat hurts.

"I mean it, Emma," she says, ignoring me. "A surprise you're going to like."

"If it involves me having to get out of bed anytime soon, I can tell you right now that I'm not going to like it. If I do anything tonight, I'll work on my story."

"This may be more important than your story. This is about you working for the hottest new magazine in L.A."

I feel suddenly alert. "What do you mean?"

"It's going to be called *Angeles*," she says. "I guess there used to be this magazine called *LA Style* ages ago? Or something? Anyway, it folded, and then there was this one called *Buzz*, which also folded, but since *Los Angeles* magazine is a bore, the city is just ripe for this. It's going to be the L.A. version, essentially, of *New York* magazine."

By now, I'm quite awake. I see the half-empty pack of Camel Lights I'd bought the other day sitting on my bedside table and reach for one, and a lighter, almost subconsciously. "Tell me more." I light my cigarette.

"Well, the publisher, Greg Rowland, has been a friend of mine for years. He lives in New York but comes here for at least a few months every year."

"Go on."

"His dad's a billionaire who invented some piece of plastic that goes into boxes or cars or something. Greg's always wanted to have a magazine, and now he's got his dad and Ron Burkle and some other people backing him."

I inhale on the cigarette and admire the smoke rings I blow out. "Is that so?"

"It is," Jessica says. "And he trusts me implicitly." She pauses.

"This may be a chance for you to kiss party reporting good-bye for good."

As I smoke, I wonder over the fact that every time it seems like things have reached their most miserable apex, Jessica swoops in and offers some bright, shiny escape. "What time do I need to be ready?" I ask.

"I PREDICT WE'LL be the reigning Los Angeles publication in a matter of months," Greg says, picking up a piece of tuna with his chopsticks. He's younger than I expected and, with his splotchy face, freckles, and red hair, resembles what you'd think Danny Bonaduce back in the Partridge Family days might have grown into if he hadn't grown into Danny Bonaduce. "The city has been all but begging for someone—anyone!—to give them something interesting to read."

I nod. "The regional magazines around here are really boring," I agree. "They always seem to have articles on, say, where to get the best shoe polish or doorknobs or some other random thing you would never want." I take a bite of my chicken.

"Exactly!" Greg says, pointing a chopstick at me excitedly. "Like I said, I imagine *Angeles* magazine will make all of them yesterday's news pretty quickly."

"When are you planning to launch?" I ask, glancing at Jessica gratefully. Greg Rowland seemed to be the real deal: he had the backing of all the media bigwigs, had mentioned well-known journalists he was planning to sign up for contracts, and seemed, in general, to be the best contact I'd possibly ever made.

"Within a few months," he says, emptying his sake glass. A few months certainly didn't sound like much time to launch a major magazine, but what do I know? I toil thanklessly on press lines with the other bottom-feeders while he's a real player in the publishing world. He glances at Jessica and then at me. "Jess told me about the story you're working on for *Substance*."

I shoot her a look but she just smiles at me innocently. "Yes, well, I'd appreciate it if you keep that quiet, as—"

"Give it to me instead," Greg says, popping a dragon roll into his mouth.

"Em, you've been able to really infiltrate our world," Jessica pipes in before I can respond. "Probably more than any other journalist before." She plays with the rice under her maki. "And you know that *Substance* isn't paying you even close to what you're worth."

"I can't." I glance from Jessica to Greg. "It's out of the question." I look at Greg directly. "I'm turning the piece in later this week."

"Turn it in to me instead."

Not knowing what else to do, I laugh. "That's crazy. I mean, I've been working toward getting a *Substance* feature for years."

"Well, it used to be a great magazine—that's for sure. But no one even talks about it anymore. Face it, *Substance* has lost its edge."

"That's not true."

Greg leans back in his chair. "If I had a story like yours in my premiere issue, I'd release it early to Richard Johnson, Liz Smith, and Gawker and make the kind of media splash that would really put us on the map."

I suddenly see myself earnestly chatting with Diane Sawyer on *Good Morning America* about my piece, and then wonder why Ethan and Mark never mentioned a press plan. Greg adds, "Jess was telling me that some of the girls you're profiling in the story actually think you're one of them."

My face gets hot at the mere mention of the topic I'd been working so hard to avoid even thinking about. "Yes, but I—"

"See, I think that's great," Greg says. "It shows that you're a risk-taker and not just some by-the-books rule-follower."

I smile at him. "I wish my *Substance* editor felt the same way."

Greg points at me. "That's what I mean when I say they've lost their edge! Face it, *Substance* has gotten stodgy." I consider this as Greg motions to the waiter for more sake. "I'm also looking for an editor in chief," he says. As the waiter fills our cups, this provocative statement lingers in the air.

"Meaning?"

"Christ, what do you think it means, Emma?" Jessica asks. "Give him the story and he'll hire you."

"Really?" I ask Greg.

"Sure," he says. He's looking at Jessica but talking to me. "Jess says you're smart and on the ball, but that you're not at a place that allows you to do what you're capable of."

"But *Substance*—"

"And look, how far are you going to be able to rise at a New York–based publication?"

"Well, once I start writing features—"

"Once you start writing features, you're going to continue to stand outside parties and accost celebrities," Greg says. "I'm offering you a chance to be on the inside."

"But honestly, I don't think I'm qualified to be an editor in chief," I protest. "I mean, I wouldn't have a clue how to create a budget and deal with contracts or any of those things."

"Emma." Greg laughs. "Haven't you ever heard that it's not good business to try to talk someone out of offering you a job?" He gulps more sake. "Besides, all of that is the managing editor's responsibility. What I need in an editor in chief is ideas, energy, and an ability to help me create an overall vision for the magazine and then find the writers who can best carry that out."

A prickle of excitement starts washing its way over my body. "When would you want me to start?" I find myself asking.

He looks surprised. "Is that a yes?"

"No. I mean, I can't back out on my editor. But I'd still like to know exactly what I'm missing."

"Well," Greg says, "I needed someone yesterday so it would essentially be as soon as you agreed. But since I don't have office space yet, you'd be working from home for the first few months—until we staff up." He sips his sake. "It's a serious job, Emma. I've been talking to the *Esquire* articles editor about it but I really need someone who's already out here in L.A."

I stare at him, marveling over the fact that a publisher would really give such an important position to a person who'd spent the better part of her career asking people like Omarosa how she prepared for an evening out. Then again, maybe this is simply how the other half has always lived: while some people try to keep their heads above water in the gossip ghetto, others weigh amazing opportunities over dinners at Matsuhisa. I envision myself collecting a National Magazine Award for the prostitution piece and dedicating it to Greg for being "the one who took a chance on me." To buy some time, I say, "I'm really flattered but—"

"She'll come around, just give her a day or two to think about it," Jessica says, kicking me under the table and potentially causing a permanent Louboutin heel indentation on my upper arch.

My foot throbbing, I shoot Jessica a dirty look. "I'm really flattered," I repeat dumbly.

Greg nods and smiles. "Good, you should be," he says. He wipes his mouth with his napkin. "Now, will you excuse me while I visit the little boys' room?" He stands up, and as he strolls away from the table, I turn to Jessica.

"You can't make a decision like that for me," I hiss. I'm surprised by how angry I feel. "I've made promises. You don't understand."

"I'm just trying to help you stop selling yourself short," she whispers back. "His magazine is going to be huge."

"You don't have to whisper—he's in the bathroom," I snap in a normal voice. "And I get what a great opportunity this is—and appreciate your introducing me to him—but this is for *me* to figure out, you know."

Jessica's eyes flare and she sniffs loudly. *I wonder if she's on coke now,* I think, and the thought suddenly sounds appealing, which terrifies me. Before I have time to worry that my coke indulgence may have been more than just a one-time experiment, Jessica says, "And here I thought *you* were supposed to be the one with the good breeding."

I hate it when Jessica mentions the different ways we were raised or has a sort of too-awestruck appreciation for wealth or cultivation. She'd once referred to a certain restaurant we passed as "fancy," and I'd internally cringed, pained as much by my own snobbery as I was by her ignorance that saying "fancy" only underscored how not fancy the person using the word was. "What's that supposed to mean?" I ask.

"It means that the guy's taking us out to dinner. I was just trying to help you be polite."

I look at her—the almond green eyes, the permanent smirk etched into her face—and feel like I'm seeing her as a stranger would. I suddenly remember Antonio calling her a cold-hearted bitch. "He doesn't have to pay for dinner," I say. "I'm happy to—"

"That's not the point, it's just—"

Before I realize it, Greg has slid back into his chair. "Looks like I'm breaking up something pretty interesting," he says. "Fighting over who gets to take me home?" He and Jessica both laugh, and I suddenly feel ashamed and embarrassed. He gazes at me coolly. "Just so you have all the information," he says, "I should tell you that I'd be paying you a base salary of a hundred thousand. Plus another ten grand for the story."

I want so much to not be impacted by this number, but I am. He's talking about the sort of money that would put me on par with all those people my parents are always comparing me to. But at the same time, I know I can't just yank the story from Ethan when it's scheduled to run in the September issue. And *Substance* is a proven entity, whereas Greg's publication is still just an idea. Besides, I have too much residual anger left over from my little exchange with Jessica—who's now grinning at me as she strokes Greg's arm—to do exactly what she wants. But what's worse—Jessica's need to control everything or Claire and the triumvirate of girls who believe that anyone who doesn't have a husband and a fetus growing inside is somehow an inferior person? At least Jessica is genuinely interested in helping me out. "Let me think about it," I say, as Jessica squeezes my hand under the table.

chapter 19

MATT LEANS OVER the passenger seat to give me an appreciative glance. "You look hot," he says through the slit in the window of his Mercedes. I open the door and slide in, trying not to be bothered by the fact that he didn't ring my doorbell or even get out of the car. *But that would have been obsequious and annoying,* I remind myself. *Matt's smooth.* "The movie's supposed to be a piece of shit," he adds as he starts the car.

"That's what I heard, too." I don't mention to him that I'm supposed to be on the press line for the premiere we're on our way to, and that, per Jessica's advice, I'd simply decided to blow it off when Matt invited me as his guest. I likewise don't inform him that my prostitution story is due in a few days and so what I really need to be doing tonight is finishing the first draft. I also don't explain that the anxiety I'd had about him had returned—multiplied by about a hundred—since the minute he'd called me and extended this invitation.

"Won't be the first crappy movie I've seen, certainly won't be the last," Matt says as he runs a red light. I tug on the slit of the skirt I'm wearing, trying to calm down by reminding myself that I'm different now than I was when I was first involved with Matt. I'd been studying, after all, at the altar of Jessica—the woman better at making men fall for her than anyone I knew—for a month and a half. When Matt and I dated before, I now see, I'd had everything mixed up—like a stereo with the red speaker cord plugged into the black part and the black cord attached to the red. I'd been a bundle of neediness and insecurity, and he responded to cool indifference. I was determined to show him how independent and confident I could now be.

"I've sat through worse, I'm sure," I say. While Matt had taken me to events before, he hadn't deemed me premiere-worthy until tonight. Since this movie—yet another *Charlie's Angels* sequel, the kind of thing I'd rather tear my eyeballs out than see—is a legitimately enormous, A-list film, the fact that he now sees me as an acceptable plus one in this department more than makes up for the dreck I was going to be sitting through.

"You just can't be too disgusted when you hear me kiss Drew's ass and tell her how brilliant the movie is," he says.

He cares what I think of him, I think. Out loud I say, "I wouldn't expect anything less." It surprises me how steady my voice sounds.

He smiles, and then laughs. "You know, I'm glad we ran into each other again."

Channeling Jessica, I ask in what I hope is a coy tone, "Is that so?"

"Yeah," he says. "I guess I thought you were a little—I don't know—too nervous or innocent or something—before. But you don't seem that way anymore."

I take a deep breath. "Um, thanks," I say. Then I add, "For noticing."

Matt reaches over and strokes my leg but doesn't say anything else. And though I want to jump in and start a conversation in order to put a dent in the silence, I remind myself that if I really was as indifferent to him as I'm trying to act like I am, I'd be perfectly comfortable not talking. I always think I have to perform skits or do flips or be outrageously amusing in order for people to continue to want me in their company, but Jessica had once told me that no one really expected much from those around them and I should just calm down. So I watch the city pass me by and remind myself that he thinks of me as relaxed now so I might as well try to act that way.

"IT WAS A fucking masterpiece," Matt says, kissing Drew Barrymore on both cheeks.

She beams. "You think so?" she asks, looking absolutely thrilled. "The critics have been a little brutal."

"Fuck 'em," Matt says. "They're all fat player-haters, pissed off that their Ivy League educations don't even net them enough to cover their mortgages."

"That's why you're on my team," Drew says, grinning. "You always know exactly what to say." They continue to chat and it occurs to me that now would be an ideal time to show Matt how little I care about him. I take a step toward the bar but Matt grabs my hand and gestures toward the tables filled with platters of prime rib, salmon, and chicken.

"You hungry?" he asks. Before I have a chance to answer, a fleet of suit-clad agent types descend upon him, saying things like, "Sixty million this weekend, for sure," and "Sixty? More like a hundred," all with congratulatory and self-congratulatory tones, like Matt himself wrote, directed, and developed the movie, and they, too, were somehow intrinsically involved in its creative process.

"Fuck the critics," Matt says in response. "They're all fat player-haters, pissed off that their Ivy League educations don't even net them enough to cover their mortgages." One of the guys slaps him on the back while I decide that there's nothing wrong with him repeating a good line and that I might, in fact, do this myself without even realizing it. "You know Emma, right?" Matt says to the group. The guys all greet me, and one of them—a shiny-looking guy wearing a leather coat—shakes my hand.

"You pretty proud of your boy?" he asks. I nod, relishing how the words "your" and "boy" sound together. A WireImage photographer breezes up to our group and says, "Hey, Matt, can I take a couple shots of you? And maybe later a few with you and Drew?"

For a second, I think Matt's going to reach over and pull me into the picture and I fantasize about photos of the two of us appearing in the *Hollywood Reporter*'s party page tomorrow—"Ten-percenter Matt McCarthy and gal pal, journalist Emma Swanson"—and how I'd explain to people that although the "gal pal" label was a bit premature, I was certainly willing to entertain the notion. But two of the guys move closer to him so I step away as if I'm actually not interested in being shot. Then I walk over to the bar, noticing out of the corner of my eye that Matt is continuing to smile for the WireImage guy and seems to be oblivious to the fact that I'm not by his side. As the bartender hands me a drink, Rebecca sidles up. "Hi there, Emma," she says coolly.

"Hey, Rebecca," I say. "How are you?" Completely sober and without Jessica by my side, I don't feel nearly as powerful as I did the last time I saw her.

Suddenly, Brooke makes her way over to us. "Where's Jessica?" she asks, wrinkling her nose. Before I can respond, Matt appears.

"Brooke, Rebecca," he says, giving each of them a kiss on the cheek as he hails the bartender. "Do you want a drink?" he asks me. I point to my martini as Brooke looks from Matt to me with amazement.

"Are you here . . . together?" she asks, glancing conspiratorially at Rebecca, but Rebecca is waving and making the "call me" gesture to someone across the room. I nod and add a tiny shrug, putting on such a solid act of pretending that Brooke and I never discussed Matt—or his predilection for women like Jessica—that I essentially believe it myself. I can practically see the wheels in Brooke's head spinning as she tries to determine whether I've somehow joined Jessica's ranks and she should snub me or if I'm now Matt's girlfriend and she thus needs to be jealous. "Really?" she asks.

Once Matt has his drink and turns around to face us, Brooke focuses her increasingly beady eyes on him. "So how long has this been going on?" she asks Matt, gesturing from him to me. Figures. Here I am using everything in me to show how indifferent I can be toward Matt and I have Hollywood's biggest busybody putting pressure on him to define the nature of our relationship.

"This? What? We're at a premiere," Matt says as I smile and try to look blasé. Even though I shouldn't be hurt by Matt's response—*What the hell is he supposed to say with Brooke bombarding him like that,* I think, *especially when they used to date?*—I feel just the slightest bit miffed. Matt looks at me. "Why don't we go sit in that corner booth?" he asks, gesturing his head toward the back of the restaurant. "I want you to meet Drew's publicist."

I smile. With that "I want you to meet," Matt had restored

all my confidence in him—and, in a roundabout way, myself. Brooke, now looking openly hostile, throws a fake smile on her face.

"Have fun," she says, as she takes a step back. Rebecca blows air kisses at us. As soon as we're a few feet away, however, Matt suddenly stops and drains his glass.

"Sorry—I just had to get away from them," he says, and I try not to care that he doesn't really want to introduce me to anyone. Glancing up at the entrance, I see Steve and Celeste walking in and instinctively turn in the opposite direction before they notice me. After all the consoling Steve had done when Matt dumped me, I have to imagine that I'd be in for a hell of a "what are you thinking getting mixed up with that guy again" lecture tomorrow if he saw us together right now. Steve just wouldn't, I decide, understand the recent changes in my life.

"Oh, the riffraff have invaded," Matt says, gesturing to two guys in Hawaiian shirts that I recognize as *Access Hollywood* cameramen. I see Jack make his way inside, grinning from ear to ear. "Do you want to get out of here?"

"Yes, please," I say. *It's much easier,* I think, *to act indifferent without other people around reminding you that you're not.*

"GOD, IT'S GOOD to be home," Matt says as he pulls into his driveway. We never discussed my coming here with him but it was all part of my plan to prove to myself that having sex with a guy didn't cause you to lose your power over him, so I actually appreciate the fact that he didn't even consult me on the matter—*almost,* I think, *like we're a couple simply returning to our place after a night out.*

As I remembered, his house is tacky and expensive-looking—lots of black leather couches and sharp lines—and at first I blame the decor for the fact that I don't feel particularly comfortable right now. Watching Matt pour a scotch as he examines his mail, I try to come up with something to talk to him about. *What do I most want to know about this man?* I think, racking my brain for some of the thoughts I'd had when I was so obsessed with him. Finally, I simply ask, "Do you have TiVo?"

Matt looks up and smiles. "Now, what would we need TiVo for?" he says as he walks over and picks me up.

"You won't be able to carry me!" I protest as he hoists me over his shoulder, showcasing strength I never knew he had. As he lumbers toward his bedroom with me in his arms, I laugh, realizing that I feel carefree for the first time all night. I congratulate myself for finally being in the moment but then realize that if I'm congratulating myself for being in the moment, I've clearly come out of the moment, so I instead I silently beg my brain to turn itself off. He tenderly tosses me onto the bed and collapses nearby.

"Isn't this better than any TV show?" he asks. I can't help but notice that he has bad breath but then tell myself that he had a long day and just had to schmooze his way through a premiere so I shouldn't be so judgmental. He leans in and I want so much for us to have one of those utterly passionate kisses—like the kind from that famous photo of the soldier and nurse at the end of World War II—but instead it's cold and dry and awkward. I decide that I'm really going to own my sexuality the way Jessica seems to own hers, even though I'm not remotely clear how to do that. By really concentrating on what he's doing to me? By moaning more? He's suddenly removing my pants and his own and I'm marveling at how fast this is all going before I realize I'm not the slightest bit turned on. I'm worried that Matt will think there's something sexually defective about me when he feels how dry I am but he either doesn't notice or simply doesn't care because the next thing I know, he's putting on a condom and thrusting into me in this very quick, almost jackhammer-like way that I don't particularly like. *Tell him to go slower,* I think, instantly deriding myself for thinking this and not saying it out loud and thus not doing even a semi-decent job of owning my sexuality. I start to wonder if sex is as complicated for other people as it is for me when I suddenly imagine Jessica in the throes of ecstasy. Disturbed, I shake the image away.

After it's over, Matt cuddles up to his memory foam pillow and immediately starts snoring. I just look at him, marveling that someone can fall into slumber roughly 3.3 seconds after his head hits a pillow and pondering how empty I feel. I remind myself that this is what I wanted, but I suddenly can't think of one reason why I liked Matt in the first place. It's as if some power switch inside of me has been turned directly from on to off and I instantly see that it wasn't Matt I was obsessing over all this time but the idea of Matt—and what his approval of me implied. Matt himself, I realize, doesn't do a thing for me. It then occurs to me that I might be certifiably insane.

I get up and start pacing around his house, trying to identify the unpleasant feeling I'm having. *It's guilt!* I decide, realizing, as I stand on his balcony, that this is the first time I've had sex outside of a relationship. Whoever said guilt over sex was reserved for Catholics obviously hadn't taken into account how horrible giving up your body to feed a part of your ego could make you feel. I wander back into the bedroom, gathering my clothes and calling a cab as Matt continues to snore. I have this strange, unfathomable desire never to see him again, and realize that in the past few minutes, I've somehow sailed past indifference into actual disgust. *Am I disgusted with him or myself?* I wonder as I wait for the cab, knowing that it doesn't really matter.

chapter 20

THE RUSSIAN WOMAN looks at me strangely when I follow Jessica into the laser hair removal room.

"You want I do removal, too?" she asks.

"No, I—"

"She's my personal assistant, Milla." Jessica pats the woman—Milla—on the shoulder and winks at me. "It's imperative that she's with me at all times."

Milla shakes her head and holds up a pair of glasses. "I have only two pair glasses to filter out laser light," she says. "One for me."

Jessica grabs the glasses from Milla. "That's okay," Jessica says as she puts them on and lies down on the treatment bed. "Emma can keep her eyes closed."

I know it's strange that I'm in the room while Jessica is having her armpit hair lasered off but when she had stopped by this morning, I'd taken a break from working on the story to tell her about my abysmal date with Matt—essentially informing her that I hadn't felt like I had anything to say to him before, during, or after we had sex. She insisted I come with her to her appointment so I could give her more details, but the sad fact of the matter was that there wasn't really anything left to say about Matt and me.

"So what have you decided to do about *Substance*?" Jessica asks as Milla rubs an icepack on Jessica's right underarm.

"I haven't." I cross one of my legs over the other. "I left Ethan a message and he hasn't called me back."

"Really?" Jessica asks and I feel certain that she's raising an eyebrow underneath those laser-proof glasses. "When was that?"

"A few days ago."

"Well, if I was passing up the biggest opportunity of my life solely out of devotion to a man I'd met three times, I'd certainly hope that he'd respect me enough to return my call."

I sigh. "Look, he's a busy guy. I'm not his only writer. And I don't even know what I'm going to say to him when he does get back to me. 'Um, hey, Ethan, you know that story that you're expecting me to turn in over the next few days—that one you begged the editor in chief to let me do? How would you feel if I gave it to a different magazine instead?' "

"Another magazine that will pay you ten times what he is," Jessica says.

Milla snaps her fingers. "Ladies. No chitterchat while I do the laser, yes?"

"Oh, sorry," I say. Milla puts on her glasses as I sit back in the chair and close my eyes, wishing I could be more like Jessica and not worry so much about loyalty or doing the right thing and simply surrender to the better opportunity.

As Milla turns the laser off, Jessica says, "Look, success is more a function of continued common sense than it is of genius."

"What are you talking about?"

"The Chinese engineer An Lang said it, and he's right. A lack of common sense may well be your problem."

This annoys me. "Who says I have a problem?"

"Oh, Emma." Jessica laughs. "You have a lot of problems."

"What?" I ask, angrily rising out of my chair.

"Come on, I'm just playing," Jessica says, smiling at me. She looks at Milla. "Aren't I just playing, Milla? You know how silly I can be."

Milla nods as she rubs ice on Jessica's other underarm. "You very silly girl," she confirms.

Jessica laughs. "What did I tell you? Milla speaks the truth. You can't take me seriously."

I sit back down as Milla snaps her fingers at us again. They both put their glasses back on and Milla starts up the laser. As soon as Milla turns the machine off, Jessica sits up. "Look, let's go out with Greg later. Maybe he can give you advice on how to talk to Ethan." She stands up and adds, "Assuming, that is, Ethan ever calls you back."

"I can't." Jessica and I make our way toward the reception area. "Family dinner tonight—to discuss Lilly's impending nuptials." I make a face as we walk out the door. "Not that I'm looking forward to it."

Jessica presses a button on her keychain to open her car door. "Well, why are you going, then?"

"What do you mean?" I ask as we get in her car.

"You're not contractually obligated and they're not paying you. You have a lot of work to do so you can meet a major deadline. You're flung into a major depression whenever you're around—or even talk to—them. So why put yourself through it?"

"Look, don't you feel guilty when you don't see or talk to your family?"

Jessica snorts. "Fuck no. My dad was nothing but an impregnator, really." Something about her voice, despite how cavalier the tone, sounds almost innocent. "I think the last time I saw him, I was seven. And my mom—well, she makes me feel like shit. I don't like to feel like shit. Thus, I don't see her. One plus one really does equal two sometimes, Emma."

I stare at Jessica as she drags on her cigarette and adjusts her rear-view mirror. Maybe it really is that simple: they make me feel like shit and I don't like to feel like shit; therefore I don't have to go. Quite suddenly, I feel incredibly angry at my family. "You know, if I have to hear about Lilly's fucking royal life one more time, I'm going to upchuck salmon all over them." I'm not sure when I went from being a person who doesn't swear to someone who does, but saying "fucking" right now feels so good that I add, "The fucking salmon my mom never seems to remember I hate."

Jessica laughs. "Atta girl. You're growing up before my very eyes." She exhales a line of smoke. "See, I thought you were getting better when you realized what a bore McCarthy was," she says. "Now I know for sure."

Hearing Jessica's praise makes me feel confident enough to be completely honest. "It sounds ridiculous, but the idea of telling my mom I'm not coming to dinner scares the shit out of me," I say.

I expect her to laugh or tell me how silly that is but instead she just nods coolly. "Be scared. You can't help that. But don't be afraid."

I look at her. "What's that supposed to mean?"

She laughs. "It's from a Faulkner story, 'The Bear.' He was talking about how animals can smell when you're afraid—but people can, too."

I repeat, "Scared but not afraid. Got it." And then, rather

abruptly, the thought of being truthful with my family makes me feel empowered—almost high. "I can do this," I announce as Jessica pulls up at my apartment.

"Want me to come in?" she asks. "For moral support?"

"Yes." I wonder for a split second how I did anything before I knew her. "That would be great."

"WHAT'S WRONG, EMMA?" Mom asks even though all I've said is, "Mom?" The woman has an incredible talent, when she applies it, for deciphering the tone of my voice and knowing when I'm about to say something she's not going to like.

"Nothing. I just wanted to let you know that I'm not coming to dinner tonight."

"Why?" she says, sounding so shocked that you'd think I'd just informed her that I'd had a sex change and was moving in with my transgendered girlfriend, Sam. "What's going on with you?"

I feel my defenses kick into overdrive but take a deep breath and force myself to plunge forward. *I'm perfectly justified in doing what I want,* I think. "What's going on with me is that I don't feel like it." I pause for a second and then add, "Sometimes I get sick of listening to all of you salivate over Lilly—and her life with Felipe—and I need a break from it." Mom doesn't say anything, but sighs in a way that manages to make the tiny sliver of pride I was developing start to dissipate into a miasma of guilt. "Seriously, Mom," I say, forcing the words out now. "I'm tired of feeling like I never measure up."

"That's ridiculous, Emma," Mom says. "I honestly have no idea what you're talking about."

"You can drop the act, Mom. Stop trying to pretend you don't get it."

There's a pause where I picture her holding the phone away and looking at Dad or Lilly—someone standing nearby, who's watching intently and horrified on Mom's behalf by whoever it is on the other end of the phone that's making her so upset. "I don't know what's gotten into you," Mom finally says, her tone more sad than angry. "What happened to my little girl?"

"I'm not your little girl anymore, Mom," I suddenly explode. "Don't you get that? I'm an adult and living my own life!"

"Is this what you call living your own life, Emma? Verbally abusing me and insulting Claire and the rest of the girls at her tea party?"

"Jesus Christ!" I yell, realizing that Claire must have called my mom and confided in her about what happened. "You and Claire are now talking shit about me?"

"Honey," Mom says. "Claire is your best friend. And we're both worried about you and who you're becoming."

"Claire isn't my best friend!" I yell, somewhat hysterically. "No best friend would fucking tattle on me to my mom!" I realize that I sound like a child, but the rage flooding my body has stopped me from caring. "I don't know where you and—"

"If you're going to yell at me and use that kind of language, I'm going to have to hang up," she says in a composed and concerned voice that seems to imply that I'm a lunatic who's just escaped from the local asylum and she's the one motioning for the doctor to put me in a straitjacket.

I'm seething now. "I'm not fucking—"

"Good-bye, Emma," she says, and then adds before she hangs up, "This makes me very sad." Click, and then dial tone.

"Good-bye!" I yell, slamming the phone back into its cradle. I look up. Jessica's staring at me, smoking, with a bemused look on her face. "Canceling on family dinner didn't go so well," I say, realizing that my throat hurts from shrieking.

"Yeah, well, the people who've had you under their thumb your whole life don't tend to react well when you figure out that the nail polish they're wearing is making you suffocate."

For some reason, this strikes me as incredibly funny. I laugh—a slow, guttural cackle that's as satisfying as a long-anticipated sneeze. My phone starts ringing. "Let me guess," Jessica says. "Mom again?"

I see that it's an unknown caller and shake my head. "If I know my mother, she won't talk to me until I come running back to her and apologize." I answer the phone, hear a woman say my name, and immediately recognize the cranky, dissatisfied voice of the *Substance* editor who handles party reporting. "Hi, Lauren," I sigh. I roll my eyes at Jessica but she's already on her own phone and doesn't notice.

"I'm afraid I've got some bad news." Lauren pauses. "I'm going to have to cancel your event coverage contract."

I'm simultaneously shocked and not remotely surprised. I'd barely been doing the job for months now and the truth is, I've been terrible at it from day one. "Right," I say.

"Your reporting on the last few parties has been undeniably shabby and I haven't even received anything from you for the *Charlie's Angels* premiere," she continues. "The way I see it, you've left me with no other options—"

"It's okay, Lauren," I surprise myself by saying. "I get it."

"Well," she says, sounding slightly confused, "all right, then." She pauses. "Um, I guess we don't really have anything else we need to discuss."

"No, we don't," I say. "But good luck with everything."

"You—"

"Bye." I place the phone down and look at Jessica, who's now done with her phone call. "I've always wanted to be able to wish someone 'good luck' just before I thought they were going to say it to me," I say. I'm feeling strangely calm. Motioning for her to hand me a cigarette, I add, "Wow, that felt good."

"You got canned?" she asks as she lights me up with her Zippo.

"Yup." I inhale on my cigarette, and then slowly blow smoke out. *I don't have a job,* I think. The thought, surprisingly, doesn't induce a panic attack.

"That's amazing." She grins.

"How so?"

"Emma, *Substance* would never want to run a story by someone whose contract they just canceled."

"I don't know about that," I say. "Event coverage is a completely different department. Ethan probably doesn't even know."

Jessica shakes her head. "Jesus, how many excuses are you going to make for that guy?" she asks. "Of course he knows. And if you mattered to him at all, he would have gotten in touch with you before she did. Why do you think he's not calling you back? He's screwing you over." She stands up. "The only thing you can do, as far as I see it, is give Greg the story, take the job with him, and let Ethan find out the way you just learned about your situation: from someone else."

My head feels like it's spinning. "I should call Ethan again."

Jessica laughs. "Oh my God, you're really determined to screw yourself over, aren't you?"

I watch her put her hand on her hips and take in her self-assurance. "Do you think?"

"I know. If you insist on getting in touch with Ethan, do it later. Because I have something far more enjoyable for you to do."

"What?"

"Do you know who Rob Silver is?"

"Of course." Rob is about as close as you can get to being a celebrity in this town without actually being a celebrity: he's created and produced more hit dramas than almost anyone else so he's regularly profiled in newspapers and magazines, and he dates enough actresses that he's covered somewhat religiously in all the gossip pages.

"Well, apparently he saw you at that premiere you went to with Matt the other night and thinks you're hot," she says.

"He did? He does?" Steve had introduced me to Rob at a party a few years ago, and he'd acted as indifferent to me as someone might be to a wallpaper pattern they'd looked at every day for the past twenty years. Hearing that he'd finally noticed me somehow causes all my anxiety over the Ethan situation to immediately dissipate. "How do you know?"

She grins. "Well, he figured—correctly—that because of my relationship with Matt, I'd know who you were, so he just called and asked me about you. And I took it upon myself to set the two of you up."

"Are you serious?"

"He wants to meet you tonight."

"Tonight?"

"Yes, tonight. Which means that you need to call Greg, accept the job, then show up at the Chateau Marmont at nine thirty to meet Rob for some event."

"But my deadline—"

"Emma, you don't have to worry about your deadline anymore." She smiles. "You're doing the story for Greg now. He'll let you have more time, trust me." She raises an eyebrow and adds, "I gave Rob your cell."

I nod, feeling completely overwhelmed. Not sure what else to do, I simply ask, "What's Greg's number?" Jessica recites it to me and I dial. When I get his voicemail, I say, "Greg, it's Emma. I'm calling to let you know I'm accepting the job and giving you my story. I just need a few more days before I can turn it in." I leave him my number and look up at Jessica, who's now standing by my door.

"Nice work." She smiles. "Now, if you'll excuse me, I have to go home and bathe in gold."

"Excuse me?" I glance at my shelf and see the Ursula Elise Marc Jacobs bag Jessica gave me that day at Fred Segal. Tonight, I decide, I'll wear it out.

Jessica starts walking toward my front door. "Bernie gave me a bubble bath he got in Japan that's filled with actual specks of gold. It's time I tried it."

"You're something else." I laugh. "Enjoy being coated in gold."

"Oh, I will. As Dorothy Parker said, 'Take care of the luxuries and the necessities will take care of themselves.'"

"Ha." I smile as Jessica lets herself out. Then I lean back on my couch, thinking that Rob would actually make a far more impressive boyfriend than Matt. And we could be quite the power couple—the editor in chief of L.A.'s hottest new magazine and a big-time producer. I imagine a photo of our wedding in the *New York Times* Style section where I'm wearing flowers in my hair, an *In Style* piece on our Hollywood Hills home, the two of us laughing at an inside joke at the *Vanity Fair* Oscar party. *Maybe,* I think, *it's time for my gold bath*.

"UM, I GUESS I'll have another Amstel Light," I say to the bartender, with another glance around the outdoor bar. It's five minutes before ten—that is, twenty-five minutes after our arranged meeting time—and there's still no sign of Rob. The event is, however, lousy with magazine people—two *Us Weekly* freelancers are talking to David Spade to my left and the *Vanity Fair* West

Coast bureau chief is chatting up a *Substance* feature writer near the entrance. I smile at the bartender as he slides the beer over, wishing the drink somehow had the power to help me remain invisible until Rob showed up.

As I curse Jessica for not picking up her phone the three times I've called her in the past twenty minutes to ask her for Rob's cell phone number, I look around the patio and decide to give the guy another ten minutes. If he still doesn't show, I'll leave, assume I'm being stood up, and never let Jessica arrange a date for me again.

But, oh God. I suddenly see Brooke sitting at a table about twenty feet away with a girl I don't recognize and the gorgeous MTV correspondent Adriana Lopez, and I realize a new level of horror has just been added to the equation. I avert my eyes as quickly as humanly possible but it's too late: Brooke's face alights with recognition and she motions me over to her. *Christ,* I think. If there's anything more humiliating than being stood up, it's being stood up and then spotted in this situation by someone who had the ability and resources to broadcast that fact to the world at large.

"Emma!" she yells, gesturing me over to her again. Then, so loudly that I'm certain she can be heard in Los Feliz, she bellows, *"Are you here by yourself?"*

I nod and she continues to madly insist with her hands that I come say hello so I regretfully approach their table. "Hi, Brooke," I say. "How are you?"

"You know Meredith, right?" she answers, gesturing to the woman I don't recognize. She and I both nod—in Hollywood, everyone's always pretending to know people they don't and feigning that they don't know those they do. "And have you ever met Adriana?" As I shake my head, Brooke adds, "Isn't Adriana even more stunning in person than on TV?" Without waiting for me to answer, Brooke continues, "Are you all alone?"

"I'm waiting for someone," I say, "who's late." The last thing I want is for Brooke to invite me to sit down, as I can only guess that now that I'm not with Jessica or Matt, she'd quiz me incessantly about my relationships with both of them. And I'm not too eager to explain who I'm meeting, either. It's all too easy to imagine Brooke breaking into frenzied whispers once I walk away about how I used to be this kind of clueless party reporter and now I hung out with a high-class call girl and various successful Hollywood men, breaking these facts down until they were bite-sized, gnawable bones they could all swallow.

"That sucks," Brooke says, clearly assuming I'm not meeting anyone who's worth registering on her radar, and then her attention is diverted by the sight of Matthew McConaughey walking by. "Matthew!" she yells, and then points at herself. "Brooke Howard from Howard Productions? I met you through Gus?" As Matthew gets caught in Brooke's web, I feel relinquished, so I make my way back to my place at the bar, where I sip my beer and feign contentment.

Just as I've decided to give up on him—a good hour after our scheduled meeting time—I see Rob walk down the outdoor stairs of the hotel and toward the courtyard. *He probably has a really good reason for being late,* I think, as he looks over at me and raises his hand in greeting. We smile at each other as he approaches, but then, of course—

"Rob Silver!" Brooke shrieks. "There you are! I've been leaving word for you! Has your assistant not been telling you? And, oh, you know Adriana and Meredith, right?"

I watch and smile patiently as Rob stops and gives them all cheek kisses. *He'll say hello and move on,* I think. But when his greeting turns into a full-blown conversation, I simply stare at him, dumbfounded, pretending not to care that he's standing there telling them some story that is making the girls—and Adriana in particular—laugh hysterically. *Is he honestly going to make me continue to wait for him?* I think incredulously, pretending to look perfectly entertained by myself until he eventually meanders over.

"How are ya, babe?" he says, leaning in to kiss my cheek. No "I'm so sorry I'm over an hour late and stopped to talk to those girls for way too long." No "Thanks for coming to meet me at the last minute." Nothing. He looks at the waiter. "A Tanqueray martini," he says, as he sits down.

"It's after ten thirty," I respond, unable to hide my annoyance. When he doesn't say anything, I look down at my watch and point to it.

"You're not going to give me some major guilt trip right now, are you?" he asks, sounding just as irritated as I feel. "Because the parking situation here is a nightmare."

Sighing, I consider telling him he's an asshole and sauntering past the triumvirate of girls—who would, at that point, surely be watching with mouths agape—to my car. But then I realize it would be far easier to calm down and just have a drink with the guy. *What would Jessica do?* I wonder, before realizing that she'd probably have left an hour ago—assuming she hadn't refused to meet at the bar and insisted on being picked up in a town car instead. I debate my options. And that's when I see, walking toward me, the only person who could make the Brooke sighting seem like a welcome respite: Ethan.

"Hey, Emma!" he exclaims. A woman I've seen with him at various events is by his side.

Oh God. Oh God. Oh God. "You never called me back," I say softly. It's the only thing I can think of.

Ethan furrows his brow and then seems to realize something.

"You know, our office voicemail has been on the fritz all week. What's going on?" He motions to the woman with him. "By the way, this is my wife, Laura Adams," he says. "Laura, meet Emma Swanson, the party reporter I was telling you about who's doing the prostitution feature."

I shake Laura's hand while glancing at Rob. He's waving at someone across the room and apparently not remotely interested in what I'm doing. "Nice to meet you," I say, feeling like I might collapse into a puddle of guilt here in the outdoor bar area of the Chateau Marmont.

"So how's the story shaping up? Are you going to be able to turn it in the day after tomorrow?" Ethan asks.

I close my eyes, tell myself that this will hurt less if I get it over with quickly, and say, "I'm giving it to another magazine." *It's his fault,* I think. *He insisted I do the story his way and hasn't been checking in with me about it.*

"What are you talking about?" Ethan seems confused.

"Well, a lot has happened," I say, not meeting his eye. I pause dramatically and then look up. "Lauren terminated my contract."

He looks shocked. "Are you serious?" I nod. "Jesus," he sighs. "I'm so sorry. Well, I'm sure Mark will agree with me that what happens with the party coverage department has nothing to do with this piece."

My heart thuds. *Jessica was wrong,* I think. "Well, I didn't know that," I respond coolly, sounding more like Jessica than I ever have. "And it's too late now."

"Too late?" Ethan emits a sound that's somewhere been a laugh and a gasp. His eyes narrow as he seems to finally understand what I'm telling him. "You should have called me the second you got off the phone with Lauren."

I look down at my Marc Jacobs bag and then up at Ethan. "I would have, but I was still waiting to hear back from you."

"Christ, Emma." He's angry now. "Please don't tell me you're going to try to use that as an excuse."

I gaze at the ground. "Look, I got an offer from a great start-up magazine that involves me giving them the story," I say. "I figured you'd understand." I glance at Rob, who's now watching us with mild interest.

"What are you talking about?" Ethan's face is turning red with indignation. "What magazine?"

"It doesn't matter, Ethan," I say, positive that if I tell him about *Angeles*, he'll give me some lecture about how start-ups aren't as reliable as already established magazines. *He's had me under his thumb and I'm suffocating under the nail polish,* I think. "But that's what I'm doing."

"Emma, I promised Mark you'd come through on this." The way Ethan is looking at me makes me want to either collapse into the fetal position or scream at him. "You can't put me in this position."

I'm about to say some line out of *Jerry Maguire* about how it's show business, not show friends, but the magazine world isn't exactly show business and quoting an early nineties movie—any movie—right now probably isn't a good call. Yet I want to say something flippant that will take the seriousness out of this moment and stop making me feel like such an asshole. *Ethan should be happy for me,* I think. *A good guy would want what's best for my career.* "Look, Ethan," I finally say. "I'm sorry." I glance at Rob and then back at Ethan. "By the way, do you know Rob Silver?"

Rob holds out his hand as Ethan just continues to stare at me. "How the fuck could you do this?" he asks. I start at the word "fuck"—it's just not something I could have ever imagined Ethan saying—while Rob simply puts his hand down.

"Ethan, I—"

"Forget it," Ethan says, grabbing Liz, turning around, and

walking away. I feel partially embarrassed that he didn't return Rob's shake or introduce him to his wife, even though I also respect him for not caring that Rob is an important producer and behaving appropriately with him. I stare after Ethan for a second, not certain what to feel.

"Dramatic guy," Rob says. This makes me laugh, and I'm suddenly grateful for his presence. "Doesn't sound to me like you did anything wrong," Rob continues. "In my business, that kind of thing happens every day between and among friends and everyone knows it just goes with the territory."

"You're right." My guilty feelings begin to evaporate as I down the rest of my beer and place the empty bottle on the bar. I notice the bartender standing there expectantly, so I order a martini. "He really did make far too big a deal about the whole thing, didn't he?" I can't seem to resist the opportunity to be told again that I'm right and Ethan's wrong.

"Yeah," Rob says. "He needs to get a life." I smile at Rob, thinking that I really shouldn't have jumped to the conclusion that he was horrible solely because he was so late. "By the way," Rob adds as he glances at his watch, "don't just order a martini or they may give you some shit kind of gin. You really should have specified Tanqueray or Sapphire."

"Oh," I say. I wait for something else to come out of my mouth but it doesn't.

"And hey, would you mind if we went over and joined Brooke and them? I have a project that would be perfect for Adriana if she wants to make the leap from hosting to acting."

chapter 21

ETHAN IS OBVIOUSLY one of those people who wants to keep you down," Jessica says as I turn right on Beverly. We've just left the Ivy, where we had dinner with Greg to celebrate my having accepted his job.

"I guess," I answer. She and Greg had spent the bulk of our time together trashing Ethan and insisting that he was a selfish ass for not understanding my decision to go with the better opportunity. And while I desperately wanted to believe them, somehow the more they railed against him, the worse I felt.

"Oh, I have an idea—let's go to the Mosaic." Jessica lights a cigarette.

"Where?"

"The Mosaic Hotel. They have a sake martini that's out of this world. Plus, we may run into Philip, my most idiosyncratic Hollywood player of all."

"The last thing I want," I sigh, "is to meet any more of your Hollywood players."

Jessica readjusts the rear-view mirror so she can see herself and then applies lipstick. "Just because Rob was an asshole doesn't mean they all are." She rubs her lips together. "Oh, turn right here."

"I don't know about that." I follow her directions, reflecting on my joke of a night with Rob. I'd agreed to join Brooke, Meredith, and Adriana at their table, but had managed to say no when he asked me afterward if I was interested in coming home with him. "I'm definitely never letting you set me up again."

Jessica laughs. "You just expect too much from guys in this town, Emma." She sprays perfume on each of her wrists. "You have to accept the fact that men in the entertainment business are barely human."

"Not all of them." I think about Nick, the producer Jessica and I met the night we did coke. Although I'd surely never hear from him since I'd blown him off entirely to go talk to Matt, he was inarguably sweet and genuine.

"Trust me—all of them," she says in a tone that annoys me. "Oh, and make a U-turn so you can valet."

I do as she tells me. "Who's Philip, anyway?" I ask as I pull up in front of the hotel.

Jessica smiles. "Have I never told you about Philip?" she asks. "He turns up here sometimes. And he's very generous: he essentially buys me an entirely new Rick Owens wardrobe every time I'm with him—even though he's usually too coked up to do anything." She laughs. "Basically, I spend a few hours with him every couple of months where he smokes coke, looks through his blinds, and worries that the FBI is coming after him. And in exchange, I get a year's worth of amazing outfits." She sounds unmistakably proud of herself.

A valet parker rushes up. "Really?" I ask. "Do you ever—I don't know—feel bad about that? Or, I mean, tell him he should probably be spending his money on rehab or something instead?"

Jessica opens her door without responding. As I join her at the hotel entrance, she lights a cigarette. "Don't you and I live in the real world, Emma?" she asks.

"What's that supposed to mean?"

She looks at me. "Do you really think I should feel bad for the guy? Or put his needs before my own?"

"I don't know, I just—"

"Is that what you do with Antonio?"

I start. Jessica and I had never spoken about Antonio—I had no idea she was even aware of the fact that I knew the guy—and, quite honestly, I had almost forgotten about his existence altogether. "What are you talking about?"

"Have you ever told him you think he should go to rehab?" Instead of answering, I reach for her cigarette. I inhale deeply, feeling grateful for this distraction, however toxic it is. "Be careful what you judge, Emma," Jessica says, grabbing the cigarette back from me. "Because whenever you point a finger at someone, there are always three pointing back at you." I don't say anything and just watch her step on her cigarette. Then I let her lead me inside, even though I'd told Greg I'd get the story to him in the next few days and what I want more than anything is to go home, sit down, and reflect on how fast everything has been moving lately.

"WELL, LOOKY WHO'S HERE," Jessica says when we enter the bar area. She tilts her head in the direction of a dark-haired girl sitting away from most of the crowd, and I realize, when I follow Jessica's gaze, that it's Amanda. How the hell did Jessica see her from the entrance? I gesture to a table on the other side of the room but Jessica stares at Amanda and waves enthusiastically until she looks up. Dear God, no.

Then Jessica starts pushing me in Amanda's direction and, before I realize what's happening, we're standing in front of her. "Hey there, Mandy," Jessica says, and I want to fucking kill her. Amanda looks at us in semi-horror; in a battle to determine who's most disturbed by this turn of events, Amanda and I would probably be neck-and-neck. I hadn't spoken to her since she and Kristi had invited me to the "lucrative" party and I'd begged off with a migraine, even though she'd called me a few times since. Now that I didn't have to adhere to *Substance*'s rigorous fact-checking process, I had planned to just use whatever information I'd gotten from her and Kristi and simply deal with whatever repercussions came up later. "Oh, hi," Amanda finally says to me. "I didn't realize you guys were, like, hanging out." She completely ignores Jessica and I feel like I'm in high school again, or on an episode of *The Hills*.

"There's so much you don't realize, Mandy," Jessica says, and then turns to the bartender and orders two sake martinis. I feel sweat begin to gather under my arms and silently pray for Jessica to stop antagonizing Amanda so we can just get our drinks and move somewhere else.

Ignoring Jessica, Amanda grabs her purse and looks at me. "You know, why don't we catch up another time?" she says and I'm flooded with relief. "There are a lot of bad vibes everywhere." She stands up just as Kristi—who seems to be coming back from the bathroom—walks into the bar area.

"Hey, there," Kristi says sweetly to me.

Then Jessica bellows, "Yeah, she'll catch up with you another time, Mandy. So she can get some more information for her story."

Oh, fuck, no. My heart feels like it plummets from my chest to my stomach. *This can't be happening,* I tell myself. "What's she talking about?" Amanda asks me.

"I—" I start to say. I'm about to tell her that Jessica is just confused and then ask Jessica to be quiet but before I can—

"Oh, wake the fuck up, Mandy," Jessica says. She glances at Kristi. "You too, professional sycophant." Her eyes flick over to me. "Just take a look at her." I don't move as all three women stare me down. "You really think she's one of you?" Jessica's eyes look almost feral. "Emma—with her private school diplomas and barely hidden smug superiority? You really think she seems like the kind of girl who'd fuck for money? Look at her I've-never-wanted-for-anything eyes." Amanda and Kristi seem to be taking in everything they possibly can about me as I try to wrap my head around the fact that I'm the person being talked about. I feel my hands shaking. "Check out her posture," Jessica continues, "and how refined she is. Have you ever seen her so much as snap a piece of gum or speak with anything but perfect grammar?" The thought that everyone uses the phrase "begs the question" incorrectly pops into my head and I feel so lightheaded and overwhelmed that I'm about to mention that just as Jessica laughs. She accepts her sake martini from a bartender who seems to be putting ample effort into looking like he's not paying any attention to us and adds, "She's not like you. And the fact that you believed she is means you're even more idiotic and delusional than I've always thought."

For a few seconds, nothing happens. Then Kristi turns to me. "She's full of it, right?" she asks.

My heart is pounding so loudly that I wonder if she can actually hear it. "She's drunk," I respond. "She doesn't know what she's saying."

"Oh, come on, Emma." Jessica sighs and I beg her with my

eyes to stop what she's doing. Instead, she takes a sip of her drink and adds, "Just fess up—you're going to have to at some point, anyway."

"Here's the thing," I say. I feel like everyone in the bar—in Los Angeles, in the world—is staring at me. I look first at Amanda and then at Kristi. "Jessica's right," I finally say. "I'm not really one of you. I am doing a story. But I didn't know how else to approach you guys. I want people to see the truth about what you do—how much more complicated you are than you seem and—"

"Christ, Emma, isn't it time you stopped the bullshit?" Jessica asks.

Kristi crosses her arms. "So everything you said was a lie?" Her ski button nose is twitching ever so slightly and I want to be a different person—the kind who would take her in my arms, apologize for being such a coward, and tell her that she didn't deserve this or, even better, the kind who would never have done this in the first place. I can't seem to make words come out of my mouth at all. I look at Amanda, who won't meet my eyes, and it occurs to me how much she must regret ever warming up to me that first night. Her well-honed bitchy demeanor was created and designed precisely to keep people like me away. To my utter shock, a tear runs down my face—an errant one that seems to have slipped out despite the fact that I hadn't granted my system permission to release it.

"Dear God, let's not get weepy about the whole thing," Jessica sighs as she gulps down her martini and places the empty glass next to my untouched one on the bar. "Face it, girls, you were had. Wasn't the first time, certainly won't be the last." She tosses a fifty-dollar bill on the bar and turns to me. "Now can we get out of here before their stupidity becomes contagious?"

• • •

"WHAT?" JESSICA SAYS while I drive in stony silence. "So now you're giving me the silent treatment?"

"I'm really not sure what to say." As we sit at a light on Santa Monica Boulevard, I reflect on what an odd coincidence it is that we ran into Amanda and Kristi—and consider the fact that perhaps it wasn't a coincidence after all. "Did you know they were going to be there?"

"What are you talking about?" Jessica lights a cigarette and flicks ashes out the window.

"I don't believe that our running into them was just a random thing." My voice sounds as shaky as I feel.

She laughs. "Oh, so now I'm stalking them?" She snorts. "Get real."

I don't say a word, just reflect on how Amanda and I "happened" to see Jessica that day at Bloomingdale's. "I'm trying to get real, Jessica. I really am."

"What the hell does that mean?"

"I don't know."

"That's all you have to say about what happened?" she asks, laughing cruelly. "You're 'trying to get real'?"

"What am I supposed to say? I feel really bad for lying to them."

"You've got everything all mixed up, Emma." Jessica sighs. "You don't feel bad for lying to them—you feel bad that they found out. And that was something you were going to have to deal with sooner or later."

Gazing at the Trader Joe's on the left-hand side of the street, I consider Jessica's words. I have to admit that, in addition to the guilt and shame and horror coursing though my system, there's also a smidgen of relief. *They know what's going on,* I think. *I don't have anything I still need to confess.* "But did it have to be like that, Jessica? Wasn't that unnecessarily harsh—even for you?"

Jessica tilts her seat back so she can stack her feet on the dashboard. "Look, who cares? We both know you'd never really find the balls to tell them yourself. I did that to help you."

"But you humiliated them! Now they could stir up trouble and—"

"What, tell people?" Jessica asks with a laugh. "Hookers who probably never made it past the ninth grade are going to find an effective way to retaliate?"

"I don't know, but—"

"What planet are you living on, Emma? They're disposable. Don't you get it? People like Amanda and Kristi are meant to be used in just the way you used them." I remember how desperate Kristi looked when she was frantically calling clients in order to make enough money to buy the bracelet. For a second, I fantasize about smashing into the car in front of me and seeing Jessica fly through the windshield. "If you start giving yourself some massive guilt trip," Jessica continues, "then you're as pathetic as they are." She flicks her cigarette out the window and I resist the urge to tell her that I know someone who got a five-hundred-dollar fine and a stern lecture from a cop about California forest fires for doing just that.

chapter 22

JESSICA PICKS UP a nectarine, squeezes it, makes a face, and then puts it back down as we walk through the Larchmont Farmers Market. Watching her express her disdain for the discarded piece of fruit, I wonder how she managed to get me to come here with her.

I had woken up this morning entirely drained by life in Jessica's orbit. After weeks of feeling her influence over every thought I had and decision I made, I was suddenly both desperate to get away from her and terrified of what that might actually be like. But then she'd called and told me how sorry she was for being "such a drunk bitch" last night, sounding so small-voiced and sweet that I'd actually, for the first time since we'd met, felt something close to pity for her. And when she'd asked me if I'd go with her to an outdoor market to help her find some exotic spice she needed in order to make a certain dish for Bernie, I'd found myself saying yes when I meant no.

As I catch up to her, I gaze at all of the pesticide-free produce and bean sprouts from local farms that seem to make up the market and suddenly find myself thinking that I should buy everything here so I can launch myself into a new, healthy life. If I had a hemp skirt, organic acai necklace, and whale therapeutic back bench, I think, I wouldn't be feeling loaded down with shame and guilt. But then Jessica starts pushing me along to a booth that sells spices and I realize that whatever my problem is, a whale therapeutic back bench probably isn't going to help it.

"Do you have harissa?" Jessica asks the man selling spices and he nods. She yelps in excitement just as I notice a fifty-something woman who's bulging out of a pink Juicy sweatsuit ambling over—her friend, a woman in a spandex workout outfit, holding her arm.

"Come on, Paige, forget it," the woman's friend says as they step in front of us. "You're only going to make yourself crazy." Jessica moves aside to let them through, but the woman—Paige—suddenly stops in front of Jessica.

"You're trash," she spits out.

My heart seizes but Jessica looks at her calmly. "Excuse me?" Jessica says so dispassionately that it seems possible she really hadn't understood her or noticed her razor-sharp focus, and maybe just thought this random woman was searching for a trash can. Jessica hands the spice vendor a twenty-dollar bill.

Paige stares at her. "You heard me."

A wry smile slides across Jessica's face. She looks Paige up and down. "Save it for your husband, honey. I'm not the one who vowed to be faithful to you for the rest of your life." She takes a step away and tugs on my sweater as an indication to keep walking, but I feel unable to move.

"How do you live with yourself?" Paige asks Jessica's back.

Paige's face is a morass of plastic surgery and despair, which, next to Jessica's preternatural perfection, seems especially cruel.

Jessica, already on to the next vendor, calls back to me, "Come on, Emma!" Afraid to look at Paige, ashamed not to, I hurry over to Jessica without glancing back. "So you have to finish the story later?" Jessica asks, her red and blotchy chest belying her calm tone. She raises an eyebrow so high that I can see it over her oversized glasses.

I nod, then look at my hand as it reaches out for a lavender candle and notice that it's shaking. "Um, who was that?" I ask.

Jessica shrugs. "Someone's wife. Not my problem." She smiles. "I don't let myself get mixed up in domestic disputes."

"But—"

"You know I have Greg wrapped around my pinkie if you want an extension." She smiles, clearly wanting to change the subject.

"I don't want an extension," I snap. I'm suddenly flooded with annoyance over the way Jessica was treating my new job like it was some trivial appointment she'd arranged and could reschedule at any moment. "I like to meet my deadlines."

Jessica's face folds into a smirk. I look away from her, over to an area of the farmers market where masseuses, acupuncturists, and nutritionists have set up camp and are hawking their services. Looking closer, I spy Danny standing at a booth with a "Free Adjustments" sign behind him and, in the span of about three seconds, I move from happy to concerned to horrified to hoping I can look away before he sees me. No such luck.

"Emma!" he yells. "What are you doing here?"

I walk over to him, Jessica trailing behind, judgment and disapproval emanating from her. Her disdain for the nectarine was surely nothing compared to her feelings for a back-cracker trying to drum up business at a farmers market. "Shopping," I say to Danny as he leans in to give me a hug. Even though I already know the answer, I ask, "What about you?"

Danny lowers his voice. "Well, this isn't totally kosher since I don't have my degree yet, but a guy from my school gave adjustments here all the time before he graduated and he was drowning in clients by the time he was ready to practice." Danny points cheerfully to a chiropractic bed that's unfolded next to the sign.

I try to focus on taking in his easygoing, innocent energy. *If I were around him all the time, he might rub off on me and I wouldn't be so awful to Mom, Claire, and Ethan,* I think. For a second, I feel like I might burst into tears.

"Come on, Emma," Jessica says as she tugs on my sleeve. "We're going to be late to that thing." I smile with embarrassment, knowing that Jessica sounds exactly like what she is: a girl making up an excuse to get away from a guy. She fixes Danny with that look of hers that somehow manages to be both welcoming and off-putting. He ignores her and smiles at me.

"How's your African violet?" he asks. "Have you killed it yet?" I'm unable to meet his friendly grin. "Haven't seen you in the store," he continues. "Let me guess: your Diet Coke addiction has you in its grasp." He laughs.

"Something like that."

Noticing that I'm not moving along despite her best efforts to make me, Jessica extends a hand toward Danny and says, in a somewhat haughty voice, "I'm sorry, I don't think we've been introduced. I'm Jessica. Now how do you two know each other?"

Danny's eyes focus on Jessica's upper lip and he suddenly looks alarmed. "Hey, you're bleeding," he says. I glance over at her, expecting to see a tiny cut on her face—and am shocked when enormous streams of blood start gushing out of her nostrils.

Jessica holds a hand up to her nose calmly. "No big deal," she says as blood continues to pour down onto both her dress and the ground. Despite how cavalier she sounds, her eyes are tiny balls of fear. I feel other people start to look over.

Danny reaches under his booth, pulls out a stack of paper napkins, and steps up to Jessica to put them under her nose. "Here, come and sit down," he says as he leads her to the chiropractic bed. "Lean forward." Jessica does as she's told. "Now, can you hold the napkins and keep pinching your nose while I go get a cold towel?" Looking shockingly subservient, Jessica nods.

"Let me," I say to Danny. He nods and I rush over to the pizza place next to the market and ask for a cold, damp towel. I don't know if they're used to nosebleeds around here or what, but the Italian-looking kid behind the counter simply runs a red-and-white checkered linen napkin under the faucet and hands it to me without asking any questions. I thank him as I rush back to give Danny the towel, which he puts around her nose after removing the clump of blood-soaked napkins.

"I need you to hold that tight so the blood clots," Danny says, and Jessica nods. I don't think I've ever seen her be so quiet or attentive. Within seconds, however, she removes the towel from her face. "The bleeding stopped," she announces, standing up.

"You sure?" Danny asks.

Jessica nods. "Thank you so much," she says, rather suddenly the picture of calm confidence. She squeezes his arm. "You're the best."

Danny smiles but doesn't seem remotely impacted by Jessica's touch. "How do you feel?" he asks her. "Because you look a little pale. You may want to take it easy for a few more minutes."

Jessica laughs. "I'm great!" she exclaims unconvincingly. For the first time, I realize why she may not have made it as an actress. She looks at me. "I seem okay, right?"

Something—or rather, everything—about her doesn't seem at all okay but I can't put my finger on what's off so I just say, "I should take you home."

Jessica nods and then looks at Danny. "You're a doll," she says to him. "Can I do something to thank you? Pay you? Maybe I can—"

Danny shakes his head. "Don't be silly," he says. "Just take care of yourself." He turns to me, smiling. "But *you* can do something for me," he says. "Let me take you out tonight. No Whole Foods coffee. No chamomile tea. A real date." He smiles, and I notice for the first time that he's missing a tooth in the back part of his smile. Had I been so distracted by the gap that it had blocked me from seeing this other blank space? And come to think of it, what was so wonderful about that gap, anyway?

"I—" I start to say.

"She'd like to," Jessica interrupts, stepping forward, her previous gratitude toward Danny now a distant memory, "but she has a big story to write."

Danny seems to physically wilt, and I want to tell him that I'm turning the story in tomorrow and could go out with him any night after that. But I don't. "I understand," he says, and I'm immediately flooded with self-hatred for not just forgetting about the fact that he's cracking backs on a Los Angeles street and that I could never be his plus one at any fabulous event, and simply surrender to his sweetness.

"Thanks for today," I say. I lean in to hug him but he stiffens. "See you soon."

I'M PULLING UP in front of Jessica's apartment when she turns and looks at me pleadingly. "Look, can I come over for a while? I just don't feel like being alone right now."

From the moment we'd walked away from Danny at the farmers market, Jessica had been chattering up a storm—about how she wanted to buy a Todd Goldman lithograph that said "Spooning Leads to Forking," about how she couldn't decide whether she liked Dolce or Geisha House better, about how Dr. Tattoff on Wilshire was putting all the other tattoo removal places out of business—about anything, it seemed, but her bloody nose and what had just happened. Now that she'd stopped talking, however, she looked terrified.

"You know I need to turn in the piece by tomorrow," I say. I expect her to again offer to call Greg and work out an extension for me but she doesn't. Glancing at the bag of spices sitting on her lap, I ask, "And aren't you supposed to be making dinner for Bernie?"

"Not for a couple of days," she says, somewhat sheepishly. "I was going to practice first." I nod. "You don't have to talk to me," she continues. "You can do your work. I just don't want to be alone right now."

Without saying anything, I start the car again, deciding that I'm allowing this not because I can't say no to her but because I can't say no to someone who looks as forlorn and helpless as she does right now. When we get to my apartment, I put her in my bedroom with a stack of magazines, a glass of orange juice, and the remote control.

Then I finally sit down at my computer and look at what I've written of the piece so far, instantly deciding that I don't think the direction I'm going in will give me the opportunity to encompass everything I've learned. Over dinner, Greg had told me that he trusted me to do the story however I wanted to, and I realize that in trying to fit in all the details about what the men buy these girls and how the girls justify it, I've lost sight of my thesis: that these arrangements simply mimic the relationships between men and women in the world at large. Every woman alive knows what it's like to use her sexuality to get something she wants. But I've learned over the past couple months that when she starts to give that more value than it deserves—deciding, essentially, that this is all she has to offer, or at least the best of what she has to offer—she passes into a sort of no-return zone. What had to happen, I wonder, to cause a girl to make that choice? Or does she first decide to cross the line and then change as a result?

That, I realize, is what I want the piece to address.

"Hey, Emma," Jessica says, appearing in my doorway. "I don't mean to bother you."

I bury a sigh. "What is it?"

"Can I ask your opinion on something?" She holds out her cell phone. Without waiting for an answer, she continues, "Will you listen to a message for me?" Jessica loves to have me read her e-mails and listen to her messages, and I was starting to feel like she didn't count something as a real experience unless I had read, listened to, or heard every detail about it. I try to hide another sigh as she gives me the phone.

"Press one," she says, staring at me anxiously. "I just want you to tell me if this sounds like a girl calling her boss or like a girl calling her boss *who she's also fucking.*" I press one and shoot her a quizzical look. Jessica's messages are almost universally from men trying to get her to go out with them or thanking her for an amazing night. "It's Bernie's voicemail," Jessica says, smiling with just the tiniest hint of shame. "I figured out his code."

"What are you talking about?" The message starts to play and I press one again to give me time to absorb what she's saying.

"I tried the obvious things—his home phone number, some variation on the number of his favorite football player, what have you, and nothing worked. But voilà! One—two—three—four!" She grins. "Who knew Bernie was such a simple man?"

Horrified, I hand the phone back to her. "You mean you've been listening to Bernie's home phone messages?" I ask, incredulous.

"Oh, no!"

"Good—you had me worried."

"His cell," she says quietly.

"Jessica! Why?"

Now she looks defensive. "Oh, come on. Don't tell me you've never done the same thing."

"I haven't." I'm not sure if I'm more disturbed to hear that she's hacking into someone's voicemail or that she assumed I had as well.

"But you've wished you could, right?"

I remember those nights I obsessively Googled Matt. "Maybe," I admit.

"Well, I just had the balls to follow through." She shrugs and I'm annoyed by how she always seems to twist my words into what she'd like them to be. She gives me the phone again. "Just listen, please."

I press one. "Hi, it's Wendy," a girl's voice says. "I'm not going to be able to get back from New York in time to cover your phones tomorrow so I'm having the intern Rachel do it. I hope that's okay." I look at Jessica as I automatically delete the message.

"Oh, shit!" she screams. "You didn't just delete it, did you?"

I nod. "Why does it matter? Isn't that better than pressing save? I mean, if Bernie is picking up his messages and listens to a saved one he hasn't heard before, isn't he going to get suspicious that someone is listening to his voicemail?"

"Oh, shit," Jessica says, clasping a hand over her mouth. "I didn't think of that."

I put the phone down and give Jessica a once-over. My earlier hunch that something was wrong with her is developing into something of a conviction; Jessica, who thinks of everything when it comes to her manipulation of men, down to what color mascara gives off the subliminal suggestion of power, didn't consider the fact that Bernie would notice if he had saved messages on his voicemail that he hadn't saved himself?

"Jessica, I'm worried about you." I hand the phone back to her.

"What are you talking about?" She immediately looks angry. "Nobody ever has to worry about me."

"How much coke are you doing?"

Jessica's nostrils flare as she gazes at me, incensed. "Jesus, Emma," is all she says.

I decide to try a different approach. "When did you start listening to his messages?"

Jessica shrugs. "A few days ago. Maybe a week. I don't know. That's not important." She starts pacing. "The point is: what do you think of the girl?"

"I think she sounds like she works for him."

"But didn't she seem a bit *too* comfortable? You know what I mean? 'I'm not *going to be able to.*' '*I'm having* the intern do it.' "

I sigh. "Honestly, you're acting crazy. Do you know that?"

"Plus, why is she calling the *boss* on his *cell phone*?" she continues, completely ignoring me.

I take a deep breath. "Jessica, you really should stop listening to his messages—if for no other reason than that he's going to figure out what you're doing."

Jessica sticks her tongue out at me and I can tell she's disappointed by my response. "I sometimes forget how *serious* you are." She does an odd little curtsy. "Anyway, I'll leave you to do your *serious* work."

As she returns to my bedroom, I try not to seethe over the fact that she's somehow managed to make me feel like I'm the one who's done something wrong. I'm about three paragraphs into my new version of the piece when she wanders back in again, absentmindedly holding the glass of orange juice I gave her.

"Matt just called," she says. "Your plan to act indifferent to him must have worked because he wanted to know why you left his place when he was sleeping."

"He's asking you that now?" I ask, surprised. It had been weeks since we'd gone to the premiere and I hadn't heard from him.

"Yep." Jessica puts the glass down. "Maybe it will help you to talk about it—with your piece, I mean," she says. I can tell she's trying to manipulate me—that she feels like chatting and will say anything to get me to participate—but figure she may have a point.

"I don't know," I say as Jessica sits on my couch. "Being around Matt that night—and Rob, when I went out with him—just made me feel really . . . empty. Alone. Probably because I suddenly saw that the only reason I was interested in either of them in the first place is that I thought I could feel powerful by proxy." I shake my head. "It's like my subconscious decided that if I could somehow earn the admiration of a guy the world deemed that important, then I'd finally be impressive." I reach for a cigarette.

"I get it," Jessica says, nodding sympathetically. "That's really the only thing these guys are good for. It's like they stopped developing as human beings as soon as they got successful, and everybody here is so obsessed with becoming associated with them that they don't care, or even notice."

I nod. "The only guy I met recently that I really liked—who actually activated that 'I'm interested' part of me—was the one from the night we did coke," I find myself confessing. "Nick. Do you remember him?" I'm embarrassed to admit it. I mean, I'd talked to him, high as a kite, for less than an hour—only to completely desert him for Matt. But in retrospect, my conversation with him had all the comfort of my interactions with Danny, along with a lack of concern over things like a supermarket job, roommate, or missing teeth. I sigh. "I really regret blowing him off for Matt."

"You're not being serious, are you?" Jessica asks, her body instantly more alert than it's been all day, her ever-arched eyebrow seemingly higher than ever.

"I know, it's ridiculous," I say. "I barely know him."

"It's not that." She looks at me. "Emma, he's a working guy."

"I know, a producer," I say, but when I catch her eye, I suddenly understand exactly what she means. Rage and something else—horror—starts flooding my body. "Don't tell me you—"

"You can't be mad at me." She gives me her most winning smile. "You needed a confidence boost. I thought—"

"You thought what?" I ask, standing up.

"Nothing, silly," she says, not looking remotely impacted by my flash of anger. "He's a friend from way back and I just figured it would do you some good to have a hot guy hit on you."

I want to slap the smugness off her face. "You *paid* a guy to hit on me?" I ask, incredulous.

"First of all, he did it as a favor—for free." The corners of Jessica's mouth are turned up encouragingly, like she knows I'm going to appreciate how funny this is any minute. "Second—and I've told you this before—we create our own desirability. You were stuck in this place where you didn't believe you were worthy of any male attention. I figured if I arranged it so that you could have some, then you'd start being able to use the confidence you got from that to genuinely attract men on your own."

"*Some?*" I ask, my entire body suddenly filling with cold rage. "You mean Matt? And Rob? That was all shit you *arranged*?"

Jessica stands, too. "Oh, don't turn this on me," she says. "I was trying to help. I shouldn't have told you, but I couldn't bear to watch you go around thinking you'd really screwed things up by not paying enough attention to Nick—whose real name is Don, by the way, and who's as much a producer as I am the Duchess of Windsor."

Tears start stinging my eyes as I look at Jessica, now defiant and self-assured. "What's wrong with you?" I ask her. "Seriously? How could you do that to me? I feel like a fucking idiot."

Jessica's eyes flicker with anger. "What's wrong with *me*? What the hell is wrong with *you*? I mean, aren't you Miss I'm-so-open-minded-I-don't-judge-people-who-take-money-for-sex? *I'm* the one who should be upset—with the way you're so disgusted by the notion of having been hit on by a working guy. I guess I'm really getting an idea of what you actually think of me."

"Jesus, Jessica," I sigh, knowing she's twisted my words and too exhausted to bother fighting with her about it. "Maybe you should just go home."

"Come on, Emma," she responds, her demeanor instantly softened, her voice suddenly tender and soft. "It doesn't have to be like this. You're my best friend."

I close my eyes, my mind reeling from the last part of her statement. The truth is, since alienating Claire, everyone I worked with, and my family, Jessica wasn't just my best friend—she'd become my only friend. "I need to go lie down," I say. "Please just let yourself out."

"You can't be serious. I—"

"Good-bye," I say, dramatically turning and walking into my bedroom. I lie down on my bed and listen for the sound of Jessica leaving but don't hear anything. She's probably writing me some note about how much I'm misunderstanding the situation; I want to tell her not to bother but then I realize that I simply don't have the energy. When I hear my front door open and close, I finally surrender to the crying fit that my system has been craving. As I sob, something inside of me seems to unleash and I feel like an egg that's been cracked open so that the yolk is spilling all over the place. I weep about the fact that I'd believed that Nick, Matt, and Rob were actually interested in me when they'd only been put up to asking me out, and then about how much power I've given my family—and then the entire world—to make me feel okay. Then I cry about Claire and how far apart we've grown, and about Ethan, who I screwed over at the first opportunity, and about Amanda and Kristi and how easily I'd misled them, and about all the selfish and indifferent men I've wanted for purely superficial reasons. The whole weeping jag feels out of control, like I just have to surrender and let my body expel everything hysterical until it's all gone.

And yet, amid all my misery is a feeling of relief. When I was little and would get upset, my mom used to say that I was "watering the garden"—that I needed to cry now and then to continue to give life to the parts of me that were withering. "Please start growing now," I say out loud, not sure who I'm talking to, what I mean, or if I'm half losing my mind because I'm speaking out loud when I'm the only one in the room.

"HOLY SHIT," I SAY when I press the space key on my computer keyboard and notice that the screen is blank. It's now a little after nine p.m. and, feeling refreshed after my crying jag—and the nap that always seems to follow any extensive sob session—I'm finally sitting down to write the piece once and for all.

But I hadn't been counting on any technological mishaps. Plugging and unplugging the power cord, I determine that the machine is completely dead despite the fact that the power light is on. I take a deep breath and remind myself that one hysterical meltdown for the day is plenty.

Holding my finger on the POWER button, I will the system to pop back to life, but nothing happens. The computer is completely dead. What the hell am I going to do? I briefly consider apologizing to Mom and asking if I can use her computer—or Lilly's laptop—before rejecting that concept outright. I can ask to borrow a friend's computer. But then I remember that I've alienated all my friends except for Jessica—and now I've probably alienated her. I try to remain calm as I consider taking the computer to the Mac store—those Genius Bar guys can supposedly fix anything—or plopping myself down at a Kinko's or some sort of Internet café with computers for rent. But who knew how long the Mac store would take to repair something? And there was no way I'd be able to write a three-thousand-word story surrounded by club kids printing up flyers and dreamers xeroxing their screenplays. Besides, the soon-to-be editor in chief of a major magazine could hardly be conducting her business from a Kinko's or Mac store. I decide to call Greg, thinking that he'll have to understand these circumstances beyond my control.

"Hi, Emma," Greg says when he answers the phone, not sounding terribly thrilled to hear from me but not thoroughly annoyed, either. I've only called him a few times and he's always had the same I'm-quite-busy-but-willing-to-listen-to-what-you-have-to-say tone. "What can I do for you?"

"Well," I say, suddenly nervous. I can hear people in the background on his end. "There's been an emergency. My computer—it's completely dead. I don't know what happened. I mean, it's a few years old but I've never had problems with it before and—"

"And why are you calling *me* about this?" he asks. His voice has made the transition from distracted to irritated.

"It's just that I'm going to have to figure out some new kind of computer situation and it might take me a few days—"

"Emma, my editor in chief needs to be more on the ball." He sighs. "You're supposed to be the one *dealing* with situations like this, not bothering me with them."

I'm suddenly filled with shame. *He's right,* I think. "I'm so sorry. I guess I'm just asking for an extension on the deadline because—"

"The answer, I'm afraid, is no," he says. "I've been telling the investors about your piece, explaining that it will be the cover story of the first issue, and they're looking forward to reading it. I really can't put them off any longer."

"I see," I say, feeling thoroughly panicked but not wanting that to seep out in my voice. "I understand."

"Once you turn it in, we can talk about getting you started on your editor in chief duties," he says. Before I can respond, he adds, "Thanks, Emma," and hangs up.

I blink, telling myself that there has to be a solution, as I walk over to my coffee table to pick up my cigarettes. Underneath the pack sits a note. "Emma," it reads. "I hope we can work through this. Just remember, if you ever need anything, I'm here." It's signed with an enormous "J." I sit down and sigh, knowing that I need to separate from Jessica but simply unable to think of anything else to do right now besides dial her number.

"Jessica," I say when she answers. "I need something."

chapter 23

I'D JUST INTENDED to ask her if she could loan me her computer. But I hadn't expected her to be so kind and compassionate—which seemed particularly soothing after Greg's abrasiveness—and how willing she'd be to help me after I'd been so dismissive of her earlier. Amazingly, Jessica actually had a brand-new Apple laptop that Bernie had gotten her—the exact same one he'd given her a few months earlier—still sitting in the box, which she insisted I keep, at least until I figured out what was wrong with mine.

By the time I got the computer set up in my apartment, it was after midnight and I realized that I'd never get anything done in my thoroughly overwrought state, so I crawled between the sheets and set my alarm for early the next morning. I slept fitfully, dreaming that it was the last day of college and everyone else had all of their belongings packed while I hadn't even been to the box store to start the process.

Sitting down in front of the computer again in the morning, I wonder if I'd been too harsh with Jessica. She *had* been trying to help me with my dating life, I reason. Sure, it was undoubtedly embarrassing to have been the recipient of piteous good will in the romantic department but, I think, no one had ever gone that out of their way to make me feel more desirable before. She had, I decided, been thoughtful but misguided.

I start writing the piece, remembering everything I'd come up with before my computer died and easily weaving in a succession of thoughts I've had and scenarios I've observed over the past few months. I get so wrapped up in the process that literally an entire day passes where I do nothing but smoke and type. Once I email the story to Greg, I lean back in my chair and kick my feet up onto my desk. An amazing rush of relief floods me—the same feeling I used to have after finishing college term papers or when I turned in my *Substance* party coverage at the end of the night.

But this time, the ease is almost immediately punctuated by loneliness. A sense of completion, for me, was usually followed by the need to take care of whatever it was I'd been neglecting in order to meet the deadline. I'd always have something I needed to do—whether it was picking up dry cleaning, calling Claire back, or hitting a yoga class before covering an event that night. But sitting here at my desk, staring at the enormous, shiny new computer that I have courtesy of Jessica, I see how small my life has become. I glance at the ashtray overflowing with Winston Lights—after accepting the fact that I was officially a smoker, I'd decided to at least buy the lightest cigarettes possible, telling myself that this made my having taken up the habit not nearly as horrible—and realize that the yoga schedule I have on my refrigerator is two months old. And I can't think of one thing I need—or want—to do.

I pick up my phone. There must be someone I can call. Then it suddenly hits me with shocking clarity that the missing piece in my life is Danny. How had I managed to keep this hidden from myself? I'd liked him since the first moment I met him, I now see. I'd just been too blinded by my zeal for a bold-faced boyfriend to realize it. I light a cigarette—*what the hell,* I think, *I'm obviously not quitting today*—and wonder how to handle this realization. Should I confess my feelings to him? Apologize for turning him down yesterday at the farmers market? Do nothing? Looking around my apartment, I notice for the first time in God knows how long that it's disgustingly filthy, so I put the cigarette out and start gathering up dirty dishes, thinking that I'll just clean until I figure out how to proceed from here. After an hour of almost manic housework, my conviction that Danny is the one for me has grown even stronger, but I'm no closer to determining what to do about that so I decide to take my broken computer to the Mac store. By then, I'll surely have figured out what to say to Danny and I can go visit him at work. In honor of the good idea, I take a shower, trying to cleanse all the nicotine and anxiety and loneliness threatening to overwhelm me with a good scrub.

"HOW CAN I help you?" the guy at the Mac Genius Bar asks as he reaches across the counter for my laptop.

I point to the computer. "Please just make this work," I say. "It's never had any problems before but suddenly went completely dead last night."

He nods earnestly, picks the computer up, and puts it under his right arm. "I'll be right back," he says, shuffling toward the back room. While he's gone, the strangest thing happens. As I'm staring at two kids playing a computer game, I suddenly realize that I lost my contract with *Substance.* Of course, I'd been there for the conversation with Lauren and everything, but the fact that I don't have that job and that my dreams of writing a feature for the magazine are now officially dead and buried seems to hit me for the first time. I've somehow painted myself into a corner, with Jessica as my only friend and my entire future dependent on Greg—a guy I barely know. Thank God, I think, for Danny. The Genius Bar guy returns with a concerned look on his face, placing the computer on the counter.

"This is never going to work," he says grimly.

"What? Why? What happened?"

He looks at me strangely, and then points to the space between the *G* and *H* keys. "Something got in here and destroyed your logic board," he says, putting his nose up to it and sniffing. "It smells citrus-y." Looking closely, I notice a few tiny white specks. "If you can dry the computer off in time, sometimes you can stop whatever liquid it was from frying your system altogether," he says. "In fact, there was a kid who was just in here because he'd turned a container of Chinese food over on his mom's computer." He grins, his face inexplicably exuberant at the thought. This must count as a wild and exciting experience over at the Genius Bar. "We were able to save it," he says with pride. "So the kid doesn't have to feel bad about how much he digs mu shu pork."

As he continues to smile over this memory, I remember the glass of orange juice I'd given Jessica when she was in my apartment. I had asked her to leave, and then gone into the bedroom so she could let herself out. And, without even having to think about it for a second longer, I'm positive that she destroyed my computer on purpose. Whether it was to get me ever more dependent on her or to punish me for kicking her out doesn't matter. Standing in the Mac store, I suddenly see that Jessica has been buying and manipulating me from our first interaction. And somehow this discovery is a relief—like the tidy conclusion to a murder mystery that had once seemed petrifying but you suddenly found out was merely schlock.

"Hey, please don't shoot the messenger," the Mac Genius Bar guy says, clearly unnerved by my silence. "I just—"

"Oh, I'm not," I say. "You've actually helped clarify a lot."

WHEN I PULL UP at Whole Foods, I'm surprised by how nervous I suddenly feel. *It's Danny,* I remind myself. *He's sweet—and no one to fear.* The thought of driving away right now is immensely appealing but I tell myself that I'm just overwhelmed by the past twenty-four hours, and in minutes I can be basking in Danny's basic goodness. With what feels like excruciating effort, I get out of the car and start walking toward the entrance. I see Danny outside the store, whistling as he wheels a grocery cart.

"Hey." I walk up behind him and touch his arm. *Please be the same,* I pray. *Please treat me the same.*

He turns around. "What's up, Emma?" My heart falls: his tone is decidedly cool.

"Not much," I lie. I try not to look at the vein popping out of his arm as he stacks two carts together. "I just wanted to talk about . . . I don't know . . . yesterday and, well, everything. The way I've been." I force myself to look at him.

"You don't need to do this." Danny leans on the cart as he stares at the ground.

"But I want to." I clear my throat. "I like you, Danny. But I've just been screwed up. My priorities are seriously out of whack. Or they were. I—"

Danny holds up a hand. "Look, don't worry about it."

"But I *am* worried about it! And you don't know what I'm trying to say. Just hear me out."

"I don't need to hear you out. Because I've realized something, too." Oh, no. He finally looks at me. "You don't really see me. Maybe you don't really see anyone."

"What does that mean?" I feel a sharp pain in my stomach.

"I think you decide what roles people are going to play in your life. Or let me just keep this about you and me: I think you assigned me a part to play in the Life of Emma that I didn't have much say in."

"I don't know what you're talking about." I stare at the space between his two front teeth.

"Really? Because I think you might—or a part of you might." Someone yells Danny's name from across the parking lot and he reaches his hand up in greeting before turning back to me. "I was the guy you talked to at Whole Foods. The one who encouraged you to like yourself a little more. Who I really am outside of a few very superficial facts didn't—doesn't—really matter to you."

I look at him, desperately wanting to not understand what he's saying. But his words ring a bell somehow—a foggy bell, like he's repeating something I heard a lifetime ago or reciting lyrics from a song I've long since forgotten. And then I realize that it sounds familiar because he's stating a truth I've been doing everything I possibly can not to have to face. "But Danny, I—"

"I started wondering how you got to be this way," he continues, "trying to imagine how much a guy must have hurt you to make you so afraid to just be who you are and like who you like. And then I realized that no guy had probably ever hurt you as bad as you hurt yourself. I mean, I doubt you've ever even given a guy a chance to do that."

I nod, my heart picking up speed as I realize the truth of his words. I don't know how to respond, so I just say, "I should go."

"Yeah." He nods and, to my surprise, reaches over to hug me. I lean in, inhaling the smell of detergent and deodorant. "I think," Danny says, "you need to be with someone who cares about himself—and you—a little less."

chapter 24

PULLING UP AT THE PALM and handing my keys to the valet guy, I'm surprised by how calm I feel. After talking to Danny, I'd come home and sat on my couch, feeling like I'd reached information overload and simply fizzled out.

When Greg called and asked me if we could discuss my piece and new job over dinner tonight, I'd simply agreed and made my way over here without even stopping to consider what it might mean. But walking into the restaurant and spying him sitting in a booth beneath a wall that's painted with cartoon heads of Jack Nicholson and Andy Williams, I'm suddenly gripped with the sensation that all is not right.

"How are you?" I ask. "I hope I'm not late."

Greg winks at me—I'd never noticed that he was a winker before—and pours me a glass of wine from the bottle on the table. "It's a '95 Margeaux," he says.

"Great," I respond, despite the fact that I've never been able to tell the difference between the $3.99 stuff from Trader Joe's and the kind my mom and Lilly are always salivating over. After a pause, I ask, "So what did you think of the piece?"

"It's fine." He examines the menu. Glancing up, he asks, "Would you be interested in splitting the New York strip? I had a three o'clock meeting at the Grill and I'm afraid I overdid it."

"Sure." I take a gulp of wine.

"You should get the hash brown, too," Greg says with another wink. "It's so decadent, it looks like a piece of apple pie."

After we order, Greg gives me yet another wink. "Do you know the history behind all the cartoon drawings on the wall?" he asks. Without waiting for a response, he continues, "Back in New York in the Depression, there was an artist who'd draw in exchange for bowls of pasta." He looks incredibly proud of himself for possessing this information.

"That's interesting," I say.

"Supposedly, if you buy ten grand worth of steak here, they'll draw one of you." He glances absentmindedly at a woman in a red dress walking by, and then laughs. "I'm not so far away from that number myself."

"Greg." I smile. "Let's talk about my story—and about how we're going to proceed from here."

"Your story's fine," he says, looking back at the woman, who's now sitting in a booth across the restaurant. "I like it."

"Fine?" I ask. "Anything more? I mean, do you want changes? How did the investors respond?"

Greg scratches his head. "Hah," he says admiringly. "I like a woman who gets right down to business." He turns his gaze to me. What had happened to the businesslike tight-ass who'd reprimanded me when I'd called him during my computer crisis?

"I worked really hard on it," I say, trying to hide my frustration. From the way he's acting, I'm wondering if he even read the article at all. "It took months of research and I struggled to find the right way to approach the material."

"Good!" He smiles, sips his wine, and looks at me. "Good," he says again. "The story will be great for us."

Slightly encouraged, I smile back. "So the investors liked it?"

He takes a gulp of wine and chortles. "'The investors this' and 'the investors that.' Aren't you supposed to be leaving the business end to me?"

I sigh. "Greg, you made a big deal about how I had to get the piece in on time so the investors could see it. It's only natural for me to be curious about their response."

Greg nods as he sips his drink. "True enough," he says. Then he smiles as he looks into my eyes. "But don't you worry. They're going to love you."

"So you haven't given it to them?" I sit up a little straighter.

"Emma." He motions toward my wine. "I think you need to drink some more of that. You're acting far too somber for a girl wearing such a stunning dress."

I'd been so dazed when I was getting dressed that I'd just grabbed the first thing I found, but right now I find myself wishing I was in a turtleneck and long pants, not a black wrap-around. Torn between wanting not to be difficult with my new boss and feeling like one of the steaks on the menu, I smile uncomfortably and sip my wine. "Well, I take this job—or I will take this job—really seriously," I say.

Greg grins. "Has anyone ever told you how adorable you are when you get earnest?"

I smile thinly. "Thank you, but I think we really need to talk about work here." Realizing that I sound like Gloria Allred—or at least one of her future clients—I give him what I hope is a winning smile.

"We'll have plenty of time to discuss work, Emma," Greg says. "For now, I think we should concentrate on getting to know each other." It sounds like a terrible line from an even worse movie and I suddenly feel as if I'm being played like the world's simplest violin. Then Greg says, "I don't mean to make you uncomfortable," and smiles in such a comforting way that I think I must be jumping to conclusions about him. "I've just been in meetings about this damn magazine up to my ears and I had been looking forward to a break from talking about it."

I tell him that I understand and when the food comes, Greg changes his tone altogether, peppering me with questions about what made me want to be a journalist and where I picture myself in ten years. He continues to ask me about my interests and career aspirations for the rest of the meal and I decide that my epiphanies about Jessica and disappointment over Danny had clearly impacted my thinking and made me overly suspicious of everyone.

After Greg pays the bill and we start walking toward the front of the restaurant, however, he stops at the hostess station and takes a toothpick from the rack. "So are we taking one car or two?" he asks casually.

At first, I think he's joking, but when I glance at his face—as serious as his toothpick is sharp—I feel like I must have missed a crucial part of the conversation. "Excuse me?" I say. He opens the restaurant door and I feel a gush of fresh air as we walk outside.

"You're cute, Emma—I'll give you that." We approach the valet stand and Greg hands his parking ticket to the valet guy while I try not to panic.

I don't know what to say, so I yawn and sigh, "I'm tired."

"Oh, Emma," he sighs, and I wonder when he got so comfortable uttering my name. I don't ever recall him saying it before, and suddenly tonight it seems to be his favorite thing to do, besides winking. "I want to give you your check for the piece—but it's back at my hotel."

I look up from the ground to his face. Having that money would mean not only that I'd finally be compensated for months of work but also that I could return Jessica's computer, get a new one, and start working on ideas for *Angeles*'s first issue. Yes, he was being potentially inappropriate right now, but most people, I reason, are inappropriate at times. And just because he's asking me to come by his hotel to get my check doesn't necessarily mean he's expecting anything—even if he has punctuated this entire interaction with enough winks for me to consider the fact that he may actually have an eye twitch.

"I think I'll take my own car," I find myself saying as the valet driver emerges from Greg's Jaguar and hands him his keys. I'm as surprised by my words as I would be if I were listening to someone else talking. "Call me a control freak, but I really like driving myself whenever I can."

Greg grins as he slides into his front seat. Rolling down the window, he asks, "Does that freakiness translate elsewhere?" I try to smile as he explains that he's staying at the Four Seasons.

"I'll meet you there," I say weakly. I hand the valet driver my parking ticket and decide that if Greg makes a pass at me, I can simply rebuff him, tell him that we need to keep our relationship professional, take my check, and be on my way.

"Fantastic," he responds, winking again as he rolls up his window. As I watch him drive away, I tell my heart to stop beating so quickly. If I've learned anything from Jessica, after all, it's that men can be toyed with. All I needed to do, I saw, was stop approaching Greg from an inferior position. *I can be the one in charge here,* I think. I just need to start acting like it.

As I get in my car, I decide that going to the Four Seasons won't be so bad. Then an altogether new thought occurs to me: maybe having sex with Greg wouldn't necessarily be a horrible idea. He's not awful-looking. It occurs to me that maybe *that's* the way to put myself in the power position.

As I pull onto Santa Monica Boulevard, switch on my turn signal, and get in the left-hand lane at Doheny, I realize that my heart is now bouncing around so powerfully that it seems like it's preparing to fly right out of my chest. Taking a deep breath, I turn the radio on: Pacifica, a public radio station. I hear a man's voice and, grateful for the opportunity to hear thoughts that aren't my own, I turn the volume up.

"If you follow your bliss, you'll have your bliss," a gravelly voice says, and I increase the volume. Something about the sentence makes me feel unexpectedly comfortable, like I'm suddenly bathing in a warm bath. "If you follow money, you may lose money and then you don't even have that." My hand lingers on the volume control, and I'm suddenly gripped with a strong sense of déjà vu. "The secure way is really the insecure way," the disembodied voice continues, and I realize that I'm listening to the Joseph Campbell quote Danny mentioned—that I'm, in fact, listening to Joseph Campbell. "The way in which the richness of the quest accumulates is the right way," the radio continues.

I feel tears starting to sting my eyes as I suddenly realize that my blinker is on and I'm about to turn into the Four Seasons Hotel. And then a thought becomes so clear that the words in it feel like they're being displayed on a marquee in front of my face: I'm going to the Four Seasons so that I can be hit on, probably groped by, and potentially sleep with my future boss. I've had sex with fewer than ten men in my entire life and I'm suddenly considering screwing someone for a job.

The reality of what I've come to swiftly hits me as I brake before the turn, causing the Mercedes behind me to have to stop suddenly and the person inside to give me the finger. As a different radio voice says, "That was a recording of Joseph Campbell, but you can find this conversation and many more in 'An Open Life: Joseph Campbell in Conversation with Michael Toms,'" I almost feel like Danny's been transported into the car alongside me. I can practically hear him telling me that I need to take better care of myself.

Turning around and zooming away from the hotel, I feel like the world is actually a snow globe—and that someone has just come along and shaken it so that things look entirely different than they did before. As I drive up Santa Monica Boulevard, I know I've slammed shut one door in my life but that a small window nearby offers all the escape I need.

"I'M HERE TO SEE Jessica Morrison," I tell the doorman.

"Is she expecting you?" he asks, picking up his phone.

I shake my head as I hoist up the enormous shopping tote filled with Jessica's computer, the Marc Jacobs bag, and the other odds and ends I've accepted from her over the last few months—all of which I picked up at home after speeding away from the Four Seasons. "She's not," I say. "But I need to see her anyway."

Perhaps in response to my authoritative tone, he places the phone down. "Go ahead," he says, and I walk down the hall and ring her bell.

"What are you doing?" Jessica asks as she pulls the door open, starting the sentence before she can even see me. She seems jittery, high, and far angrier than I'd been expecting.

"I came to say good-bye," I say. "I can't do this anymore."

"Oh, please." She snorts. "Stop with the big dramatic speech, Emma. I'm just not in the mood."

For one of the first times since I've met her, Jessica doesn't seem strong and controlling and wise and beautiful, but scared and small and wired to the gills. "This isn't a dramatic speech, Jessica," I say. "I just wanted to give you your things back." I hand her the shopping bag, which she immediately lets fall to the ground.

"Oh, really?" she says, looking like she can't decide whether to be amused or alarmed.

"I know that you purposely destroyed my computer," I say.

"Jesus." Jessica shakes her head. "You really have lost it, haven't you?"

"Good-bye, Jessica."

"Good-bye?" she asks. "*Good-bye?* What kind of a game are you playing, Emma? Greg just called and told me that you were a no-show at his hotel. Do you know how your behavior made us—me—look?"

"I'm not like you." I look at her. "I don't want to do things your way."

Jessica's eyes narrow. "See, that's where you're wrong," she says. "Because you're exactly like me—you can be bought, too. You just don't think you're worth very much."

"Jessica—"

"You act like you're above it all, but you love these Hollywood guys. Is it for their souls, Emma? Is it that you think they're wonderful people? No. You want the free ride as much as the rest of us. You're just a shitty businesswoman."

I wait for a second to see if her words sting, remembering when she quoted Eleanor Roosevelt. *No one can make me feel inferior without my own consent,* I think. "Maybe that was true," I say. "But I don't think it is anymore."

"Your perfect little sister who's shacking up with the goddamn prince gets it," she continues, ignoring me. "Wake up, Emma. This is the world we live in. Stop trying to pretend it's not and accept the fact that we're all the same. You, me—every woman on earth. We're biologically programmed to use men to get our needs met."

"That's just what you tell yourself to justify fucking for a living, instead of getting a job." I can't believe how calm I sound.

She laughs. "And that's just what you say now." She smiles. "If I know you at all—and I do—your stance will change. You won't realize it—you'll tell yourself the little lies you need to in order to get by and sleep at night—but your Pollyanna world of purity and independence will only last long enough for the right guy to come along and buy you. Or for Mommy and Daddy to step in."

I feel shaky but my voice somehow sounds confident. "I sure hope not."

Jessica, perhaps surprised that I'm not defending myself, suddenly softens. "Look, this is ridiculous," she says. "What are we even fighting about?" She smiles. "Let's stop this and be friends again." She takes a step toward me.

I move back. "That's impossible, Jessica. Because, you see, we were never friends." I breath in deeply, and end up coughing—*the goddamn cigarettes,* I think. "Life rafts maybe—but not friends," I say. I take another step away. I don't feel vindictive, the way I did when I insulted Claire or swore at my mom; instead, I have the sensation that I've just been unleashed from a collar I hadn't even been entirely sure I was wearing. I gaze at her, taking in her every last feature. Despite the fact that the veil that's prevented me from seeing who Jessica really is has slipped away and all that remains is an ugly truth, she's never looked more beautiful: her face, pink and moist with surprise, appears to have just been rinsed in morning dew, and her standard jaded smirk has morphed into an expression of surprise that's softened the corners of her mouth and eyes. "Still, I agree with you: in some ways, we are all the same," I say. "We all want to connect with other people and use what we have to get what we want. I just don't want to do it your way, and it seems like you don't want to do it mine." Then I turn and walk down the hall. I don't look back, just in case her gaze somehow has the power to stop me.

chapter 25

As I MAKE MYSELF a cappuccino with Mom's extravagant Italian coffee machine, I take an enormous breath. For the first time in weeks, inhaling deeply doesn't cause a massive coughing fit—surely a result of the fact that I smoked my last cigarette over a month ago, when I was driving to Whole Foods to talk to Danny that final time.

I'd figured that Lilly would probably be in Europe by now and knew the chances of finding Mom and Dad home during the day on a weekend were minimal, so I hadn't been all that surprised when I pulled up and saw no cars in the driveway. Luckily, the hide-a-key rock was in the same conspicuous place as usual—right next to the front door—so I just let myself in to wait.

Without any people in it, the house feels enormously comforting. I walk down the hall to the back den, thinking of all the different phases the room has been through—when we first moved in and it had wall-to-wall puke-colored carpeting, when

I was in high school and an elegant leather sofabed had replaced the mauve velvet couch so we could have an extra guest room, and now, with its light brown tiles and pillows from Granada, in honor of Mom's Spanish phase. I sit down and turn on the TV—or at least attempt to. Ever since they'd gotten some new system, watching television at my parents' house had grown into an inexplicably complicated affair that involved at least four different remote controls and an endless amount of patience. After trying each of them and managing to only tune into a Spanish-language soap and a fuzzy screen, I give up entirely.

Scanning the room, my eyes land on the enormous wooden chest where Mom has always kept all of the letters, report cards, school projects, yearbooks, and programs Lilly and I collected over the years. The chest had been moved from room to room—it used to be at the foot of my parents' bed, for a while it was upstairs in their shared office—and I hadn't pored through its contents for at least a decade. When I was younger, I used to love examining everything in it, an activity my mom called "yearbooking" because it was so similar to how obsessively I combed through all of my yearbooks and stared at the photos, captions, and personal notes until the pages were practically falling apart.

Sitting on the floor in front of the chest, I wonder why seeing evidence of my existence used to be so important to me, and when it ceased to be. I hadn't so much as taken a picture, or even had a working camera, in years. As I pick up my class photo from first grade—in which I'm wearing the same dress as Katy Tam but, since I accidentally wore mine backward, no one, besides me, was even aware of the coincidence—I realize that somewhere along the way, I'd decided that I didn't really matter.

I stare at a class report from my sophomore math teacher, Mr. Horowitz, who said I was a lively student but hadn't yet managed to master fractions. Then I run my finger over my name in a program from a Crossroads dance show, read a letter I sent to my parents from camp when I was nine in which I begged them to let me come home, and pick up a notebook from high school that's filled with my name next to the names of almost every single boy in my class; I vaguely remember someone in Mr. Horowitz's class telling me that if you and a boy had the same number of vowels and consonants in your names, that meant you were supposed to be together. No wonder I'd had such trouble with fractions—I'd clearly had other things on my mind.

I then find a clump of notes Claire had passed me in different classes over the years and notice that most of them contain an undercurrent of competitiveness. Letting that relationship go—at least until I could figure out if I thought it was a friendship that could even be salvaged—seemed, for now, like the best move.

I start pulling out my past—folders, tests, notes from pen pals and, most astounding of all, old love letters. I examine one from a boy named Paul—who I dimly remember meeting at that summer camp I'd begged to be saved from—asking if I'd "go steady" with him. As I smile at Paul's letter—which asks me to check "yes," "no," or "maybe" as an answer—it occurs to me that I've had more than my fair share of attention from men over the years. I just tend to reject most of them outright—like a photographer I met on the press line for the MTV Awards ("A paparazzi guy?" I'd thought), an accountant I sat next to at Claire's birthday dinner ("As stimulating as a piece of toast," I'd told Claire when she asked me what I thought of him), and a Buddhist vegan from yoga class ("Too much of a do-gooder," I'd ultimately concluded). Clutching Paul's letter, I finally understand that I haven't actually been looking for men to have relationships with but for ones I thought I could attach myself to in order to make myself look brighter and shinier.

By the time I hear Mom's car pull up, I've got at least half of the chest out on the floor in front of me. "Well, hi there," Mom says as she walks into the den. She eyes me like I'm some kind of a feral cat who might attack her. "We saw your car."

"Hi," I say softly. For once, I'm grateful for the fact that she likes to pretend unpleasant incidents never occurred.

Dad follows her into the room and smiles at me. "I'll let you girls visit," he says before turning and going upstairs.

"You feel like a walk?" Mom asks, subconsciously turning the stereo on as she passes it and instantly filling the house with the familiar strains of classical orchestral chords. It occurs to me that she doesn't blast this music to torture me or try to show me that I'm not as cultivated as she and Lilly but simply because she likes it. I nod. "Come on," she says.

As we start walking down our driveway, Mom's golden retriever, Buddy, trailing behind, I notice how deep the worry lines in Mom's forehead have become. She's always looked young for her age but today, as we pass the Kosners' house, she seems to be wearing all of her sixty-something years. I take a deep breath and blurt out, "I'm so sorry about the way I've acted."

She surprises me by calmly saying, "I know you are."

I clear my throat. "I'm beginning to see that I've made up a story about how you guys think I'll never measure up to Lilly—and I've been blaming you for it."

Rather than looking at me quizzically or launching into a series of questions like I expect her to, she just gazes at the bougainvillea surrounding the Kosners' front fence. "Honey, you were born at a different time." She picks up and then tosses a stick, which Buddy frantically retrieves. "Back then, I was still hoping to make it as a painter—balancing art galleries with breastfeeding and—"

"What do you mean?" I interrupt her, shocked. "You never showed your work at any galleries."

She smiles wistfully. "Actually, I did. I didn't sell very much—but also never gave it much of a chance. Believe me, this was a source of serious contention between your father and me."

"But you think art shouldn't be—"

"Well," Mom says, bitterness creeping into her voice, "he told me I'd never be able to contribute even a hundredth of what he could to the family income and that I should just appreciate the fact that I didn't have to work. We fought about it all the time." Her face seems to be in a battle between appearing downtrodden and settling back into her naturally cheerful look; she frowns, making the sad side the clear victor. "By the time I got pregnant again—ten years later—I'd given up the fight and just become the full-time nanny and chef your dad always wanted me to be." She smiles wryly, watches a Lexus drive by, and then finally notices Buddy obediently waiting for her to see the stick in his mouth. She grabs it and tosses it a few feet ahead. "Lilly got a lot more of me than you did."

I meet her eyes, realizing that this is the only time I've ever heard my mom come close to admitting that she'd done anything wrong. I'd always assumed, in fact, that Thou Shalt Never Admit to Mistakes was one of the major tenets of parenting. "How come you never told me?"

"I don't know," she says. "I hadn't really thought about it until the night you got so upset and I started allowing myself to notice and feel how distant we've become." She suddenly looks indignant. "I've tried to compensate—to show you how much I identify with your struggles—but it seems like everything I say ends up hurting your feelings." She pushes the sleeve of one of her sweatshirt arms up as she gives me an impassioned look. "I want you to have a full life—with a loving relationship and good food and beautiful music. I want you to have wonderful, nurturing things around you . . . a vegetable garden, animals—all the things that matter. And it seems sad to me that you can't even consider any of that because you're always just managing to stay afloat."

"But that's just it!" I say, suddenly angry. "Those are all the things that *you* think matter. I don't *like* gardening, I don't particularly *want* a pet, and I'm not *in* a relationship. And I'm tired of feeling bad about all that."

She looks surprised. "Honey, I don't want you to feel bad. I'm just trying to help you see what I wish I'd known at your age. Life is a lot less disappointing when you have realistic expectations." She looks at me sadly, no trace of her "inner glow" evident. "And I just think that pursuing a writing career is setting yourself up for a lifelong struggle."

I nod as I remember once hearing that no one is better at pushing your buttons than the people who installed them in the first place. As we circle back toward home, I decide that it's probably best if I never tell Mom about everything that had gone on with Jessica—or what had happened since.

I wasn't sure how she'd react to the news that I'd decided to write an essay about how corrupted and confused I got while attempting my first investigative feature story without knowing what I was doing, or about the fact that I'd sent a copy of it to Ethan, along with a heartfelt note of apology. And I couldn't imagine how she'd feel if I told her that Ethan wrote back to tell me he forgave me but thought I ought to consider journalism school, that he'd recommended me to a friend of his at Columbia for an investigative journalism fellowship that would cover most of the tuition, and that I'd used the prostitution story as my application essay. As far as Mom knew, I was still spending my evenings on press lines. Since I had enough money saved to tide me over for a little longer, I figured I wouldn't need to let her know otherwise until it was time for me to get whatever odd job could sustain me until I heard back from Columbia.

Expecting my family to wholeheartedly support me exactly as I am and not who they want me to be, I now see, is as futile as waiting for Buddy to suddenly stand up and start talking. I can't change Mom or Dad or Lilly any more than I can alter Jessica or the men in Hollywood. But I can try to accept them the way they are and work on not letting what they say or do have so much power over me. While my family may not be the one of my dreams—the one that would boost me up and always tell me how much they believed in me—I was starting to realize that I might not be the daughter of theirs, either.

Mom grabs my hand and we walk like that through the neighborhood. I can tell she finds the fact that we're holding hands reassuring and it reminds me of those times she asks me to promise her that I'm going to see her soon—as if she wants validation from me that I love her despite what she hasn't, and can't, give me. For some reason, making her happy doesn't seem so difficult right now.

"HOW ARE YOU holding up?" I ask Antonio as I approach him on the basketball court.

He doesn't even seem to see me—only the box that I'm holding. "Look who's here!" he yells, a particularly pungent version of Drakkar Noir emanating from him. "Sugar!"

I'm then descended upon by a swarm of sweaty, smiling women and men—alcoholic and drug-addicted women and men, as it turns out—who all reach grubby hands into the bakery box in my arms, grab hold of the first cookie or brownie they find, and shove it into their mouths. While I have mixed feelings about feeding a slew of addicts who are in the early stages of recovery enough chocolate to see all of Los Angeles through the next few Halloweens, Antonio's drug counselor—an earnest woman who goes by the name Sage, never revealing whether that was a moniker she'd taken on or one her parents had given her—had assured me that these treats were, in fact, a good substitute for the sugar they were missing now that they'd stopped drinking.

The first time I'd visited, I brought Antonio a cupcake from Sprinkles and, after seeing how ravenously he'd consumed it—by literally squashing and mashing the entire thing into his mouth at once—I promised I'd come by every few days with different desserts. And as soon as the people from his group heard about it—and it was impossible for them not to since, as soon as the offer was out of my mouth, Antonio immediately shrieked, *"You mean you're going to bring cupcakes like these all the time?"*—I'd somehow become known around rehab as the Sugar Lady, or, more commonly, Sugar. Sage had told me that I should consider the nickname a compliment.

I was relieved when Antonio first called a few weeks ago to tell me he was in rehab. But when he explained that it was because of a "nudge from the judge"—which, loosely translated, meant that he'd been arrested for selling coke, fired from the *Post,* and was hoping this would keep him out of jail—I'd started to doubt that his time here was going to stop him from doing drugs once he was out. He kept calling rehab a "rest stop," saying it was doing a good job of teaching him that he had to "mellow out" on partying but that they had way too "extreme" an attitude here. Sage had told me privately that he was already setting himself up for a relapse when he was released and that there wasn't much she could do about it—that some newly sober people "got it" right away and others needed to "keep going back to the empty well for water."

But being in this environment—and seeing how far down people could go in their devotion to drugs—has been undoubtedly good for me. Every single time I'm here, I feel increasingly convinced that my one-time experimentation with cocaine had been more than enough for my entire lifetime.

"I can't believe you're going to graduate in a week," I say to Antonio once we're settled in two foldout chairs near the Ping-Pong table.

He bites into a brownie. "I know." He nods his head in Sage's direction. "I just wish she could stop telling me I need to take this shit more seriously. I mean, she's named after a fucking spice—what does she know?" He laughs.

"Maybe she's right," I say.

Antonio laughs again. "Listen to you! I'm going to start calling you Parsley." He hits my leg and I just smile and shake my head. Antonio wasn't interested in listening to me, Sage, or anyone else. And Sage had said that my trying to make him see how thick his denial still was would only make him alienate himself from me, and that the best way I could be of service to him was to just continue to be his sounding board.

Before I know it, Sage is telling me and the other visitors that it's time to go and I'm hugging Antonio and promising him that I'll be back in a few days with a fresh infusion of chocolate. As he walks me to the front gate, he says, "Oh, I almost forgot to tell you. Guess who's getting out of the business based on something you said?"

"Who?" I ask. "What business? What did I say?"

"Kristi," he says. "You remember her, right?"

I stop walking, completely shocked. I'd assumed he meant a reporter from the press lines. "Yeah, of course. But what are you talking about?"

"Some girl who just checked in here, Heather, is friends with her and she told me." He lowers his voice. "Actually, Heather went to college with Jessica, and Jessica helped set her up as a working girl."

"She did?" I ask. I hadn't told Antonio how wrapped up I got in Jessica's world, or, really, anything that had happened with my story and *Substance* and *Angeles*. I figured I'd fill him in down the road if he wanted to hear about it. "So what did Heather say?"

"Just that Kristi had told her that ever since some writer named Emma had said she looked like she should be teaching kindergarten, she'd been thinking that's what she wanted to do." He laughs. "So now she's going back to school for it." He smiles at me. "She was a sweetheart—always seemed too innocent for that world—so I'm glad to hear it. You know?"

"I do." I rub his head affectionately. "I do, indeed." As we reach my car, something occurs to me. "Um, Antonio?"

"Yes, baby?"

"You said this girl went to college with Jessica?" He nods. "Do you remember where she said they went?"

"Come on, you know I don't give a shit about that kind of thing."

"So she didn't say?"

Antonio tilts his head in contemplation. "No, she did—it was one of the big ones." He scratches his head. "Harvard or—"

"Yale?" I ask.

"Yep, that's it," he says as he good-naturedly punches the arm of a tattooed kid walking one of his visitors to their car. "Yale."

"Thanks," I say, wondering if I'll ever be able to understand what about Jessica was real and what wasn't.

"CONGRATULATIONS." I KISS Celeste on the cheek and put the flowers I've brought her on a table next to literally hundreds of other arrangements. "Unsurprisingly, you look better than any woman who just gave birth has a right to."

"I don't happen to agree"—she smiles sweetly—"but thanks." Glancing at Celeste's perfect blond highlights and fresh face, I wonder if she and Steve actually had a hair and makeup artist come over and spruce her up before they invited friends to come by their hospital room to visit. For however much I like the two of them, I wouldn't be surprised. I'm standing, after all, among a group of at least twenty-five of their "best" friends in what seems to be an entire wing of Cedar-Sinai dedicated to Celeste's delivery. Looking around, I spy Brooke and Rebecca across the room engaged in what looks like an extremely passionate conversation with Nicole Richie. When Nicole walks away, Brooke gazes in my direction with a confused look on her face, like I'm a mirage or a person she knew once but heard had died, and then hits Rebecca, who glances at me with surprise. They start making their way over to me but someone else sidetracks Brooke.

"What the hell happened to you?" Rebecca asks. "Did you fall off the face of the earth?"

I smile and shake my head. "No."

"But what have you been doing? Are you not working for *Substance* anymore? How come you're never out?"

I feel relieved that this line of questioning isn't making me feel insecure the way it once would have. "I'm applying to graduate school," I say. "In New York."

Rebecca looks confused. "Grad school?" she asks. "You mean film school?"

It occurs to me that I don't actually have to continue this conversation if I don't want to. "Nice seeing you, Rebecca," I lie. I gesture to the corner of the room, where Steve is showing off his baby girl to some men in suits. "I'm going to congratulate Steve now."

"But—"

I turn away but before I can escape completely, Brooke grabs my arm. "Hi, Emma," she says. "Where have you been?"

"Hey, Brooke," I say. "I've—" I'm about to say, "I've just gotten a life," but then I remember that I don't need to try to feel better than them. "I've been busy."

"Did you hear about Matt?" she asks, the look in her eyes suggesting that this is information she's quite excited to be revealing to me. I shake my head. "He's getting married!" she trills. She seems so giddy that for a second I think this is her extremely backward way of telling me that she's going to be the bride. "To Adriana Lopez. From MTV. Isn't that crazy?"

I nod. "It is."

"They're supposed to be here any minute."

"Really?" I ask disinterestedly.

Brooke, clearly frustrated by my reaction, sighs. "I heard you're not hanging out with Jessica anymore."

"I'm not," I say, briefly wondering how and where she could have stumbled across this information. I smile and thankfully lock eyes with Steve, who motions me over.

"Well, the same can't be said for Matt," I hear Rebecca add as I walk toward Steve. I ignore her.

I'M FEELING ODDLY UPLIFTED when I leave the hospital that evening. Rather than taking what Steve and Celeste have as an indication that I'll never get what I want, I'm just happy for them. And I'd forgotten how good it felt to stop thinking about myself long enough to actually feel happy for other people. As I cross La Cienega, my phone rings. I don't recognize the number.

"Hello?" I say. I only hear hysterical sobs. "Hello?"

"Emma?" The word manages to break through the crying. "Where are you?"

"Lilly?" I ask, shocked. I'd know her voice anywhere but literally haven't heard or seen her upset since we were in grade school. Sheer panic grips me—a protectiveness I haven't felt for my little sister in years. I suddenly remember how, after seeing her stub her toe when she was a toddler, I'd burst into tears right after she had—though I still wasn't sure if it was out of sympathy or because it made me feel helpless to not be able to prevent her from getting hurt. "What's going on? Are you okay? Where are you?"

"It's Felipe . . . it's over . . ." Her voice is thick and clotted, like she's trying to speak while holding her nose.

Rage starts flooding through me. "Are you sure?"

"Yes." She sniffles. "Can you come home—I mean, to Mom and Dad's?"

"I'm on my way." I want to kill him, tear him apart, royal limb by royal limb. You don't make a nineteen-year-old girl fall in love with you, convince her that you want to spend the rest of your life with her, and then walk away.

"Thank . . . you." She stifles a sob. "I don't know who else to talk to."

"Everything's going to be fine," I say. "I'll be there in twenty minutes." I'm stopped at a light on Beverly Boulevard, watching a driver emerge from a Maybach limousine. He's in white tie—literally wearing a suit and tails—and I wonder what over-the-top movie star insisted on dressing a driver in such a get-up.

Lilly sniffles. "I feel better knowing that you're coming."

"Just do me a favor and don't come to any conclusions until I get there, okay?"

"Okay."

I hang up the phone and suddenly realize that the woman in the stunning off-the-shoulder aqua-blue gown exiting the limo is Jessica—looking as gorgeous as I've ever seen her, her skin tan and radiant, her makeup perfect and her hair gathering around her face in delicate wisps. She's smiling seductively at a man who's getting out of the limo and walking over to her. As I see their lips connect for a deep, passionate kiss that puts the World War II soldier and nurse to shame, I think that if I didn't know better, I'd swear they were some picture-perfect couple off to have a night as flawless as all the others that made up their idyllic existence.

I shake my head. The light turns green so I watch them through my rear-view mirror as I race toward home.

acknowledgments

Bought only exists because many years ago, I was assigned an investigative feature by Andrew Essex (alas, no longer a magazine editor) on high-class prostitution in Hollywood. Six months of infiltrating that world seriously opened the eyes of this sheltered Marin girl. (Sitting in a most definitely unhinged pimp's apartment while he demanded money I didn't have in exchange for information, interviewing a porn star who did "side work" as a prostitute as she stripped at the Spearmint Rhino, and getting hold of the contents of a laptop belonging to a former partner of a madam who was locked up in a Cuban jail were among my midadventures.) This is all a long-winded way of thanking Andrew, who encouraged me to turn all that I'd unearthed into a bigger project—though I don't think he (or I) ever imagined it would be a novel.

Thanks as well to Pilar Queen for selling the book and everyone at Harper Perennial—from Cal Morgan and Carrie Kania to Michael Signorelli, Robin Bilardello, Rachel Chubinsky, and Nicole Reardon—for working with me on it. Robert Palmer, Andrew Brin, and Alec Shankman read various and sundry drafts and offered up encouragement I definitely needed. Nicole Balin, Jennifer Belle, and Neil Strauss chimed in with astute input, and Vanessa Grigoriadis and Dufflyn Lammers saved me with their suggestions for improvements. But it's John Griffiths who deserves the bulk of my gratitude for taking the book apart by its tendrils and then painstakingly explaining to me how he thought I should put it back together (and then proceeding to send me roughly ten thousand articles over the next few years about prostitution, in an effort to show me how endlessly "zeitgeisty" my topic was). Thanks as well to the indefatigable and endlessly supportive Cathy Griffin for putting the word out before the final version was even on the page, Jayson Barrons for ingenious help on the marketing end, Eric Weis for line editing, and Elise Nersesian for coming up with the final title.

I'd also like to thank the girls who told me their tales, most of whom would surely rather not be named here. Always remember: you're not the only ones who have been bought.

ALSO BY ANNA DAVID

PARTY GIRL

A Novel

ISBN 978-0-06-137400-5 (paperback)

Celebrity journalist Amelia Stone is the quintessential Hollywood party girl, but when her high-rolling, cocaine-fueled lifestyle spins out of control, she makes the drastic decision to end her drug abuse. When she sinks a new job with a major magazine to report on her wild exploits, the lure of her former lifestyle begins to pull at her. So Amelia must choose: will she save herself, or salvage her reputation as the ultimate party girl?

"David's debut novel combines a candid picture of addiction and recovery with scandalously funny, only-in-LA adventures." —*Redbook*

"At once uproarious and poignant, Anna David's portrayal of the experience of addiction and nuances of recovery is the most accurate I have come across."
—Dr. Drew Pinsky, addiction expert and host of *Loveline*